Nora,
The Ape-Woman

BY THE SAME AUTHOR

Homo-Deus
The Human Arrow
Ouha, King of the Apes
Pharaoh's Wife

Nora,
The Ape-Woman

by
Félicien Champsaur

translated, annotated and introduced by
Brian Stableford

A Black Coat Press Book

ISBN 978-1-61227-403-4. First Printing. May 2015. Published by Black Coat Press, an imprint of Hollywood Comics.com, LLC, P.O. Box 17270, Encino, CA 91416. All rights reserved. Except for review purposes, no part of this book may be reproduced or transmitted in any form or by any means, electronic or mechanical, including photocopying, recording, or by any information storage and retrieval system, without permission in writing from the publisher. The stories and characters depicted in this novel are entirely fictional. Printed in the United States of America.

Introduction

Nora, la guenon devenue femme by Félicien
Champsaur, here translated as *Nora, the Ape-Woman*,
was first published by Ferenczi in 1929. It is a sequel to
the earlier novel *Ouha, roi des singes* (1923)[1] and also
gives a major role to the central character of *Homo-
Deus: Le Satyre Invisible* (1924)[2], who had also been
given a minor role in *Tuer les vieux! Jouir!* (1925)[3].

The list of the author's previous works included in
the preliminary pages of *Nora* includes sales figures to
date, which claim that *Ouha* had sold 95,000 copies and
Homo-Deus—recorded as *Le Satyre invisible*, which was
presumably the author's intended title, as—50,000. Although some earlier works had racked up sales much
more considerable than those, the figures are considerably higher than those for any of the other titles
Champsaur published in the 1920s, and the provision of
a sequel to both must therefore have seemed an attractive
proposal. The resultant text did not do nearly as well,
however, and might have been thought by contemporary
readers to have taken the evident bizarrerie of the two
earlier novels a step too far.

All three of the novels making up the peculiar triad
completed by *Nora*, as well as the other novel featuring
Homo-Deus in a cameo role have been largely eliminat-

---

[1] tr. in a Black Coat Press edition as *Ouha, King of the Apes*,
ISBN 978-1-61227-115-6.
[2] tr. as "The Invisible Satyr" in the Black Coat Press volume
Homo-Deus, ISBN 978-1-61227-351-8.
[3] tr. as "Kill the Old: Enjoy!" in *Homo-Deus, q.v.*

ed from modern awareness, along with their author. *Nora*, however, has attracted some belated critical comment of an entirely negative kind, having been explicitly condemned by some recent critics as an offensively racist text. Brett A. Berliner, for instance, in "Mephistopheles and Monkeys: Rejuvenation, Race and Sexuality in Popular Culture in Interwar France,"[4] begins his article with the statement;

"In 1929 Félicien Champsaur, a Rabelaisian author of much pulp fiction, published *Nora, la guenon devenue femme*. The cover illustration of Champsaur's book featured a svelte black woman wearing nothing but a banana skirt, looking not unlike the African-American entertainer Josephine Baker, who, just a few years earlier, had taken Paris by storm." Having explained Nora's genesis by means of the transplantation of "the ovaries of a Russian ex-princess," Berliner concludes his first paragraph with the judgment that: "Nora evolved into a brown-skinned woman—symbolically, Josephine Baker."

The subsequent commentary on the plot of the novel, including various quotations, suggests that Berliner had read it and had access to a copy of the book, but it is worth noting that the front cover (attributed to "Endré") actually depicts a white woman who does not resemble Josephine Baker, save for her hair-style, and although there are two internal illustrations by Charles Naillod that are reminiscent of Josephine Baker, neither of which features a banana skirt, the other internal illustration and the back cover (by Lucien Jaquelux) also depict a white woman. The text initially describes Nora as having "bronzed" skin in the first chapter, but offers a some-

---

[4] in the *Journal of the History of Sexuality* vol. 13 no, 3 (2004),

what confused account thereafter in which several different colors, including black, are deliberately confused. The most significant datum to emerge from that confusion, in fact, is that her complexion has a faint bluish tint that licenses description of her as "la danseuse bleue" (the blue dancer)—a phrase whose repeated use suggests that the character owes at least part of her inspiration to one or both of two famous paintings featuring that formula in their titles, one by Edgar Degas and the other by the futurist Gino Severini.

In addition, although Nora's mother was an orangutan, there is a strong possibility that her father is the white American scientist who has adopted her and given her his surname, Abraham Goldry; he sometimes denies the biological kinship (with a furious blush) but his closest associates have no doubt of the fact, and attribute his reaction to shame, or, more generously, to his being "in denial." Nora's counterpart within the plot, Narcisse, is the son of a native black woman and the part-human orangutan Ouha—but he is the only character in the plot to have any such relationship, and he is treated far more sympathetically by the author than any other character.

The first chapter of the novel, in which Nora is introduced, features a minor character whose sole purpose is to make a speech arguing that "we are all apes," thus summarizing the moral of the tale, which is the very opposite of the xenophobia that Berliner tries to foist upon it. The plot continually draw comparisons between the hybrid apes Nora and Narcisse and the "fully human" characters—every single one of whom is white—always suggesting that the supposed "superiority" of the latter is false, and consists largely of a hypocritical denial of their animality, particularly in respect of their sexual impulses. If evaluated in accordance with its own assertions, therefore, the story is anything but racist, and conspicuously refuses even to be "speciesist" in its evaluation of the claims of civilized white men to be superior to other races.

Having said that, it is necessary to agree with Berliner that Nora's first appearance on the stage of the Folies Bergère is, indeed, strongly reminiscent of Josephine Baker's debut there in 1925 (following earlier performances at the Théâtre des Champs-Élysées), when she performed a so-called "*danse sauvage*" wearing a skirt made from a string of artificial bananas. One reference in the description of the dance to Nora being in the midst of "the other negroes" forming her supportive chorus suggests that Champsaur did see that performance, and is adapting a journalistic description of it, in a somewhat slapdash fashion, for his own description of Nora's "*ballet nègre*." It is vital to realize, however, that in doing that, Champsaur had not the slightest intention of insulting Josephine Baker or the chorus, and that Nora's actual symbolism within the story is in no way relevant to the career of the American dancer, or to black people in general. The fact that Nora's performance is a *ballet nègre* is attributed in the story to the fact that she learned to dance in Cuba, and it is useful for modern readers to bear in mind that the phrase *ballet nègre* was a general term for a style of dancing, which was not intended to be pejorative (it was subsequently used as the title for the African-American modern dance company founded by Katherine Durham in 1930).

Josephine Baker did cause a sensation when she appeared at the Folies Bergère, but it is worth remembering that the reason she took that job (breaking her previous contact in order to stay in Paris rather than continue touring) was because she found far less racism in the French capital than she had encountered elsewhere, especially in her homeland. She was not the first part-negro dancer to appear on the Parisian stage wearing an extremely scanty costume and dancing *ballet nègre*. She had been preceded by Aïcha Goblet, who appears in a cameo role in a scene in *Tuer les Vieux! Jouir!* set in the Café Rotonde, where Champsaur used to hang out with Picasso and Modigliani, both of whom used her as a model; the scene not only establishes that Champsaur knew her, but that he was entirely sympathetic to her, and it serves to allow the narrative voice to defend her against unjustified moral suspicions; it illustrates that racism was by no means absent from the Parisian social scene in the 1920s, but also that Félicien Champsaur was a fervent opponent of it rather than a collaborator.

Perhaps, viewed in retrospect, it was a *faux pas* for Champsaur to borrow aspects of Josephine Baker's dancing to characterize Nora's, but it ought not to occasion the blanket condemnation of the book—which is otherwise totally innocent of any accidental racist suggestion—or of its author, who was one of the least xenophobic of his generation. It is, admittedly, difficult for a reader who has not previously read both *Ouha* and *Homo-Deus: Le Satyr invisible* to get a grip on the text, but that does not excuse the kind of gross misrepresentation of which Berliner is guilty. Champsaur would have been deeply mortified to know that the work had given rise to such criticism—all the more so because there are many so aspects of the book that really are intended to shock and offend, albeit in a very different cause, fiercely attacking the hypocrisy and folly of the arrogance of supposedly-superior "civilized" (white) humans.

In order to understand Nora's actual symbolism it is helpful to refer back to two of Champsaur's earlier novels, both published in 1888: the two that did more than any others to make him famous and to establish his narrative method and style. The first, *L'Amant des danseuses, roman moderniste* [The Man Who Loved Dancing-Girls; a Modernist Novel] is a relatively earnest psychological study of the erotic attraction of the world of the theater in general, and dancers in particular, which uses a painter as a central character, clearly based on Edgar Degas, although the fascinations credited to him are largely the author's own, and insofar as the narrative is critical of the character's obsession, it is a kind of self-criticism without any intention to insult Degas. The second, *Lulu, roman clownesque* [Lulu; a Clownish Novel] is a study of a dancer, couched as a sentimental comedy, in which the dancer explicitly becomes a symbol not merely for the eroticism of her art and the fickleness of womankind, but for the essential spirit of the city of Paris. The narrative goes even further than that in its extravagant climax, when the lover that Lulu finally chooses from among her various suitors is revealed to be an incarnation of the divine "Eros-Bacchus," who subjects her to a metamorphosis described in the relevant chapter-title as an apotheosis, represented by the illustrator Louis Chalon in an image entitled "L'Assomption de Lulu" [The Assumption of Lulu], which transforms her into the "ange d'acrobatie" [angel of acrobatics].

Nora brings Lulu's lyrical symbolism back down to earth, making the dancer an ape rather than an angel precisely in order to fit her into the context of evolutionary history and the true nature of the simian and human species, as suggested by modern science—a long-term fascination of Champsaur's, as illustrated by his early short stories "La Légende du singe" (1876; tr. as "The First Human" in *The Human Arrow* [5] and "Le Dernier homme" (1885; tr. as "The Last Human" in the same volume). As with Lulu, Nora's principal function within the plot is to be an object of sexual desire, and an archetypal embodiment of the very essence of sexual desire; amour, however, is no longer imagined in the present novel as something intrinsically divine, but as something intrinsically animalistic, and so deep-seated that even a scientific genius like Homo-Deus, let alone a litterateur whose trade is romance, cannot hope to escape it entirely. *Nora* is a story of the triumph of that animality, but it is also a story that attempts to argue, very fervently, that it is a triumph of which we ought not to be ashamed, and which even scientists ought not to regret.

Insofar as *Nora* has a plot—and, like many of Champsaur's later novels, it is something of a slapdash hotchpotch, thrown together at the whim of a mind that has more than a hint of butterfly about it—that plot is concerned with the scientific modification of species by means of surgery, and the possibilities inherent within that surgery of the enhancement of the human condition, ultimately extending as far as the creation of the superhuman and conquest of death. In that respect, the story takes a great deal of inspiration from the contemporary exploits of Serge Voronoff, who is one of its leading characters, forming a quartet with Abraham Goldry, the anthropologist earlier featured in *Ouha*, and Marc Vanel (alias Homo-Deus) and Jean Fortin, the two biologists and psychic scientists featured in *Homo-Deus: Le Satyre invisible*.

---

[5] Available in a Black Coat Press edition, ISBN 978-1-61227-045-6.

Serge Voronoff (1866-1951) was born Samuel Abrahamovitch in Russia, but went to Paris at the age of eighteen to study medicine, and was eventually naturalized as a French citizen in 1895. As a student he worked for a time under one of the leading physiologists of the era, Charles Brown-Séquard (1817-1894), the pioneer of xenotransplantation, who claimed shortly before his death to have injected human subjects with extracts from the testicles of guinea-pigs and dogs, that the injections had resulted in observable rejuvenation, and that he hoped they might also result in an extension of longevity. Subsequently, Voronoff also worked in collaboration with a younger student, Alexis Carrel (1873-1944), who was similarly interested in the possibility of xenotranplantation, and whose work was eventually to help pave the way for actual organ transplantation, although he became far more famous in the short term for his work on tissue cultures, enabling cells to develop in vitro.

Voronoff was independently wealthy, but he also attracted considerable research funding in 1917 from a wealthy American socialite, Evelyn Bostwick, who worked as his laboratory assistant at the Collège de France before they married in 1920. Her connections in high society helped Voronoff to become famous—or at least notorious—and to reap massive publicity for the hopes that he based on the possibilities of xenotransplantation, taking up exactly where Brown-Séquard had left off. After several scientific publications of a more general kind he published *Greffes testiculaires* [Testicular Grafts] in 1923 and a report of *Quarante-trois greffes du singe à homme* [Forty-Three Grafts from Monkeys to Humans] in 1924, and then followed them up with *Étude sur la vieillesse et la rajeunissement par le greffe* (1926;

tr. as *Rejuvenation by Grafting*), which is an exercise in self-publicizing futurology rather than a scrupulous report of his research findings. Those findings were never published in a form that would be considered today to be full and adequate scientific reportage.

In consequence of their somewhat equivocal reportage, there is little hard information as to how many animal experiments Voronoff carried out between 1917 and 1929, or what the results of those experiments might have been, let alone how many experiments he carried out on human beings and what their effects were. Hindsight, judging by the example of further experiments, suggests that the claims he made about the success of his grafts must have been wildly exaggerated, reflecting his optimism rather than his evidence, probably because he fell for his own patter rather than because he was a calculated charlatan. How many grafts of simian testicular material he had carried out on human subjects prior to 1929 remains unclear, but what is perfectly certain is that by that date, everyone in Paris believed that he was doing such operations on a regular basis, and people were eagerly searching high society for signs of youthful behavior in aged individuals who might—behind a shield of strict confidentiality, of course—have been his clients.

Voronoff's work obtained a vast amount of press coverage, and provided the basis for several works of speculative fiction, almost all of them mocking or grimly hostile. Of all the writers of such speculative works, however, Félicien Champsaur was probably the only one who not only knew Voronoff well—he met him socially not merely in Paris but also on the Riviera, where they both had second homes (one on either side of the Italian border)—but might well have contemplated seriously the possibility of becoming one of his clients. Born in 1858, Champsaur had edged into his seventies by 1929, and as a relentless lifelong debauchee, he was probably painfully aware of the declining effects of age.

Obviously, Champsaur must have had Voronoff's consent to use him as a character in a book, and Voronoff, well aware of the potential publicity value of an account that was not overtly hostile, might well have encouraged him to do so fervently. As to whether or not he offered Champsaur a free rejuvenation treatment in return—and whether, if he did, Champsaur accepted the offer—we can only speculate. All we know for sure is that Champsaur died in 1934, no younger than he had been in 1929, and all we can really deduce from the pages of *Nora* is that if he did think seriously about acquiring such a graft, he was very hesitant about it, not merely because he was squeamish on his own account but because he would have felt extremely guilty about the cost of such a sacrifice to an innocent ape. Unlike most of Voronoff's clients, Champsaur believed sincerely that the brotherhood of man ought to extend to the great apes, and that employing them for the purposes described and practiced by Voronoff was morally dubious in the extreme.

The character featured in *Nora* who is faced with the decision as to whether to risk the rejuvenation treatment is, like Champsaur, a famous writer and a relentless but discreet debauchee, but Champsaur went out of his way to avoid the possibility that readers might identify the author with his character—so far out of his way, in fact, that he explicitly based the character in question on another writer, in such a way as to make the representation unmistakable. Even before the supplementary details began to accumulate, the mere name of the character—Ernest Paris—would have been highly suggestive to contemporary readers, who would immediately have drawn an analogy of nomenclature with "Anatole France," (Jacques-Anatole Thibault, 1844-1924) who had worn the mantle of his country's leading novelist for at least two decades before his death, and had won the Nobel Prize for Literature in 1921. In the novel, Edgar Paris is 80, the same age as Anatole France had been when he died; he lives at the address at which Anatole France was then living; and many other calculated similarities are dropped into the plot before it reaches a climax that is a straightforward account of Anatole France's funeral—until the moment when Nora and Narcisse get involved in the obsequies, in their own distinctive fashions.

Although no sensitive reader could sincerely believe that Champsaur's portrayal of Nora was intended as an attack on Josephine Baker, it is difficult not to see the portrayal of Edgar Paris as anything but a scathing assault on the late Anatole France; it is, in its way, quite savage. What is more, Champsaur had form in that regard. The same chapter of *Tuer les Vieux! Jouir!* that leans over backwards to be sympathetic to Aïsha Goblet contains a remarkably bilious speech—presumably written almost immediately after the great man's death—made by the heroine of the novel, attacking Anatole France's morals with a great deal of aggression and contempt. That speech is, however, elicited by a question as to whether she would ever contemplate marrying a artist, and follows critical comments on the morals of various other men of genius who number among her literary heroes. Significantly, however, the last word in curled-lip contempt and implied unthinkability comes in the brief sentence with which she concludes her tirade against artists: "Why not Félicien Champsaur?"

In reading the portrayal of Edgar Paris, therefore, it is as well to bear in mind that he and Champsaur had a great deal in common. In terms of their tastes, their interests and their politics they were so similar that they would surely have been very good friends had they not had the additional similarity of being notoriously spiky personalities, whom even their friends found difficult to like. The one great difference between them, however, of which Champsaur was doubtless painfully aware, was that Anatole France was much more highly-regarded as a writer, and justly so. Champsaur knew full well that Anatole France was a genius, and that he was not; that must certainly have increased his jealousy immeasurably, but the fact that Anatole France was the man that he would have dearly liked to be might also have had another effect: the consequence that, if he ever did sit down to ask himself, seriously, whether he ought to submit himself to Serge Voronoff's rejuvenation treatment, he might well have posed himself the question: "What would Anatole France do?"

And that, in a nutshell, is half the plot, and perhaps more than half of the *raison d'être*, of *Nora*.

The fact is that Edgar Paris is only superficially similar to Anatole France, in spite of the wealth of surface detail supporting that appearance. Apart from his infatuation with Nora, there is one other symbolic detail which differentiates him severely from that model; in the story, Edgar Paris is struggling ineffectually with a novel that he has been planning to write for years, entitled *Le Vrai Jésus*, a historical novel that will reveal the "real" (i.e. non-supernatural) character behind the Biblical legend. So far as we know, Anatole France had no such project on his mental drawing-board when he died—but a year after publishing *Nora*, Félicien Champsaur published *Le Crucifié*, a historical novel speculatively revealing the "real" non-supernatural character of Jesus. Deep down, where it counts, Edgar Paris is not Anatole France, but Félicien Champsaur—who was, like many sarcastic cynics, routinely harder on himself than he was on other people, and was doubtless proud to be his own worst enemy as well as his only true and wholly sympathetic friend. (He was, of course, a lover of paradox too.)

One thing that Anatole France would not have done was write *Nora*—or, at least, if he had written something remotely akin to it, it would have been a very different book. It would have been much more stylish, must more delicate and much more coherent. Champsaur's style is often brutal, and when he strives for oratorical effect he routinely seems pompous and unconvincing—and the fact that he puts most of his speeches into the mouths of characters who are condemned for being pompous and unconvincing does not serve to exonerate him entirely from blame. He is far more accomplished at indelicacy than delicacy, and although that is not always a fault, by any means, it is not necessarily a virtue either. Nor is the uneven, patchwork quality of much of his later work entirely a bad thing, but one is bound to suspect that it owes more to carelessness and ineptitude than to calculate contrivance. Champsaur's indelicacy and inability to maintain a coherent thread of plot or argument for more than a few hundred words do, however, give his later works an intriguing brio and garish surreality that is far from unappealing, if they are read in the right spirit.

In conventional terms, *Nora* is a considerably poorer novel than *Ouha*, the last book Champsaur wrote that looks as if it were written to a plan and might even have gone through more than one draft, and in terms of imaginative reach it does not measure up to *Homo-Deus: Le Satyre invisible*, on the ideas of which it is largely parasitic. It is best regarded, in fact, as a belated and patchy addendum to the two earlier novels, and readers really ought to read the other two novels first if they hope to get anything out of it at all, but it does have its moments, and it certainly displays a magnificent bizarrerie with admirable flamboyance.

Although it is a book obsessed with the nature and paradoxicality of erotic attraction, *Nora* only has one really explicit scene, which describes a lesbian orgy. Although graphic even by the standards of 1929, it is not much different from any other lesbian orgy scene to begin with, but as it unfolds it undergoes a remarkable metamorphosis; as the text itself modestly points out, a lesbian orgy scene that is interrupted by the advent of an invisible man and an intelligent ape, competing for the lust of another ape reshaped into beautiful human form by Voronoffian grafts and the invisible man's skill in esthetic surgery, is "not banal."

Whatever else one could justifiably say about *Nora*, it is very definitely not banal—and that is no small triumph.

This translation was made from a ludicrously expensive second-hand copy of the Ferenczi edition.

Brian Stableford

I. The Star of the Ballet Nègre

Folies Bergère, Casino de Paris and Moulin Rouge: those three dazzling beacons fascinate Parisian and foreign moths, irresistibly attracted by the incandescence of the artificial light in which they flutter madly, without caring whether they burn their wings. Casino de Paris, Folies Bergère, Moulin Rouge! Ambiance of luxury and lust! All races are encountered there; the most various situations and the most abnormal milieux rub shoulders there, with the most disparate mentalities mixed in. Moulin Rouge, Casino de Paris, Folies Bergère! Factories of excitement! Marvelous antechambers of gallant shocks and spasms in which one dies, drowned in a minute! Pagan temples where the drugs and incense of voluptuousness burn! The most dissimilar objectives lead the two sexes there, moved by an avid desire for the noise, glare and hectic agitation favored by the sparkling décor, the magicality of the spectacle and the radiance of electricity.

In the blackness of day at the end of December, heavy low clouds have poured rain persistently over the saddened city. With nightfall, the lights come on, and Paris is reborn. Finished, the day of labor for some, of bitter hunting for others, and sinister ennui for the majority. Now is the hour of dance-halls, theaters and music halls! The men don their smoking jackets, the women make up a savant beauty; all of them rush toward the places of pleasure, the factories of stupor, the department stories of worse-than-naked—in order, at the end of the day, to distract themselves, to relax, to forget cares, to silence, sometimes, the inhibiting voice of conscience and, in a general fashion, to escape from oneself for a few hours.

That evening, at the music hall of the Folies Bergères, the première of a new revue, with *ballet nègre*, was attracting All Paris and the birds of passage, cleverly lured by intensive publicity. A hint of mystery, relative to an unknown star, was exciting curiosity. Brought to Paris by the celebrated actress Cécile Borel, who had discovered her during her last tour of North America, the young half-caste was, according to the press, exceptionally original, and promised the public the revelation of an unusual talent, or, at any rate, a strange, disconcerting beauty.

It did not require anything more to fill the hall to bursting, and there was everything in that gathering: aristocrats, clubmen, politicians, well-known doctors, rich manufacturers, artists, rich foreigners, resident aliens sparkling with jewelry, and the nouveau riche, arrogant in order to seem distinguished. On the feminine side there were renowned actress in the theater and on the screen, sacred or consecrated prostitutes, trendy socialites and good-time girls in search of lucrative adventures. Figures of luxury, lust and the all-too-necessary superfluous: a bizarre crowd, very mixed, emanating the special magnetism of places of amusement.

In one front-of-stage box: Cécile Borel. Her imposing beauty is enlivened by a gleam of triumph; she is the focal point of the audience's gaze; is it not to her that that the alluring promise of the unusual—ardently sought but rarely encountered—is owed?

By her side, another beauty, much younger and less made-up: Miss Maud Macfield, an American billionairess of fantastic caprices, a frantic tourist for whom the small globe no longer has any secrets. By yacht, airplane, auto and sleeping-car, she has gone twice round the world, leaving memories of an exaggerated whimsy everywhere. She was at the gala première at the Folies Bergère that evening in order to support, with Cécile Borel, the Parisian debut of the bronzed dancer Nora, whom both of them were pushing hard, with their money and their connections.

Behind the two women, slightly dissimulated, Monsieur Ernest Paris of the Académie Française, the celebrated litterateur of the genre and the genius—is it necessary to spell it out?—admired by all: Ernest Paris, the king of the audience, at least in the domain of letters. The witty malice of his eyes, the final youth in that antique man, attenuates the sensuality expressed by his equine and faunesque mask, the heavy gourmand mouth and the long prominent nose.

The opposite front-of-stage box is occupied by four men, three of whom, at least, are "aces" of science: Dr. Jean Fortin, the high-browed image of the seeker, whose audacious and disconcerting discoveries have rendered him popular. By his side Dr. Serge Voronoff, the Agni of extinct virility.[6] In rear, a tall dark-haired fellow, well-balanced, with extraordinarily beautiful eyes, most impressive, above all, because of their metallic and hypnotic gleam: Dr. Marc Vanel, Homo-Deus, the mysterious individual around whom strange and fantastic legends circulate, who has studied psychic sciences in the hermetic realm. Further back, an unexpected and discreet

---

[6] Agni is the Hindu god of fire, acceptor of sacrifices, eternally young because his fire is reignited every day. He has two heads, one symbolizing immortality and the other the mystery of life.

fourth occupant: Georges Clemenceau, whose presence the public explains by virtue of his well-known long friendship with Dr. Fortin.[7]

Then, at hazard, the roaming opera-glasses of a spectator might discover a hundred other faces more-or-less notorious and transitory; there is an entire top drawer at the Folies Bergère this evening.

The curtain has just fallen on the first act, and the star, Nora, so widely and well advertised, has not yet appeared. The revue, exempt from banality, justifies its success. The exotic rutilant scenery, the artistically-contrived costumes, the joyful types of the actors, the frenetic or soothing music, form an ensemble evoking, in an agreeable and nostalgic manner, those mysterious lands of perfume, sunlight and dream, of which those who have visited them retain the charmed memory, like delicious vanished kisses.

Interval chatter. People are talking almost everywhere, not about what they have just seen but the *ballet nègre*, and the surprise, Nora, who is discussed in more than one conversation in complete ignorance.

In the front-of-stage box, Ernest Paris comments on the desire of that public, ready to give the ovation of its applause to a new idol.

---

[7] Georges Clemenceau (a.k.a. the "Tiger") died on 24 November 1929, which might have been before the publication date of the novel, but it must have been written while he was still alive. Champsaur had known him for a long time, and thought highly of him. There is no way of knowing for sure whether he obtained Clemenceau's formal permission to employ him as a character (Clemenceau burned all his private correspondence before his death) but it is probable that the great man was aware of his employment, and approved of it; it is possible that it arose from a conversation between the two men.

"Fortunate women! Not twenty years old, they only have to appear to plunder success. We poor men of letters only reach it after a great deal of hard work, when we can do no more with it."

"You have glory, Master, and the world salutes your genius. How many yearn to match you?"

The white-haired old man with the equine profile smiles. "Nothing is worth as much as being twenty years old, an aviator and beloved by women."

"What!" says Cécile Borel, laughing. "You'd still like to steal hearts?"

"No need to steal them when your name is Ernest Paris. They come to you."

"If I took you at your word, Miss Maud," says the old man, "you'd be trapped."

"How long this entr'acte is," interject the actress. "I'm in haste to see my Nora make her entrance."

"Hey!" says Ernest Paris, "I can see 'the Tiger' sitting opposite, behind our mutual friend Dr. Jean Fortin—yes, the former President of the Council, Georges Clemenceau."

"Oh, I'd like to be introduced to him. Can you do that, my dear?"

"Perhaps…some time…but not here."

In the gallery, Patrice Montclar, the dramatic author, runs into an old comrade of his generation, Maurice de Fédraudy.

"What is the doyen of the Comédie-Française doing at the Folies Bergère?"

"Learning his métier ape-fashion," says the actor, laughing. "And I'm not alone here. Who among us isn't more or less an ape? Humans will always have something of the ancestral in them. We're all apes, from the artist like me, a grimacer of passions, to the parliamentarian who earnestly repeats the same hollow phrases at the tribune, heard all the way from Mirabeau to Jaurès. Other apes march in line, head to the right, head to the left. And those same apes kill one another with enthusiasm, as their forefathers have always done. Mussolini apes Napoléon."

"You're forgetting the best: the pope and his cardinals.

"Let's not touch on those. They teach us the first grimaces, and we only let loose the last.

A young actress who was with Montclar: "You haven't dared to compare our smiles with your grimaces."

The doyen continues: "Because I've only been talking about males. But she-apes play artfully with the human heart: it makes one afraid. The most beautiful grimaces, truly, are those that we command."

"You're not very amiable today, Master Ape. Has someone trodden on your tail?"

"It's starting again. I love the harmoniously cacophonous and scatterbrained sounds of that jazz overture that's beginning. Let's get back to our seats."

The curtain rises on the second act, especially contrived, it appears, for the unknown star. On the edge of a tropical forest, an inviolate refuge of wild beasts, negroes of both sexes are crouched, singing to the accompaniment of an unfamiliar music: first a grave and monotonous chant; then a frenzy of rage makes them rise to their feet and gesticulate savagely, only, without transition, for them to resume their heart-rending plaint and fall back into their weary poses. Fatalistic resignation after impotent revolt! A moving symbol of a race that has groaned under slavery and whose suffering and rancor are expressed in those old songs, devoid of rhythm but poignant, which only negroes, perhaps by atavism, are capable of singing without the emotive character being diminished.

Suddenly, arriving like those magical characters who surge forth from a trap-door, a bizarre individual whom the troop of negroes surround and welcome, is quivering on the stage.

A black bird, a sylph or a woman?

She dances, bounds, spins, capers with vertiginous rapidity, followed in her evolutions by a hallucinating jazz. Then, suddenly, that Beast—pink, yellow, brown, blue...yes, blue—is immobile, in the hieratic pose of an idol, in the center of the other prostrate, adoring negroes.

And the opera-glasses are focused: it's evidently a woman, but how original! She is naked, save for a string of bananas that girdle her, an ivory necklace circling several times, falls beneath her young breasts; long pendants hang tremulously from her ear-lobes, refining the face, which is illuminated by two beautiful, ken and mobile eyes, and the white, sharp teeth of a wolf-cub. The body is svelte and graceful, an admirable living statue—disquieting too, because an indefinable but undeniable animality emanates from it, which is slightly disconcerting. She astonishes, charms, galvanizes.

The idol has resumed her dancing, furiously. Is it dancing or acrobatics, which the most skilful fairground performers could not contrive but which she executes with the ease of a frightful flexibility? Her blue, maroon body, with unexpected movements of the hips, writhes in a thousand fantasies rich in sensations, which suggest a versatile spirit and strike the most unexpected, the most grotesque and the most vivid—and perhaps, sometimes, the most obscene—poses. But of that has nothing learned, nothing imposed, and seems instead to be the frolicking of a young animal amusing herself, without worrying about anything whatsoever—and giving the audience imperishable moments, with the bronzed gleam of her agile and sensual person, which overturns the traditional esthetic installed thus far in the minds of spectators of civilized dancing.

One is no longer in the theater but in the most secret and the most distant nature, in the mysterious bush, and the virgin forest, where that woman was dancing as a young wild animal bounds.

Dr. Jean Fortin said to his neighbors, Clemenceau, Mark Vanel and Voronoff: "We did well to come; I believe that's our girl."

Where does that black bird come from? From what primitive hut lost in the tropics? Hidden in the leafy branches of a fallen tree that garnished almost one entire side of the stage, an enormous orangutan, with a abrupt leap, falls alongside the dancer, and seizes her in its arms, while the horrified negroes, with irresistible expressions, run away howling.

A struggle is engaged between the jungle monster with its partner, until the latter escapes, leaps, grips the rim of Cécile Borel's box, and with surprising agility, aiding herself with her undulous hands and her intelligent feet, she turns, almost falls, catches herself magically by one foot, and arrives thus, bimane, quadrumane, in front of the box where doctors Jean Fortin and Marc Vanel, on their feet, wonderstruck, have followed the extraordinary acrobatics.

But the huge orangutan has hurled itself on its prey, who struggles and recommences her frantic writhing, hectically. Then, holding her at arm's length and making use of the fallen tree like a trampoline, it carries her away—and disappears, superb and victorious, into the profound forest.

And there was delirium in the hall. Never had such an ovation been seen before. The star unknown twenty minutes before was now famous; and Cecile Borel was exultant. When, in response to frenetic recalls, Nora returned to the stage, she turned toward the associate of the Comédie-Française. On a whim, Nora had adorned her young nudity with a girdle of multicolored feathers, which undulated gently at each of her acrobatic gestures; but her skin appeared troubling, strange, pink, bronzed, all caressed with somber azure, like that of a blue dancer. In that fashion, she appeared as a great bird of prismatic adornment, whom a malicious enchantress had transformed part-way into a woman. A charming spontaneity caused her to prostrate herself, hands extended, palms open, as if she desired to offer to Cécile Borel and the American woman the homage of the victory that she had just carried off.

"My dear friends, it's a real find you've made there," Ernest Paris said to them. "But fundamentally, what is this Nora? Woman or ape? I haven't yet made up my mind."

"Me neither," replied the actress, smiling.

Meanwhile, on the other side, in the doctors' box, a veritable emotion was added to the enthusiasm that was transporting the hall.

"Dr. Goldry will be glad to know that we've found 'his' girl—who's also a little ours."

"All that remains now to marry her off," said Clemenceau. "It won't be very easy, in that naked profession."

"Perhaps we can utilize her for further experiments," said Marc Vanel.

"When one creates a new plaything," said the facetious Jean Fortin, "it's necessary to amuse oneself with it or break it to see what there is inside." He turned to Clemenceau. "How do you find the new star, Georges?"

"Disconcerting. Is she a woman or an animal?"

"Say: a she-ape who has become a woman, and you'll have the truth of it."

II. A Corner of the Veil

The performance of the revue and its fantastic *ballet nègre* attracted increasingly enthusiastic crowds to the Folies Bergère. Success, for a ballerina, is not limited to the theater; on the artistic side, there is the woman and the attraction of a unique personality. Nora was not a conventional beauty, to be sure; she was better, for she symbolized marvelously a kind of animal voluptuousness, ancestral and vicious.

One sensed that that body, so supple and simultaneously so muscular, must be a splendid instrument of lust. Thus, love letters, flowers and jewels showered the artiste. Nora was not grimly virtuous, and her temperament, which was rather ardent, was not opposed to encounters in which her pleasure and interest had everything to gain. On the advice of her friend Maud, however, she made the decision to find and adopt a first rate maintainer, and her choice fell on Jules Ducon, one of those whom it is conventional to call the *nouveau riche*, because the World War permitted them, thanks to furnishing materials of war, to multiply a hundredfold in five years of excessive wastage, a capital that was already very tidy.

Jules Ducon was certainly not an elite intelligence, not even in the second rank, but he had what is called, a trifle lightly, "a genius for business." In ordinary times, he would doubtless have prospered, but would have taken twenty years to amass a few hundred thousand francs; in five years of war he had heaped up millions. Still young, he was fifty in 1928. Prudently, as soon as hostilities ended, he had liquidated his francs and sent his capital abroad in order to convert it into dollars, still equivalent. Then he traveled, made his world tour, and eventually returned to Paris, where, henceforth, he could live handsomely on dollars when the victorious franc was no longer worth more than four sous, and lead a sumptuous life.

From then on he was at all fêtes, and did not refuse himself any fantasy, even the most costly—fantasies which, in any case, did not surpass a meager radius; Jules Ducon was too ignorant and too inartistic to spend his money on intellectual pleasures. For a being thus made, Nora was bound to have an immense attraction: an attraction that simultaneously tempted his vanity and his love of all sensualities. He was, in consequence, one of the most ardent in seeking to obtain the favors of the star, and the latter, who was not blinded by passion, imposed her conditions, to which he subscribed immediately, with urgency. That is why Nora was installed in a charming little town house in the Rue Spontini.

For the moment, she was in the company of her intimate friend Maud Macfield, a charmer and debauched bacheloress of masculine mores. Both were extended on a low divan, covered in a sumptuous Chinese fabric, they were chatting and smoking Egyptian cigarettes.

"Yes," said Nora, "Jules is showing himself to be sufficiently generous, and I don't regret having favored him, all the more so as I believe that I'll be in Paris for some time. I've received very tempting offers from various impresarios, but I like it here, and I shan't leave France until I've exhausted all my fantasies here, even though that might perhaps annoy you, the nomad millionaires who likes to parade your pleasures across the world. Furthermore, I have a kind of presentiment that it's in France that I shall finally solve the enigma of my life."

"An enigma? A mystery?" said the American woman, interested. "What is it, then? In the six months that I've had the pleasure of knowing you, I haven't seen anything peculiar in your existence."

"How old do you think I am?" asked Nora, abruptly.

"I don't know. About twenty."

"When my father put me in the convent from which I ran away, he declared that I was ten years old. I stayed in the convent for two years, which makes twelve. Since that time, five years have gone by. I am, therefore still a minor and it's legally impossible for me to enter into legal contracts. If Paul Derval[8] hadn't been content with my physical appearance and had asked for my birth certificate, he wouldn't have hired me. To that abnormal growth, add this..."

The lovely girl kicked off the slipper in which she was shod, and, raising her foot to Maud's face, delicately took her nose between the thumb and forefinger.

"What do you say to that?"

"It's a strange anomaly...but there are, in certain individuals, such bizarre phenomena...especially in pregnant women. A *look*, as common parlance has it."

"Perhaps," said Nora, thoughtfully. "In fact, I hadn't thought of that. But there are within me aspirations to another, freer life—and more primitive too, but which attracts me nevertheless. At times I have crazy impulses to break, to bite...and, look at this!"

---

[8] The actor "Paul Derval" (Alexis Pitron, 1880-1966) acquired a part-share in the Folies Bergère in 1918 and staged revues there until his death

With her fingers, she pushed back her lips, revealing a jaw with magnificent teeth, but somewhat beyond the normal for size and strength. The canines, especially, stood out more forcefully than the rest. Nora picked up the silver sugar-tongs from the table, and without apparent effort, snapped them in two between her incisors.

"Damn!" exclaimed Maud. "I wouldn't like to be bitten by you! But that confirms my hypothesis: your mother, when pregnant, must have seen a great ape in some menagerie, In any case two prehensile feet are less important than a wine-stain in the middle of the face. But you were going, just now, to tell me your life-story. We have time—do it, and if, as you say, there's something mysterious about it, perhaps I can help you to clarify it."

"My life only really commences with my entry to the convent. What happened before that has not left me any memory. My father, I assume, was a physician, since the Mother Superior referred to him as 'Doctor.' I have even forgotten some of the events in which I took part at the convent. I learned easily, but my memory was very short, and it was only later that it began to acquire a certain fixity. Thus, all I remember about my father is his surname, because it's mine: Nora Goldry.

"It's true that the Doctor didn't come back to the convent to see me—he was traveling, it seems—but he sent my boarding fees regularly. Although I was one of the youngest pupils, I was the strongest and the most developed, and caused the good nuns considerable concern, because my intelligence surpassed the norm for girls of my age. The mystique of the milieu threw me into religious transports bordering on hysteria; the priest who confessed us every week further encouraged that tendency to religious exaltation, and I might perhaps have become a Saint Theresa or a Marie Alacoque,[9] if a fortunate children's book hadn't enabled me to escape the influence of my confessor.

"What tempted me in religion was the adoration of a beautiful Christ, everywhere displayed before our eyes in his human nudity. It was not God that I adored. The role of a supreme being making man in order to redeem a perverted humankind seemed to me rather puerile; in spite of its Christian education my mind was sufficiently critical; but I frankly adored the human form of that beautiful Christ and sensed an irresistible need to apply my flesh to it, emotionally. In many countries, all the cathedrals and all the chapels, women have a naked and suffering man to whom they can offer their desires and their unrealized dreams in that way..."

There was a brief silence, and the Nora went on:

"A little book given to me by a comrade deflected my thoughts completely. It was Madame d'Aulnoy's *Contes de fées*.[10] From then on, the beautiful Christ gave way to an imaginary being who pleased me all the more because nothing prevented me from giving him the face and form of the god of my dreams. In fact, my 'Prince Charming' didn't appear to me in velvet or silk. I repre-

---

[9] The mystic nun Marguerite-Marie Alacoque (1647-1690) was canonized in 1920, not long before *Nora* was written.

[10] The phrase *contes de fées*, adapted from the title of Madame d'Aulnoy's classic collection of 1697, was rendered into English at the time as "fairy tales" and that became a generic label for stories supposed to be of the same kind. It is, however, a mistranslation, and is more accurately rendered "tales of enchantment"—which would, in fact, have been a far better label for the genre. In the present text, I have translated *fée* correctly, as "enchantress," rather than conventionally, as "fairy."

sented him naked; but that didn't prevent me from giving him all the qualities of a prince, a friend of god.

"Oh, those enchantresses, good or wicked—how I loved them! How superior I found them to the saints who were offered to us as examples, with their futile martyrdoms and their uninteresting miracles. They, at least, were cheerful and fun-loving, they had affection for enticing princes and pretty princesses. Sometimes, they even protected a poor but handsome boy; they made him a king. I had an ardent imagination; how many themes I embroidered on fantastic adventures! I too was worthy of the sympathy of a good enchantress and the love of a king, of a Prince Charming. From then on, my religious mysticism was mingled with that fantastic world of fable. I prayed ardently to the beautiful Christ, but it was for him to descend from his cross and come with me to frolic through the world of the imagination.

"I wearied of that waiting, in which I found nothing but an exasperation of senses already awake, and since my idol was obstinate in remaining on his perch, I became determined to go into the world to search for my ideal: Prince Charming. Of the world, I knew nothing. Geographical instruction at the convent was extremely summary, my idea of it was based more on the spirit of the stories. I saw nothing there but magnificent flowers, shady woods populated by benevolent or mischievous spirits, enchantresses traveling in nacreous chariots drawn by doves or butterflies. Even the animals there were enchanted, and could speak; the streams were milk and honey. In brief, for me, exterior life ought to be a perpetual enchantment,

"I ruminated my escape. Thanks to my strength, my agility and my four hands, it wasn't difficult. One beautiful moonlit night, I climbed an oak tree whose branches surpassed the walls of the convent. I had knotted together several of the ropes we used for skipping. In a matter of minutes I was outside and set forth into the country. I had no idea of the location of the convent; all that I knew, from my companions, was that it was situated between Toulouse and Bordeaux.

"I walked until sunrise. Until then I had been following a dusty main road that did not respond very well to my caprice, but as I knew that it is by the most arduous routes that one arrives at lands of Enchantment, I was very hopeful.

"I was then in the heart of the country, a desert of rocks and clumps of woods; in the distance, high mountains were visible, where I seemed to see the silhouettes of medieval castles. I left the road to head toward those fantastic palaces in a straight line. The sun rose and became increasingly ardent. My feet, poorly protected by light shoes, began to hurt, and, very prosaically, I was drowsy, not having closed my eyes for twenty-four hours. As I came around a hillock, I suddenly caught sight of a hut made of branches and interlaced reeds and covered in thatch. I ran toward it, hoping to encounter the protective spirit I was seeking. There was no one there, but a thick litter of straw covered the floor. I fell into it, exhausted, and immediately went to sleep.

"I was woken up by a hand that was trying to be gentle. A tall man clad in a coarse jacket, knee-breeches and frayed leather gaiters was standing over me.

"'Hey, kid! What are you doing here?'

"I only half-understood his dialect. The man did not seem very old, but his face, continually baked by the sun, did not give the impression of a Prince Charming. He was more like one of those rural spirits who take on a rustic appearance to test the qualities and defects of young women they encounter.

"'My name is Nora, Monsieur Genie, and I've left the convent to look for Prince Charming.'

"The man started to laugh and sat down casually beside me. He was more accustomed to his local idiom than the French language, but he didn't have much difficulty with what he wanted to say to me. He was the initiator, my first lover. He was a herdsman in the service of his commune and was taking a flock of goats through the commons. At a certain time, when the kids were weaned, Janitou went to Bordeaux with thirty goats and sold the milk from door to door. He didn't make very much in that trade, but as he was violently smitten with me, his passion inspired him to evil thoughts. Until then he'd kept me in his cabin, bringing me bread and whatever he could steal from the farm: eggs, chickens or rabbits.

"That half-savage existence didn't displease me, and I let myself go in that sufficiently varied life, because, as well as sex with Janitou, there were crazy parties with the two dogs and the goats. Then came the time for the journey to Bordeaux. The herdsman couldn't leave me in the hut, hidden from the farmer; I went with the goatherd, sharing his nomadic life. He lodged me in the house of an old woman outside the city, and then went about his business. The sojourn in Bordeaux lasted a month or six weeks, after which he was supposed to return to the farm taking is receipts, and come back again until the milk ran out. When the work was finished, though, he didn't take the money back to his employer. He sold the goats, and with the produce of the sale we ran away to Spain.

"We lived happily for a while. Janitou bought me new clothes, and even a few pieces of jewelry. The situation improved, but it was still a long way from my dreams. When the resources diminished, Janitou took up smuggling, and I followed him through the mountains enthusiastically. Unfortunately for him, Janitou had companions, and they didn't take long to start pursuing me with their somewhat savage gallantries. Among them there was one very handsome fellow, Peppe Veno. He perceived that I wasn't indifferent to him, and proved to me that I was right to prefer him to the former goatherd. Janitou saw that; there was a fight, and the herdsman remained on the roadside, stabbed in the side. Peppe was obliged to flee, and I was devoid of a gallant.

"Oh, not for long! The brother of our innkeeper came to spend his leave at the inn—he was in the merchant navy. When he had to go back to his ship I went with him to Corogne, where it was docked. He came to an understanding with the captain, a lusty fellow, and I embarked for Buenos Aires, the destination of the voyage. During the crossing I was the queen of the ship, dividing my favors between Francesco and the captain.

"Why did I go to America? I don't really know. The desire to see something new, and perhaps to encounter, by that means, the land of my dreams. I sensed that the Enchantresses had deserted the old continent.

"Then there was a life of adventures, passing from one man to another according to circumstance: from Buenos Aires to Rio, from Brazil to Caracas, from Venezuela to the Antilles. In Cuba, I met a minstrel troop who took me with them; it was there that I acquired my first notions of dancing, for which I became passionate. With them, I set out for Mexico, where dancing is considered as an art.

"Then, there was the United States. Having left my black companions, I ran around the dives of Baltimore, dancing in sailors' cabarets. It was in one of those dens of cut-throats that William Armstrong, the great impresario from Boston, found me. From then on, there was success. Then, during her tour of America, Cécile Borel took an interest in me, and I came to Europe with her. You know the rest..."

"A beautiful life," said the American woman, "well worth the trouble of being lived. I envy you, my dear Nora, but apart from the singularity of your conformity, I don't see anything mysterious in your existence, and it would be easy enough to find your family by writing to the convent."

"But I don't know the name of the convent; all that I know is that it's located in Gascony. Then again, do you think that my father would be very pleased to find me again as I am? No. Besides which, I've lost all memory of him. Later, if I make myself an honorable life—in terms of social convention—perhaps I'll try to find him."

"You're right—I'm glad. This way, you'll remain entirely mine."

"You're mistaken, Maud, and you're trying to mislead me. Our friendship is too recent and has too much sensuality and lust in it to last long. As I've had the frankness to confess, I've had numerous lovers, but I haven't yet loved anyone."

"What idea do you have of love, Nora? Are you searching for something other than sensual satisfaction? I desire you, therefore I love you."

"No," said Nora, "there's something else, and that something else isn't lust. It's that ideal, that labor of our spirit, that makes us seek the impossible. It's akin to the

Prince Charming and the Christ of my childhood: very pure images, with which nothing imperfect is confused. They're within me: that's what love is."

"A love that isn't dangerous for anyone. Your flesh is too vibrant to be content with a dream."

"I recognize that, but the dream makes me scornful of the reality.

"Personally," said the American woman, "I don't fatigue my brain with that sort of metaphysics. I see a beautiful animal, and find it ravishing!"

"Because you've never been in love. So long as I live, I shall love my Prince Charming."

"And as you'll never find him, you'll continue to love with your senses."

"One only loves with the mind; the other thing is animality."

"But it's unhealthy, what's happening to you. I no longer recognize you today."

"It's remembering the past that's enlightened me. I've seen myself again, I've relived the sensations of old, and that has opened my eyes. I understand the ideal love of those religious fanatics better now; in their chastity they find a tenderness stronger than their bestial sensuality."

"Of which you oughtn't to deprive yourself. You're beautiful, mad and desirable, O brown flesh."

Nora shook her head. However, she allowed the American with the exquisite face—who was proud of her legs, of which her short skirts allowed the sight of her full and shapely knees—to draw her, like a little girl who has been hurt, over her thighs, muscled by sport.

III. Little Borneo

The place chosen by Doctors Voronoff and Goldry was an area east of Beaulieu, along the long high rocky cliff that borders the Great Blue, sometimes along the seashore and sometimes a kilometers distant from it. In one of those gulfs of the Riviera the American had established his refuge. The cliff, between one and two hundred meters high, forms an uninterrupted line all the way to Eze, which town and the ruins of its ancient château are its terminus. In the distance, and even higher, a second barrier rises against the east wind known as the Mistral: the Tête de Chien and La Turbie. It is a true *cagna*,[11] as they say in the region. In that already wooded retreat, Abraham Goldry had found a few hectares; nothing could have been more suitable for his plan.

It is well-known that, after the war, an immense quantity of materiel remained available—for example, immense metallic hangars that had served as shelters for dirigibles. It was, therefore, merely a question of reassembly; Goldry had been spoiled for choice. Only the end walls required more work, and with the necessary manual labor, the American had succeeded in erecting his simian refuge within a year.

---

[11] In Italian *cagna* means "bitch," and as La Turbie is close to the Italian border, all the more so as it is dominated by the rocky outcrop known as the Tête de Chien [dog's head], that would presumably be what the locals mean by it; the word, however, also exists in French slang, adapted from Vietnamese by colonial soldiers to refer to a dugout.

The works had been concluded four years ago, and the stud-farm—there is no other term to describe it—was in full production. Under metallic hangars twenty-five meters high, large trees and thick bushes, lianas, palm-trees and bamboos made a veritable tropic forest; the glazed roofs above the cages, also protected by grilles, allowed the air to be renewed and the heat to be maintained.

The cages were vast and well-lit, furnished with a comfort appropriate to their inhabitants. Because of the simian spirit of imitation, one central cage, visible from all the others, served as a school; servants clad in ape-skins combed themselves, brushed themselves and made the necessary ablutions there. Thus, in less than six months the residents were neat and rid of all vermin. A healthy and abundant nourishment, ropes, balloons and gymnastic apparatus maintained activity and merriment. So, the result was marvelous, and as soon as the second year—it requires six or seven years to grow to adulthood—the refuge was augmented by baby orangutans.

It was decided between the four doctors that the orangutans would be reserved for the mysterious important experiments, and that only chimpanzees and gibbons would be used for the grafting operations.

Dr. Fortin had notified Goldry of his arrival with Georges Clemenceau, the man who had been, for some time "the Savior of the Fatherland," so the American, highly distinguished, clean shaven, with that air of youthfulness that men of his nation conserve until advanced age, was waiting for them at the railway station. They climbed into the limousine, and in a matter of minutes, they were transported to the "paradise of apes." After the good lunch demanded by etiquette, Fortin,

Clemenceau and Goldry—Marc Vanel, busy in the laboratory, had asked to be excused—went out of the residential block by the back door and immediately found themselves in the forest.

"To every lord all honor," said Goldry. "First I'll show you my pupils, my orangutans."

A narrow path, perfectly maintained, plunged into the undergrowth, zigzagging somewhat, as if in order to be better hidden. Exotic trees—banyans, giant flamboyant magnolias, palms and bamboos—were combined with local ones: mimosas, climbing roses and arbutus. One advantage over virgin forest: no masses of detritus, dead wood or marshy areas encumbered the floor; on the contrary, fresh streams ran in all directions, vivifying grass of luxuriant thickness.

"But it's a veritable Eden!" exclaimed Clemenceau. "What a retreat for parliamentarians!"

"They'd rob our inmates," said Fortin. "That breed of ape is rather inconvenient and useless."

"I've been one," sighed the ex-President. "What a waste of time! That's what I think, in the twilight of life."

"There's our first cage," said Goldry. "Follow me."

Suspended from an enormous cedar, an iron ladder permitted climbing up to the thicker branches, extending horizontally seven or eight meters above the ground. There was a little platform there, and immediately facing, a footbridge leading to a gallery that went around three sides of the cage. The latter was ten meters square, giving a surface area of a hundred square meters. Six meters high, its summit reached the roof of the metallic enclosure. Climbing plants wound around the bars, hiding them almost entirely.

Doctor Goldry set out along the footbridge.

"You can follow me," he said. "My boarders are used to visitors."

The cage contained an orangutan couple, a two-year old male and a baby whose mother was still breast-feeding it. When the newcomers appeared, the two adults advanced and shook Dr. Goldry's hand.

The young orangutan was capering around the ropes that gave the illusions of lianas, being woven of green-dyed hemp; he stopped his game in order to leap on to Jean Fortin's shoulders; then, removing the worn beret that the doctor was wearing, he put it on his own head. That action appeared to irritate the father; he snatched the beret away from him and returned it to Dr. Fortin, who had approached the mother and was examining the infant.

As for the father orangutan, he appeared to strike up a conversation with Goldry, in which gestures played a greater role than words. Clemenceau was able to assure himself, however, that the articulated vowels were combined in some forty different words.

As soon as he went in, the statesman had experienced the malaise that all humans feel in the presence of those primates; they seem to be a kind of caricature of what we are. But that impression was rapidly overcome, and he took a keen interest in what he saw.

He drew closer to Dr. Fortin. "Well?" he said. "Are the mother and child doing well?"

"The infant is better," the scientist replied. "Teething's beginning—that's a critical moment for anthropoids. Look—the mother understands that I'm interested in her child."

Delicately picking up the little ape, Dr. Fortin sat him on his arm and stroked his head gently. The little one then emitted a kind of continuous purr. The mother took the doctor's hand and licked it.

"When I talk about them, I daren't say 'those animals.' See how easily these individuals have become accustomed to us, and what affection they seem to feel for their jailers. I believe that after two generations, we'll be able to give them the freedom of the refuge, and they'll return to their cages freely, which have become their homes. We have twenty more like this one, fourteen of which are inhabited. Soon, Dr. Marc Vanel will introduce you to a few subjects in psychological progression."

"Damn!" said Clemenceau. "You don't have the intention of making humans of them?"

Fortin smiled strangely, and winked at Goldry. "Do you remember, Georges, what you saw three days ago at the Folies Bergères?"

"Yes…but you're making fun of me."

"That's what you're going to see…Goldry!"

"What?" said the latter. "What is it?"

"I've found Nora. Monsieur Clemenceau can confirm it."

"Where? Are you sure?" Goldry stammered, hastening toward Fortin.

"Absolutely certain," he replied. "She's a woman now, but she hasn't changed so much that I, her creator, couldn't recognize her. Your daughter in now a star of the Parisian theater, and she's in the process of making her fortune—and that of her manager."

"What are we going to do, then?"

"Let her live her life, of course! What right do you think we have to intervene? She's a minor, but so what? It would be quite an affair to reconstitute her past in order to establish your rights. It would take less time to reconstitute another woman with a selected little ape."

"Oh!" Clemenceau put in. "Don't you think that humanity is bestial enough already?"

"Our dream," said Fortin, "is to regenerate the human species by renewing its vigor from the source."

The ex-President of the Council shrugged his shoulders. "Amuse yourselves, Messieurs les Scientists—but what's the point?"

The aged Dr. Fortin placed his hand on Clemenceau's shoulder. "You're a man of great intelligence, Georges. You're a physician, a man of letters, a politician—what do I know? But have you never revolted against the impotence of our comprehension before certain enigmas? Humans have penetrated everything—or, rather, made use of some of the creative or constitutive forces of our world. Today, we're beginning to perceive that life isn't concentrated on our globe, but that it extends throughout the universe, and that the universe is nothing but an ensemble of actions that are intimately connected with one another. For a long time, Terrans have believed that they were only linked to their own solar system, but now, with the revelation of cosmic waves, we have the proof that the universe has a binding force, that nothing is isolated in the ether that we call 'space.'

"Well, that which we can't comprehend, because our brains are not yet sufficiently developed, a superhuman might be able to decipher, tearing away the veil that masks the great mystery: the *why* of what *is*. What's the point of showering ourselves with marvels, if we don't know the reason for being? Every one of the creatures that populate the earth is a composite of other creatures. Nature—or, if you prefer, the creative force, the spirit, the soul of our globe—has had its infancy, its adolescence, its maturity. In what phase is it presently? We can't tell. In any case, it seemed to have proceeded from the horrible, the infamous and the monstrous to increasingly harmonious forms. Human beings, which we have the vanity of considering as the most perfect of those works, have taken thousands of years, perhaps hundreds of thousands, to become what they are today. Will they need as many more for their intelligence to comprehend the work in its totality?

"That can't satisfy contemporary humans. Their duty is to hasten, to accelerate the work of nature, and, if necessary, to bring it forward. And that's what my collaborators and I are trying to do; and, not being able to work with human beings—we'd be prevented from doing so—we're working on apes. The results we've obtained encourage us to persevere. You've seen Nora, the ape changed into a woman; we're going to continue, this time with a male, and who can tell what we'll obtain?"

"You're frightening, my dear Fortin! Two centuries ago, you'd have been burned as a sorcerer."

Goldry had drawn closer again. "How do you find our boarders, Monsieur le Président?"

"They're well on the way to reproduction."

"You've only seen my children, the orangutans of Borneo. Now I'll show you our breeding-stock destined for Voronoff's grafts: a few chimpanzees and fifty gibbons, experimentation having shown us that the results of virilization are the same by means of the latter."

The three men, Clemenceau, Goldry and Jean Fortin, came down, after having taken their leave of the orangutans, who escorted them very politely to the door.

Having gone back into the forest, they continued along the little path all the way to the extremity of the domain. That was where the dwelling of the quadrumanes was located: a residential block in brick, with a vast cage behind it, eight hundred square meters planted with trees and bushes. A clear stream leapt from rock to rock over a bed of sand and pebbles. Covered food-troughs were set here and there. Thus installed between the building and the cliff, forming a cul-de-sac, the apes lived in a constant temperature between thirty and thirty-five degrees; in case it dropped too far, the building could be heated.

As among the orangutans, the visitors were able to penetrate without danger, but here the apes seemed more suspicious and only allowed themselves to be approached fearfully. There, as everywhere else in the establishment, the greatest cleanliness reigned. Clemenceau remarked to Goldry, however, that some of the inhabitants seemed somewhat melancholy, and kept themselves apart from their joyful companions.

"They're our invalids," the American replied, "those who give humans their gift of energy. We prepare them in another lodging, because we've noticed that their presence makes the others suspicious. Voronoff doesn't want to kill them, for he hopes to be able to restore their virility, or to utilize them for other experiments...

"Look—there's a couple of chimpanzees who are particularly affectionate; they never quit one another and their arms are always linked. Several times already, the male, who is magnificent, has been chosen by clients, but Dr. Vanel has opposed it, so much does the attachment of those two individuals surpass the norm of simian sensibility. We call them Romeo and Juliet."

47

Abraham Goldry summoned the two quadrumanes, who immediately came closer, and gamboled around the doctor; he stroked them and gave them a few dry cakes.

"Humans are singular animals," said Fortin. "Look at Goldry, who has no wife or child; he's created a family and he loves his apes as if they really were his children. It's true that, if what he says is reliable, one of those orangutans, Narcisse, is the son of his great friend Ouha, the king of the apes, just as Nora is the daughter of a she-ape and Goldry."

Goldry's face had become crimson. "You know, Dr. Fortin, that that joke..."

"There's no shame in it, my friend. Personally, if I were certain of the result, I'd inseminate a crocodile or a rattlesnake. The truth is that our friend, during his sojourn in Borneo, was forced to yield to the lubricity of a female orangutan, and while he was collecting the orphans of Ouha's kingdom, he believed that he recognized his former mistress among the mothers whose offspring he removed. Not banal, eh, that story!"

"And the young Goldry?" asked Clemenceau, to tease the American.

"Narcisse, do you mean? You'll see him shortly."

"If I can ever lock you in with a she-ape, Fortin...!" snorted Dr. Goldry.

"There's no need to lock me in—I'll go of my own accord."

They visited the cage in detail, and the ex-Premier admired its features.

"It is, decidedly, all that a quadrumane could desire."

"Now we only have the study rooms to visit," said Dr. Fortin. "Here ends the Paradise of the Apes."

IV. Notes on Four Scientists

1. Abraham Goldry

In 1913, Dr. Abraham Goldry, an American subject and distinguished anthropologist left Philadelphia, where he was an honorary professor—Goldry did not actually teach; after having moved up through the university ranks, being rich, he had devoted himself entirely to research—in response to an invitation from a friend who had taken up residence in Borneo in Oceania with his daughter Mabel, Abraham's goddaughter. In order to convince her godfather to make the journey, Mabel had written to tell him that, thanks to the presence in Borneo of a young black woman named Dilou, they had captured an adult orangutan of remarkable intelligence. Dilou, the daughter of a coastal planter, had been abducted by the great apes and had lived with them for several years, and it was in order to get her back that the orangutan had allowed himself to be captured.

What luck for the anthropologist! He departed immediately for Borneo. The great ape charmed him, and he soon became his intimate friend; then, one day, Ouha-that was the orangutan's name—had escaped, abducting the woman again. They had pursued him; then, a Homeric struggle had commenced between the humans and the apes commanded by Ouha, which concluded with the defeat of the white men and the abduction of Mabel.

They could not leave the young woman in the hands of the ape. A great expedition was organized, which had no better result; many men were killed and Goldry was taken prisoner. Ouha, recognizing his old friend, had spared him and imprisoned him in a cave. There, the doctor had dressed in the skin of an orangutan killed in the battle and had become a kind of adviser to the simian monarch, to whom he rendered great services in wars with other tribes of apes—martial successes that had given Ouha the ambition of expelling all the humans from the island.

In the meantime, Mabel's father, Harry Smith, aided by a few friends, had resolved to make another attempt to rescue his daughter, and, force having failed, to employ cunning. This time, in fact, they succeeded, and brought Mabel and Goldry back to Riddle Temple. In the course of their captivity, the two prisoners had been obliged to submit to the consequences of their fatal situation; Mabel had become one of Ouha's wives, and had formed a sentimental attachment to him, and Abraham had been obliged to accept the caresses of a young she-ape, the widow of the orangutan Kri-Kri, whose skin he had been forced to put on.

Furious, Ouha had organized an army of three hundred orangutans and had marched on Riddle Temple in order to recover his wives, Mabel foremost, and a young Malay named Rava. The king of the apes had not anticipated the rainy season, though, and almost all of his army had perished miserably during the journey. When he finally reached Riddle Temple he only had thirty soldiers left; even so, he had engaged in battle, and had found death there, but taking Mabel and her father with him.[12]

---

[12] This is not what actually happens at the end of *Ouha*; it is not clear whether the text is merely simplifying in the interests of brevity, or whether the shocking conclusion of the novel is being censored from the account.

Goldry thus remained the proprietor of Riddle Temple. Should he return to America and attempt by all possible means to pursue his studies on the simian origins of humankind? The defeat and death of almost all the adult males of the orangutan tribe left the city of the apes defenseless. It was, therefore, the ideal moment to attempt a new expedition, with every change of success. Goldry organized a troop and, at the head of a hundred well-armed men, he had traversed the virgin forests yet again and invaded the orangutans' territory.

The battle was fierce; the young males and the females fought desperately to defend and project their offspring. In the end, however, the white men had the advantage of fierce, and Goldry returned to Riddle Temple with thirty young apes, including a son of Dilou and Ouha, and also a young female snatched from the cadaver of Kri-Kri's widow, who posed, for the doctor, an anguishing enigma of possible paternity.

To remain at Riddle Temple with that whole menagerie would have constituted a permanent danger; the females and a few males who had escaped the massacre had taken refuge with another tribe, and had recounted their misfortunes. All the orangutans of the island made the decision to vanquish them, determined to regain possession of the orphans. It was a war of skirmishes, because the anthropoids now feared the firearms that killed at a distance, but woe betide any man who strayed far from the temple! He was never seen again.

2. Serge Voronoff

Goldry, a member of several academies, and especially occupied with primates, had been in correspondence several times with the celebrated surgeon Serge

Voronoff, and was not unaware of his work on regeneration by glandular grafts.

The importation to France of thirty orangutans was bound to be of immense interest to Voronoff. Goldry wrote to him, and an active correspondence ensued, which resulted in the foundation of an establishment, a veritable stud-farm, for the elevation and reproduction of apes. Voronoff recommended a region to him, which, in terms of temperature and the purity of the atmosphere, seemed to fulfill all the necessary conditions for the establishment of a simian colony. It was in a corner of the Côte d'Azur, east of Beaulieu, near Eze.

Once the establishment was completed, Voronoff and Goldry immediately occupied themselves with their boarders, most particularly with the son of Ouha and the daughter of Kri-Kri's widow, and perhaps the American. Those two subjects seemed more progressive than the other orangutans.

In the meantime, Voronoff had occasion to remove the ovaries of a Russian ex-princess who wanted to amuse herself a great deal without running any risks.[13] The expert surgeon then had the idea of allowing the young she-ape to profit from that windfall. He therefore had Nora brought into the next room, and carried out the double operation very adroitly.

The result, for the young orangutan, was surprising; her intelligence increased in a sensible manner, and when she reached the age of two—the age of puberty in

---

[13] In an era when contraception was awkward and unmentionable, it was rumored that many women of high status but loose morals employed hysterectomies as a means of solving the problem.

the apes—her menstrual discharges, which in apes, are white, became red.

3. Marc Vanel

At that time, a friend of Goldry's came to visit Little Borneo, that being the name by which the establishment of the Côte d'Azur was known. And, quite naturally, Goldry introduced Nora and Narcisse—the son of Ouha and Dilou—to Marc Vanel, the fantastic scientific genius. The latter than had the idea of attempting one of those fabulous experiments that made him a kind of sorcerer or demigod:[14] to transform the she-ape into a woman, thus accomplishing in a few months, the work into which nature had put thousands of years!

A tempting project for that formidable intelligence!

A mysterious conference took place between Drs. Vanel, Goldry, Voronoff and Jean Fortin; from that collaboration a marvelous phenomenon was born: the fantastic ballerina Nora, who became, as soon as she made her debut at the Folies Bergère, one of the queens of Paris.

How? By what means?

But one fact summons another. Before going any further, it is necessary to say that Marc Vanel, a universal scholar, had a mind capable of resolving all the enigmatic secrets of nature. A pupil of Jean Fortin, the

---

[14] At this point the author refers the reader to *Homo-Deus, le satyre invisible*. As with *Ouha*, however, his brief synopsis of the earlier novel leaves out the actual conclusion, which seems to have been completely erased from the "history" assumed by the present novel, along with two of the characters featured therein.

young scientist had left France following a disappointment in love; the precocious misanthrope drowned his sorrows by traveling. He spent ten years roaming the world, particularly in India, where he was initiated into all the mysteries of the fantastic practices of fakirs and yogis. Then he returned to Europe, where he undertook research into the invisibility of certain substances. He reasoned that, if certain solid substances like sand and potassium can give birth to a transparent substance, such as glass, water or atmospheric air, then it was possible to attain the invisibility of the human body.

The research was long and difficult, but it finally succeeded. Since then, Marc Vanel merited his nickname, Homo-Deus: the man-god, the invisible being who, like the creative will, could make his efforts felt without being seen.

4. Jean Fortin

Marc Vanel then returned to Paris with his formidable secret, and entered into collaboration with his former science teacher, Jean Fortin. Fortin too was a scientist of unlimited genius. He had, most of all, made a specialty of the psychic sciences, aided, and perhaps overtaken, by his daughter Jeanne, an elite individual, a veritable personification of science.

The association of those three monstrous intellects had inevitably led them to carry out fantastic experiments. They resuscitated a cadaver, and did it so well that they attracted the fierce hatred of a trio of bandits. One night, they were attacked at Dr. Fortin's house at Saint-Cloud, the *Red Nest*. The battle was desperate on either side; the three bandits perished, but Jeanne Fortin was mortally wounded.

It was then that in those three unparalleled minds the formidable thought was born of vanquishing death. With the will-power of her father combined with her own, Jeanne caused her spirit—her soul, her self—to pass into that of Marc Vanel, her spiritual spouse.

"Death is vanquished!" Vanel cried, when he sensed his soul, his mind, doubled by that of Jeanne Fortin. That is why, from time to time, Marc Vanel will address Dr. Fortin, in the course of this story, as "Father."

Such was the quartet of fantastic doctors—Marc Vanel, Jean Fortin, Serge Voronoff and Abraham Goldry—who undertook the strange metamorphosis of Nora, the ape who became a woman.

V. How to Make a Woman and a Man

Drs. Georges Clemenceau, Jean Fortin and Abraham Goldry had retraced their route in an inverse direction. To the right of the main house were the workrooms, where all the most modern methods and instruments were employed, as well as an immense laboratory for chemical manipulations and the utilization of cathode rays. Nothing was lacking, even an observatory—which, however, had nothing to do with the aim of the establishment.

"Who can tell?" Fortin had said one day. "One of our orangutans might become a great astronomer."

On perceiving the individual who came to open the door to them, Clemenceau took a step backwards. There was good reason: an orangutan nearly six feet tall stood before him, and greeted him with a respectful: "Bonjour. Monsieur le Président."

Reassured, the excellent and ferocious gentleman with the abundant white moustache burst out laughing.

"Damn! What's this new masquerade?"

Marc Vanel came forward "Excuse me, Monsieur le Président, for not having accompanied you, but I was completing an experiment that could not be postponed."

"It would be for me to apologize if I had disturbed you, but I didn't think you were so facetious..."

"Oh, I understand your error. Permit me to introduce Monsieur Narcisse."

"Narcisse!" murmured the former President of the Council.

"Delighted to meet you, Monsieur Clemenceau. I have a book about you by Gustave Geoffroy,[15] which I found very interesting." And he extended toward the visitor a hand that was twice as big as one of his.

"But...but...am I mad?" said the other, alarmed.

"Not in the least, my dear Monsieur. My genre of beauty seems strange to you, but what do you expect? An orangutan, in spite of being named Narcisse, can't resemble an Antinous."

"An orangutan? You? But you can talk..."

"I can talk and I can think, thanks to Monsieur Vanel."

"Truly, I'm wondering whether I'm really awake, or dreaming."

"We're going to explain all that," said Vanel. "Let's go into my study. In the meantime, Narcisse, you can finish making a clean copy of the notes that we were in the process of sorting out."

Narcisse bowed, and sat down tranquilly in the mobile chair in front of a vast desk.

"Let's begin at the beginning," said Marc Vanel, when they were all comfortably seated. He addressed Jean Fortin: "It appears, Father, that you've found Nora?"

"Yes, now an accomplished woman, and furthermore, a choreographic artiste at the Folies Bergère. A great personality, a star."

---

[15] *Clemenceau* (1918). Geoffroy—whose name was more usually spelled Geffroy—had previously written for Clemenceau's newspaper *La Justice*, and Clemenceau appointed him as director of the Gobelins tapestry factory in 1908.

"I believe, since you know Nora and have admired her with us at the Folies Bergère, that it's with her story that it's appropriate to begin. According to what our friend Goldry has told us, this Nora is his own progeniture, with a she-ape with whom circumstances put him in relationship on the island of Borneo, just as Narcisse is the son of a native woman named Dilou and a heroic orangutan, Ouha, nicknamed the king of the apes.

"When Goldry came here, on the advice of our friend Dr. Voronoff, Nora was scarcely two years old. At that time, Voronoff had to perform an ablation of the ovaries on a slightly mad Russian princess. He decided to take advantage of the opportunity to graft the princess's ovaries into the young ape. Shortly afterwards, in my turn, I entered the lists. A kind of phenomenon had occurred within the young ape after the operation; her vitality had increased, her hair became longer and more supple, her intellect, above all, was superior to that of all her peers. It was a marvelous experimental field, and I took care not to miss it. To make that sketch into a woman—a true woman—seemed to me to be desirable, and I devoted myself to it with enthusiasm.

"Once, my father and I had succeeded in creating arterial blood by means of a tissue culture. This time, it was necessary for us to find the formula of the primordial atom—the atom constitutive of every living thing...let us say, in parenthesis, that everything of which the earth is comprised is alive; death does not exist; everything is transformed; nothing is created from nothing, and in the same way, nothing is destroyed..."

"There are, however, dead things," Clemenceau interjected. "Minerals."

"Minerals, like everything else: debris of beings that have been. Time is nothing in the ensemble of phenomena that rule the planet. It requires thousands or hundreds of thousands of years for a mass of vegetation to become peat, as many for that peat to become coal, and similarly for porphyry or granite to become what they presently are."

"But what about rocks of a plutonian nature, vitrified issues of the molten earth?"

"La la! Don't get carried away! If the center of the globe were molten, it would be considerably dilated, and in consequence, less heavy than it is; in the same way that making glass requires sand and potassium, to make granite or any other vitrified stone requires vitrifiable matter. Soft beings produce hard bodies like coral and seashells. Those are the foundations of the solid part of the globe, and there is no other. In the beginning there was nothing but living matter, a primordial atom that was, and still is, the basis of everything that exists.

"Thus, there's no need to seek elsewhere for that microcosm; it is in everything and everywhere, in ourselves as in a tree or a blade of grass. It was sufficient, therefore, once it was found, to isolate it and care for it, as one develops parts of organs in culture media; as with an arm or a piece of meat, once can continue to nourish it, and even to progress it, cell by cell. The soil itself is something living; it contains billions and billions of micro-organisms that work for plants, preparing their humificatory aliments."

"The primordial atom is unique," said Clemenceau, gravely. "Just as an early Christian said 'I believe in God,' it's an act of faith in science."

"But its combinations," Dr. Vanel went on, "are innumerable, and as life develops on the globe, the atom combines with its own residues to form the primal infusoria. Let's not follow that gradation—you're familiar with it. Let's return to the organic cell that I needed in order to modify a living bring.

"In sum, it was necessary for me to do, in a few months, the work that nature accomplishes in thousands of centuries. I was in the presence of a two-year-old ape—which, in terms of simian growth, corresponds to the age of ten in human growth. That constituted a further difficulty, since, for what I wanted to do, I would have required a much younger child. Let us take, in thought, a human being and observe her growth, her development. By what strange phenomenon does that individual grow and develop? It's evidently by the gradual augmentation of organic cells—but what gives birth to those cells? Is it uniquely nutrition, or do we possess special organs that spread those cells within the body in some fashion, augmenting strength and stature? Yes! And those organs are the glands, the glands whose importance was neglected for so long, which are the source of our physical progression—and, can I affirm here, our psychic progression, since Nora is the proof of it."

"Then Nora, the ape who has become a woman, is really the daughter of science?"

"To describe to you all the operations, all the manipulations, grafts and inoculations we carried out would be rather tedious, my dear President, because all of that could only be done with infinite precaution. The main thing was the intellectual progression, because it was able to aid the physical progression powerfully, via magnetic suggestion. We know now that the concentration of thought toward a unique end can influence an organ to the point of modifying it. The difficulty, in my case, was procuring the pineal gland of a living man or woman and grafting it on to Nora's brain.

"Finally, I found what I needed; one of the foremen who was working here fell victim to an accident; a metal plate fell and broke his back. The man was doomed. I took advantage of it, and before he died I carried out an ablation of the pineal gland and grafted it into Nora. My injured man was a mine. I also took the thyroid gland and grafted it in the same way. That was a great deal all at once, but I had no choice. Fortunately, orangutans have an astonishing resistance. To make the graft I was obliged to trepan the subject. I took advantage of it to raise the cranial cavity, in order to make more room for the encephalum and permit its development without the brain being compressed. That work was done with bone taken from a living animal. Fortunately, my ape held on, and I was able to pursue my enterprise."

"By what method did you procure the cells?"

"Oh, the simplest: the testicles of a chimpanzee, placed in the same culture medium I've already mentioned. The organ lived therein, was nourished and, on the other hand, spread its production of cells through the medium in which it existed—in sum, the same phenomenon that occurs in our organism.

"I then had a statue made by a sculptor, in accordance with the modern esthetic, and then a mold made, hollowed out in that form. That statue was the size of a ten-year-old child, the equivalent of my simian subject. Needless to say, I had to shorten the arms of my ape, Nora, by breakages, and elongate the legs by gradual traction using lead weights. The subject, in a magnetic trance, placed herself in the mold, where I compressed and softened her form, as an artist manipulates clay. At the same time, with a Pravaz syringe, I stuffed the thin parts, so to speak, with organic cells.

"That work cost me an entire year—with, of course, the aid of my colleagues, Fortin, Voronoff and Goldry. At the end of the year, however, the work was complete. Nora was born…the ape had become a woman."

"And then?" asked Clemenceau, breathless with emotion.

"Afterwards? Nora was then three simian years of age, eleven in feminine appearance. Her intelligence was somewhat in advance of her age. Goldry, her adoptive father, recognized her legally under the name of Nora Goldry; then he put her in a boarding-school with the Mères du Saint-Pleur at Gadijoz in the Dordogne.[16] She stayed there for two years; then, one night, she climbed over the wall of the convent and disappeared. And now, five years later, my father, Dr. Fortin, and I have just rediscovered her in Paris, in a music hall, the Folies Bergère. You applauded her with us."

"Marvelous!" said the Tiger, "I can't find any other word: marvelous! But that isn't all! What about the other, Narcisse?"

"Narcisse is something else, and much more interesting than making a puppet, like the majority of humans! In sum, an improved ape isn't as marvelous as you've just claimed, but to raise an ape to the dignity of a superhuman was much better: the same procedures as for Nora, but uniquely directed toward the goal of intellectual development.

---

[16] The name of this fictitious order might be derived from a story by Jean Richepin, "Le Saint-Pleur," published in the illustrated supplement of *Le Figaro* in 1891.

"Narcisse has conserved the simian appearance, but if you had looked at him more carefully you would have noticed that his forehead doesn't slope backwards, that his facial angle is the same as ours. The cranial cavity is larger by a third than ours, and two pineal glands have been grafted into his brain, plus a thyroid. In addition, I've worked on his larynx, and loosened the tongue and the vocal cords. As he told you himself, he talks and he thinks.

"He thinks! He understands me! He will be my equal, will surpass me, and will be what I desire: a superhuman. What does it matter that he's ugly? Physical beauty is only a convention, and Narcisse is a being who is advancing by several rungs along the ladder of progress..."

"The ladder of progress!" stammered the Tiger. "In the name of God! These people are driving me mad—I can feel my skull splitting."

"Well, well!" exclaimed Dr. Fortin. "The Tiger going dingo? That would be funny."

And the eccentric scientist sketched out the steps of a tango around the room. Then, stopping suddenly in front of the former President of the Council, the victor of the Great War, he said: "That's not all, my dear Georges. You don't think I've brought you here with the sole aim of allowing you to admire the establishment and those who inhabit it?"

"Why, then?" said the other, nonplussed. "You don't have the intention of taking me as a boarder?"

"No, your grimaces are too well-known. I simply thought of you in order to find a place for Narcisse. We don't want to make him a functionary, you understand, or a député. You're in the Académie but don't sit there.

Cede your place to him, make him your secretary and representative. He'll be exactly what's needed."

"Thank you, Fortin, but you're forgetting that I've withdrawn completely into the shadows. I think I have something that would suit you much better. What would you say to Ernest Paris?"

"An idea of genius!" exclaimed Fortin, tapping him on the thigh. "Voronoff is feeling him out just now for a graft. God's chamber pot! He's exactly the man we need! With him, Narcisse will find himself in an intellectual milieu, and, as Ernest Paris is becoming increasingly lazy, Narcisse will give him a hand to finish the book, *Le Vrai Jésus*, which he announced such a long time ago.

"Well, you can consider it as done. Ernest Paris can't refuse me; then again, Narcisse's physique is bound to please him, for, by contrast, that old white biped horse will look like an Apollo."

VI. Two Great Men at Liberty

The fourth night of May was particularly beautiful. So, on leaving Madame de Virmile's house, where he had spent the evening, Ernst Paris had a whim to go back to the Avenue Foch on foot. He had just met Dr. Jean Fortin, the Marquise's brother, at his old friend's house, for Madame de Virmile, in spite of her appearance of old nobility, had been born simply Fortin, of which she was much less proud than of her pearly crown. The doctor only came to his sister's house very rarely, so Ernest Paris had been glad to find him there, and it was, in sum, the pleasure of chatting one-to-one with the illustrious scientist that inclined him toward a nocturnal pedestrian stroll. The air was sweet and mild, the young leaves exuding a fresh odor of new sap. Paris passed his arm beneath that of the scientist, and they both set forth; the two automobiles followed meekly.

"It's a stroke of luck for me to have encountered you this evening, my dear Fortin, I've been wanting to see you for a long time. Why do you never come to visit me?"

"I have so little free time. It's necessary for me to be absolutely forced to see my sister over some matter of interest, and then not for long—the Marquise prefers seeing my heels to my face."

"You remind our dear Marquise of her humble origins. Did you hear her going on about the celebrations organized in Orléans and Paris from the ninth of May to Sunday the twelfth, for the fifth centenary of Jeanne d'Arc. Fundamentally, she doesn't care a fig about the Maid of Orléans, but she's made it into a question of politics, a party matter. She's more royalist than the king!"

"Yes. Once again the clergy are profiting from the occasion. So why have the imbeciles of the parliamentary swamp established a national holiday to celebrate a humble hysterical peasant whom the clergy want to make into a saint? Sanctify the Maid! It's diabolically clever."[17]

"Those people are always very strong, and our governments always cut rods for their own back. French ineptitude in full swing. The road to Reims is being marked out with plaques; statues to St. Jeanne d'Arc are being raised everywhere; flags, processions, illuminations... But you, Doctor, believe, medically, that the legendary individual was merely a neurotic, a hysteric? In any case, some people claim that a whore was substituted for Jeanne d'Arc in her prison, and that the Maid, liberated, went on to have children."

"It's obvious. Every era has individuals thus disposed, in their youth, to act beyond reason—and it still goes on. It's a kind of madness that, although innocent in appearance, can create fanatical murderers when overexcited by political passions."

"The Maid has always intrigued me somewhat. If the subject hadn't been done to death I'd have been tempted to write a few pages about her. I can't stomach all this stupidity. The pages in question remain in the limbo of my consciousness, like the book that's been announced everywhere, *Le Vrai Jésus*."

"You have a passion for stirring up all these old frog-ponds! What can these old legends, denuded of all

---

[17] Jeanne d'Arc had already been canonized, in 1920, three days after Marie Alacoque.

interest, matter to our generation, which has already learned useful things? A legend! One can dress it up any way one likes!"

"Stop there, my dear friend. Don't blaspheme against legend; that's perhaps the truest thing in the history of the world, if only because legend can lend itself to any fantasy, whereas, in order to write history, one is the butt of continual contradictions. Look, since we've put the Maid in the dock, will you permit me a few hypotheses that will link the past with our era? I'll be careful not to submit them to our lovely Marquise."

"Go ahead," said Dr. Fortin. He sensed that Ernest Paris was entirely disposed to sustain the controversy indefinitely, and did not really want to take part in it.

"Jeanne d'Arc," the speaker commenced, "whom legend credits with saving France, in fact, only saved the monarchy. After the liberation of Orléans, which wasn't very difficult, what was the first concern of God's envoy? Was it to fight the English? Not at all. It was to go and have Charles VII crowned in Reims. It was necessary, in that era when royalty had real value, for the king to be crowned in order to oppose genuine force to the Angevin dynasty of the Plantagenets. It was also to rally the French aristocracy, who, until then, had sold themselves to the highest bidder. Let's pass on. That's not where I want to get to. There was no battle between two peoples, but only a legal quarrel over succession between two feudal houses, the Valois and the Plantagenets.

"Let's suppose that the Valois had been defeated and the English—who already possessed the entire south-west of France and a large part of the north, including Paris—had been victorious. Let's look at the consequences of that apparent defeat: firstly, today, we'd no longer think that, after centuries of Roman conquest, the Gaulois were only thinking about Gaul, any more than that, later, they didn't take any account of the Frankish conquest. People adapt themselves to events and, as time passes, even everything out. Which gives us, with regard to the question of patriotism, a duration of a few centuries; at the end of that time, people have forgotten what they were and assimilated themselves to the new life..."

"Well, then," said Dr. Fortin, "Charles VII and his great vassals, vanquished and submissive to the law of the stronger, as you seem to desire, have recognized the sovereignty of English law. So what?"

"Although a people doesn't change its mores and its language very quickly, inevitably, the greater number impose themselves on the smaller. The English would be frenchified, and the French anglicized. Result: the fusion of two rival nations into a single whole, each collaborating in accordance with its genius and dominating the rest of Europe by means of a maritime littoral to which the rest of the world is submissive. It's quite evident that the north would join, spontaneously or forcibly, that industrial and intellectual nucleus; so the Belgians, the Dutch, the Danes and the Swedes fuse with the Anglo-French, and, by contact, attract the Latin peoples. What can the peoples of the center do, stifled by that iron belt? They unite with it, and the United States of Europe is realized. Consequence: all the wars of various duration are avoided, until the present day; peoples not divided by hatreds born of intestinal struggles—especially the last war of 1914-19, a war disastrous for the victors and vanquished alike; and finally, the employment of a universal language, English, throughout the world."

"You're going a bit far, my dear and paradoxical friend. If our diehard patriots could hear you…!"

"I'll go further still. If humankind were less stupid; if there weren't so many various parties; if universal egotism were replaced by a spirit of cooperation; if humankind finally understood its true interest; if we even understood our own affairs outside all our petty chapels, what do you think we would do if we were wise?"

"Speak! Perhaps, my dear, you're about to resolve a great problem."

"Huh! Unfortunately, it's only a fantasy, which would be treated humorously if I, Ernest Paris of the Académie Française, published it. Well, if France were intelligent, she would do what the Savoyards have done; she would give herself to the strongest. She would give herself to America, and by that means, liquidate her debt. Notice that if France doesn't offer herself to John Bull, she'll fall into the power of America regardless, because America, being too rich, is placing her capital in Europe and becoming its proprietor. Have you calculated how much territory England and America have bought in Europe, particularly in France, since the great and ignoble war? I'll wager it's a twentieth, and, thanks to the elevation of the exchange rate, our allies will continue. They have a stranglehold on all the markets in the world, send them up and down at will. Within a century, if we're not careful, the old world will belong to the new.[18]

"What would happen, on the other hand, if, in accordance with the hypothesis I put forward just now,

---

[18] This must, of course, have been written before the Wall Street Crash of October 1929. On the other hand, some people might contend that it happened anyway.

France offered herself benevolently to America and nailed her tricolor flag to the stars and stripes?

"Firstly, the liquidation of the debt; and then, by virtue of the attraction of our civilization, our Latin spirit, which will always be superior to all others, the fusion would take place, I believe, to our advantage. In the same way that the juice of the vine is bound to replace cold and heavy beer, the Gallic spirit will put an end to glacial and hypocritical Lutheran dogmas, to make way for the mild philosophy of our forefathers.

"There are two methods of conquest without cannon: conquest by money and conquest by religion. Religions have been killed by bigotry, by the diffusion of schisms; money alone is an uncontested master. However, money can only reign by constantly making dupes. The man who gains ruins three of four associates, often more; and America is the mistress of that order of things. Fortunes are made and unmade continually there. Why? Because her people, which was not one to begin with, being a composite of all the races of the old world, has but one aim: money; and money for its own sake, not the pleasures that it can bring.

"That young world, which does not known how to live, requires education by the old, the only one capable of idealism, of enthusiasm for the just and the beautiful. Races that have only practical ends need to be coupled with prodigal races. That's why I sustain that France ought to add herself to the United States of America, and that, if she leads the way, the other states will follow her example, and then we shall have the United States of the World!"

"I'll align myself frankly with your idea, my dear friend—but as you said just now, someone other than me might not take it seriously."

"Because people are stupid. In French blood—and, I dare say, that of all countries—successive invasions have completely drowned that of the primitive. Who among us can boast of having pure Gallic blood in his veins? All the peoples in our territory are mixtures, since the Romans issued from the Greeks to the Germans issued from the races of the North and East—not forgetting the Arabs, the Spaniards, the English and the Normans. The only pure races that still exist, very nearly, are those of Indonesia and Oceania. What sense, then, is there in our nationalism? Who can boast of being a pure Frenchman? And even then, the Franks came from Germany; the sons are enemies of their ancestors. Conclusion: patriotism is ridiculous in confrontation with reason. People quarrel and kill one another for a label stuck on a street-corner. Anyone who crosses that boundary is my enemy, and I have the right and the duty to murder him. Confess, my dear doctor, that an intelligent man cannot recognize such doctrines!"

"I agree entirely—but what you're saying to me, whom you know to be an internationalist, you wouldn't dare to write."

Ernest Paris started laughing. "Certainly not! Not like that. I'd be stoned. Which doesn't alter the fact that, if we're in a mess, it's the fault of Jeanne d'Arc!"

"Here we are at your door. I'll go back to my car. Come and see me in Saint-Cloud, at the Red Nest. I won't talk to you about some social question or other, but good scientific verities."

"That's all that raises the priority of modern humans above the animals. Intellectually, they're well below the level of the ancient Greeks and Romans."

"How do we know? We judge the ancients by the elite of the nation; it's as if one judged the French mind by the elite of ours: Voltaire, Rousseau, Molière, Rabelais, Montaigne, Victor Hugo and others. The great mass of people was doubtless no more intelligent than ours."

"I like to believe otherwise."

"Having preferences proves nothing. You're judging the minds of two or three thousand years ago. You know as well as I do, however, that there were other anterior civilizations that were worth as much."

"In sum, my dear Fortin, I think the stupid fraction of humankind doesn't merit others thinking on its behalf."

"To whom are you speaking? Marc Vanel and I have tried to take an interest in it. Pooh! I still have nausea. You know that a large part of my life has been taken up by the study of mental function in human beings. I've demonstrated to the public that the human self can be removed, displaced and exchanged between people, forewarned or not—which is to say, with their consent or against their will. Of what is the force of influence that can thus vanquish the will comprised? We've given it the name of magnetism, or hypnotism, but in reality that force remains rather enigmatic.

"There are fluidic forces escaping the magnetizer to influence the magnetized. An example: throw a stone into a pond. Ripples spread out from the point of the fall to the limits of the pool. Throw a stone into the middle of the Ocean, and the same phenomenon occurs. Produce a vibration in the air, and the same thing will happen. The vibration extends to infinity, without limits, more and more attenuated for our ears, the more distant it is from us, but having the same force everywhere that the sonorous vibration passes. Starting from that viewpoint, it might be the same with thought, with psychological force. It simply requires thought to propagate like sound, light and electric waves.

"That is, for me and my collaborator Marc Vanel, habitually very easy. Many times, Homo-Deus and I have practiced, on ourselves and others, the exteriorization of the self. It was therefore necessary to fix that exteriorization by some means, wasn't it? That means, we've found—and that's the key to our discovery: enclosed in our brain, the psychic wave that escapes, for example, from my brain, can only be perceived by a brain whose self is similarly exteriorized. Then, the two minds can enter into communication and understand one another. For them, distance no longer exists, and the undulation of thought extends without boundaries and without limits. Without limits! That's the hypothetical side of P.T.C."

"Psycho-Telepathic Communication—yes, I know," said Ernest Paris.

"The future of the science is the utilization of the formidable movement of waves that surrounds us and escapes from all living beings, and all metals. The atom itself, you know, is nothing but a movement of rays, of radiation, reminiscent, in miniature, of the movement of stars in the universe..."

Dr. Fortin perceived that Ernest Paris was beginning to become inattentive to that scientific verbiage, and was contemplating the stars amorously.

"But enough about that subject, my dear. You know that you're still expected at Voronoff's. He has an ape reserved for you. Good night, my friend. Dream of the regeneration of peoples—and your own!"

The two men, Ernest Paris and Jean Fortin, looked at one another for a moment in silence. Each one was following his own thought or dream—they were, at any rate, a long way from one another, on the deserted Avenue Foch, where their autos were waiting for them.

They shook hands, and Jean Fortin climbed into his car in order to go back to his house at Saint-Cloud, the Red Nest.

"Don't forget that Voronoff's expecting you," the doctor repeated, as an adieu to his companion.

Ernest Paris made a sign of ironic acquiescence. Fortin's auto pulled away in the direction of Saint-Cloud, and the novelist Ernest Paris, of the Académie Française, went back into his house, in the peaceful Villa Saïd,[19] to which the mild nocturnal breeze coming from the nearby Bois de Boulogne was bringing the freshness of spring.

---

[19] Anatole France lived, toward the end of his life, at no. 5 Villa Saïd, at one end of the Avenue Foch. The Rue Spontini, where Nora supposedly lives, is at the other end, within easy walking distance

VII. Nora Before Nora

One day Nora received a strange visit.

Berthe, her chambermaid, brought her a visiting card:

ABRAHAM GOLDRY
Professor of Anthropology, University of Philadelphia

"Goldry!" the dancer exclaimed; but my name is Goldry too! What if it's my father! Send him in..."

She advanced to meet the visitor.

"Excuse my indiscretion," said the doctor, bowing to the dancer. "I've authorized myself to make this visit because of a similarity of names, which, if I'm not mistaken, might renew a relationship between us broken some time ago."

"I believe so too," said Nora, "for your face brings back vague memories."

"Are you the Nora Goldry who ran away from the convent of Saint-Pleur at Gadijoz?"

"Yes," the young woman stammered. "And you must be...my father."

"No! That is to say...one never knows. But I am your father by adoption, and it's by that entitlement that I've come to put myself at your disposal, in case I can be useful to you."

"I had an instant of hope! You adopted me you say? Then you knew my family?"

"Yes...that is to say, almost."

"I don't understand—explain. What is your objective is coming to see me?"

"To assure myself that my friend, Dr. Jean Fortin, was not mistaken in notifying me of your probable identity."

"Well, now you're informed. So, what do you want from me?"

"As I told you, my dear Nora, to place myself at your disposal. I adopted you, child; will you refuse to allow me to continue the role of father that I once filled with such scant success?"

"In fact, I committed an act of ingratitude toward you—but I truly don't have the courage to regret it. In any case, the isolation in which you left me authorized it to some extent. Don't you agree?"

"I too don't permit myself the slightest reproach—but since hazard has brought us together, would you not like to have some affection for the person whose name you bear?"

"Certainly!" exclaimed Nora, extending her hand to the doctor. "I shall consider you as a father..."

"Gently, gently!" said the American. "I can't accept that title—but as your best friend..."

"As you please—so be it! You can't give me any information about my parents, then?"

"Alas, no—not at present. Later, perhaps, when you're ready."

Nora stamped her foot. "More mysteries! There's something abnormal about me. You're a doctor, you've seen me as a child, you know about *this*, and *that*." She indicated her jaw and her foot. "What can these anomalies signify?"

"Pooh! Nothing extraordinary. A simple emotion of your mother while she was carrying you. But if you would like to pay me a visit at the house of my friend Dr. Voronoff, where I stay when I'm in Paris, with his help, we can elucidate the matter. A visit to his Institute is, in any case, very interesting."

"The name of that doctor isn't unknown to me."

"He's the greatest of our surgeons, the first one to attempt the renovation of the sexual organs by grafting."

"I confess that that question doesn't interest me, and if it weren't for the pleasure of returning your visit..."

"An idea! Are you free today?"

"Yes, until it's time for the theater."

"And I'm leaving this evening to return to Eze. So, my dear child, I'll take you to lunch at Voronoff's. Don't fear being indiscreet; it's as if I were in my own home there."

"And what can be seen at your friend's home?"

"All sorts of things related to human beings. Among others, you'll see some of my boarders. I brought eight of them the day before yesterday."

"You have a strange way of talking about your patients. One might think it were a matter of dogs or cats."

"Well, it's a little like that. Come on, then—my auto is waiting for us."

"I accept—just give me time to put my hat on, and I'm all yours."

Left alone, the doctor rubbed his hands. "I think, as Fortin would say that we're going to have some fun!"

He did not have to wait long. Nora returned, clad in a short skirt and a dainty hat, ready to go out.

"Let's go, my adoptive father—take me away!"

At the Institute in Auteuil they were greeted by Dr. Jean Fortin. Voronoff was not there.

"Aha! Here's our beautiful fugitive, then! You see, Goldry, that I wasn't mistaken."

"You know me, then, Monsieur?" asked Nora.

"As if I'd made you," replied the incorrigible ironist.

"I've invited her to have lunch with us."

"Good idea, all the more so as Voronoff has been obliged to go to Orléans for an interesting operation. He'll greatly regret not having seen Mademoiselle. On the other hand, I'll have the pleasure of introducing her to Dr. Vanel. He came back to Paris this morning, and he's gone to supervise the unloading of the apes. Let's go into the dining room; he'll join us there."

During that conversation Nora admired the exquisite cleanliness of the surroundings. All the rooms and corridors that she had traversed were well-ventilated and illuminated. The walls and ceilings were covered in white ripolin slightly tinted with lilac. Flowery friezes in bright colors ornamented the walls. The doors were made of varnished pitch pine, with hinges and locks of polished copper. Everything was fresh, bright and cheerful. There was no useless furniture; the chairs were comfortable, the tables covered with plates of glass. Here and there, a few tubular crystal vases contained choice flowers, or a spray of gilded foliage.

"It's charming here," Nora said. "One senses an atmosphere of care and repose."

"It's a place of organic cures; it's necessary that the ambiance is adequate to that purpose."

The dining room was more decorative than the other rooms. Large painted panels brought an impression of spring gaiety into it.

At that moment, Marc Vanel—Homo-Deus—came in, followed by six of the Institute's practitioners in white smocks and skullcaps.

Marc advanced swiftly. "Ah! So this is our Nora! All grace and beauty! My compliments, Mademoiselle."

"Does everybody here know me, then? But I don't recognize anyone."

"But Mademoiselle," said one of the interns, "We've all admired you at the Folies Bergères."

"That's not a reason why I should by 'your' Nora. It doesn't offend me, but all the same..."

"My dear child, you're one of the family here," Dr. Fortin put in. "It's our friend Goldry who gave you his name, but Marc Vanel and I have the same rights to your recognition."

"And that's why," Dr. Goldry added," I can't claim for myself alone..."

"In sum, I'm a lost child that you collected and adopted?"

"That's it, exactly. You're the child of four fathers, for Voronoff is one too."

"Really?" said Nora laughing. "Will it stop there? What about these gentlemen?"

"We, Mademoiselle, are merely your admirers."

"And now the acquaintance is made," concluded Dr. Jean Fortin, "to table, my friends!"

In her capacity as an artiste and a good companion, Nora quickly acclimatized to that picturesque milieu, so full of merriment, and it was a charming lunch. The three doctors examined the young girl carefully, but surreptitiously, especially Marc Vanel, whose faunesque gaze undressed her, but Nora, full of joy, was joking with the six young men, and did not notice anything.

"It's curious," she said. "Who would suspect that this is a place of suffering, a hospital? I can't get over it."

"But it's not at all what you think, Mademoiselle. A clinic, an Institute of renovation, of rejuvenation, is not a place of suffering, even for our simian inmates, to whom we gave all possible wellbeing."

"Oh yes—I have it now! I remember having heard mention of Dr. Voronoff's method. It appears that he removes the you-know-whats from monkeys to give them to deprived humans, in order to restore their virility." She laughed and added: "Poor animals!"

"What do you expect? Man is the master. He kills to nourish himself; can he not mutilate in order to prolong and ameliorate his organism?"

"Oh, I've known too much hardship in life, you know, to weep over the sufferings of animals. I'm scarcely interested in those of my fellows..."

"Her fellows!" Fortin whispered in Goldry's ear. "Well, old man, we'll see shortly what she thinks of them!" He turned to Nora. "We have a young chimpanzee here who is very intelligent, and of whom, without knowing it, you're the godmother."

"How's that?"

"We thought you were lost to us, so, in memory of you, we gave your name to our favorite."

"That tender thought on your part proves to me that my fathers haven't forgotten me. I'm grateful to you. On the part of men I've known a great deal of desire, but never any affection, so I can assure you that I'm very sensible to what you're telling me."

"But for your flight, child, you'd have had a great many more effects of our affection. But for myself, I made a huge mistake in counting too much on the tenderness of those ladies of Saint-Pleur."

"We'll make up for lost time," Nora replied. "Now, my fathers, introduce me to my goddaughter."

They left the table and went to the long gallery where the apes' cages were.

Like the rest of the establishment, that gallery, broad, high-ceilinged and brightly-lit, was scrupulously clean. The cages, ten in number, were green, and as comfortable as a prison can be. Thick mats of rice-straw covered the floor, in order that the animals could lie down without feeling the hardness of the floor.

In anticipation of the introduction, Dr. Goldry had furnished Nora with a few gifts to offer the young chimpanzee. The cages were full; there were two orangutans, three chimpanzees and five gibbons.

When the visitors drew near to Nora's cage, the little she-ape came forward excitedly and extended her hands through the bars. Goldry took one of them and kissed it gallantly, by which the ape seemed very flattered, for she immediately gave voice to a soft purr of pleasure.

"I present you your godmother," the doctor said. "Her name is the same as yours."

The ape immediately extended her hand to Nora, who dared not take it, but placed in the extended hand a box of bonbons that Goldry had given to her for that purpose.

Without even looking at it, however, the ape threw the box away and took a step backwards.

"You've offended her," said Dr. Goldry. "Give her your hand—you have nothing to fear."

The young woman obeyed. She approached the cage and extended her hand through the bars. Without rancor, the she-ape took it and stroked it gently. Then, without letting go of the dancer's hand, she placed hers beside it and seemed to become absorbed in their contemplation.

Nora shivered. Apart from the color of the skin, the two hands were strangely similar.

From the hand, the ape passed on to the person, and appeared very interested in that observation.

For her part, the dancer was singularly impressed by the sight of her goddaughter. She also made comparisons. It seemed to her that deep within her, a veil ripped, and that she must have lived, at one time, with beings similar to that one—but it was very vague, an impression more akin to a very old dream, of which an episode had become reality.

The she-ape was the first to return to the present moment. Releasing Nora's hand, she picked up the box of bonbons—a very elegant box sealed with a broad silk ribbon. Carefully and dexterously, she undid the large knot and folded up the ribbon, which she set down beside her. Then she opened the box, moved aside the paper flap and took a bonbon, which she ate with extreme elegance.

An angry cry attracted attention to the next cage. The chimpanzee occupying it had watched with great attention what had happened in Nora's, and, at the sight of his neighbor crunching treats, had leapt on to the bars; he held out his hands, desperate to have his share of the feast—but the indifferent she-ape did not even seem to have noticed him.

What relationship could there be between Nora the civilized she-ape and that savage? Bah! Did he even exist, for her?

Nora—the woman—was equipped with more objects. She held out to her homonym a long necklace of green-tinted wooden beads. The she-ape's first impulse was to raise the beads to her mouth, but, recognizing her error, she immediately looked at the dancer, who had a superb pearl necklace around her neck—a gift from Jules Ducon. The ape understood; she put the necklace around her neck, the green olives streaming over her breast, and the rest of the long string gathered in an amusing green pile at the confluence of her legs—which she seemed very satisfied. A second necklace, red this time, rewarded her for her intelligence. She immediately arranged it alongside the other.

That was too much for her neighbor, who let go of the bars and dropped to the floor of the case, prey to a violent nervous crisis—a futile manifestation, for Nora the she-ape did not even deign to perceive him.

"Let's pass on to other exercises now," said Jean Fortin, handing the she-ape an illustrated book.

The latter opened it and stated leafing through it, pausing over the illustrations. She obviously understood, because some of the pictures were at right-angles to the page, and she rotated them in order to see them better. Having reached the end of the book she went back to the pictures, tearing out the pages of text as she went, doubtless considering them to be useless. She dispersed them around her like a carpet, and, from time to time, raised her eyes toward the dancer, as if in quest of her approval.

And Nora the woman perceived that the eyes of Nora the she-ape were the same maroon velvet speckled with gold as her own, and found in their expression a certain relationship.

She felt an impression of malaise.

"Let's get out of here!" said the dancer, abruptly. "The sight of that woman pains me."

The three doctors exchanged glances.

"In fact," said Dr. Goldry, tranquilly, "the sight of these great apes always gives an indefinable impression of sadness at first. It seems that, through the night of time, a vague memory of our origins awakens in us. But we quickly manage to overcome it. I'm convinced that at your next visit, you'll no longer feel it—or, at least, the consciousness of the progress accomplished will render you proud of the success achieved by our race over the ancestral races."

"Doubtless you're right. Yes, I'll come back, because I want to follow the intellectual progress of my goddaughter."

"And let me hope that one day you'll come to visit our establishment on the Riviera. There you'll see my great apes, the orangutans that I brought back from the island of Borneo."

"Gladly. Now that I've rediscovered in you my true family, I have no fear of abusing your benevolence."

"You're charming," said Marc Vanel. "Here, as at Eze, you're at home."

"But Eze is a long way away, and I'm not free. The theater is a kind of slavery."

"Bah!" It can be done by airplane. "You can leave after the performance; you'll be in Eze in the morning and will be able to get back to Paris by ten p.m., before the *ballet nègre*—I guarantee it."

"Yes, that's an idea, and it doesn't lack originality."

"Any day that you like," said Vanel. "I have an apparatus of my own invention, which can do two hundred miles an hour easily."

"Agreed. I'll let you know, Monsieur Vanel. *À bientôt*, my dear fathers..."

VIII. Ernest Paris and his Secretary, Jacquot Blakson[20]

The celebrated author and academician Ernest Paris lived in Paris in a small town house in the Villa Saïd, on the Avenue Foch, and during what he called his "refreshments" he lived in his Château de La Martinière, situated three kilometers from Villefranche.[21] It was the month of November 1928, and the illustrious man of letters had come to the blue sea to relax from the fatigues of Parisian life.

Ernest Paris was then at the summit of his glory, and supported its inconveniences with ennui. He was a tall old man with a face elongated by a white beard trimmed to a point, with the eyes of a gazelle but heavy, swollen eyelids, a delicate ironic mouth and a benevo-

---

[20] In contemplating the origin of this strange name, it is useful to bear in mind that Alexandre Dumas had set a famous precedent of employing collaborators to do his background research for him and provide rough drafts for him to embellish, to whom he referred as his literary "negroes." Jacquot is the name conventionally given in France to parrots, in much the same spirit as they are called Polly in England. Champsaur dictated all his later works to a series of amanuenses, but Anatole France, although he did employ a secretary to assist him in his later years, still preferred to use a pen when composing.

[21] Neither of the actual surviving Châteaux de La Martinière is anywhere near Villefranche; Ernest Paris has probably given that name to his holiday home in the south of France in honor of the famous polymath Antoine-Augustin Bruzen de La Martinière 91683-1746), compiler of the *Grand Dictionnaire Géographique et Critique* (10 vols, 1726-39).

lent expression—but always with a hint of mockery. That day, he had forbidden his door to anyone, having made the firm resolution the day before to work—a difficult thing to do, because the crowd of curiosity-seekers, esthetes and foreigners gave him no respite.

Always amiable and seemingly welcoming, the Master often regretted all the time that his celebrity caused him to waste, all the more so as his natural slothfulness did not incite him to hard labor, but he had promised his publisher the publication of a work famous before its birth, *Le Vrai Jésus*, and in the ten years since the book had been announced, the publisher and the public had been waiting for it impatiently.

Sometimes, Ernest Paris said to his secretary Jacquot: "Well, young man, tomorrow we'll strike a blow!" But the next day, some circumstance or other prevented the beautiful plan from being realized, and the secretary, who was expecting it—a subaltern is not necessarily an inferior—shrugged his shoulders and made notes on what was said at La Martinière, knowing full well that one day, something would come of them.

Sprawling in his armchair, Ernest Paris was dreaming, and the young man—Jacquot was only thirty-five years old—was waiting, as usual, for his employer to decide to open his mouth. A large cardboard box, stuffed with notes and notebooks, was open beside him.

"Do you know, Jacquot," said the Master finally, "what's going through my mind at this moment?"

"Another feminine silhouette. Aren't you incorrigible? Why think about that, since"—Jacquot made a slicing gesture with his hand—"it's futile."

"Hmm! Not entirely. I'm thinking about Voronoff and his method of regeneration."

"Oh, well! That's all you need. And if the graft succeeds, the situation here will no longer be tenable; I'm handing in my resignation in advance."

"Come on, my lad…at least wait until I've completed my *Vrai Jésus*. That work will be original—you'll see."

"I'm certain of it, although I find it strange to write a book about an individual to prove that he didn't exist. Anyway, at the rate we're going, the book won't exist anymore than the true or false Jesus."

"One can't always be working, damn it. Thus, today, I feel fatigued."

"Not astonishing. I left you yesterday evening with the Marquise de Virmile. That woman will kill you!"

"What does it matter if one dies of beauty? And then, *that woman*, as you call her, has great qualities…for her age. Tell me, what age do you think she is? She's still attractive…so?"

"I'm the same age as her daughter.[22] Draw your own conclusion!"

"Damn! Damn! One wouldn't think it. But she has a great deal of experience; that makes up for it. By means of her linguistic audacities, the Marquise always attains her goal."

"Tastes and colors one can't dispute. In any case, today you're worn out."

"Really? Is it as obvious as that?"

And Ernest Paris, getting to his feet swiftly, went to look at his old equine face in a superb Venetian glass

---

[22] This is the only reference in *Nora* to Huguette de Virmile, whom Marc Vanel married at the end of *Homo-Deus: Le Satyre invisible*, and who would be much younger than thirty-five in 1928 if the two texts were consistent.

placed above a sideboard opposite the large window that illuminated the room.

"Hmm! Indeed! I'm decidedly not reasonable. I definitely need to go to talk to Voronoff."

"And that's what you call being reasonable? We aren't going to do anything today, then?"

"But my friend, you can see yourself what a state that old she-ape has left me in. If you're up to it, you strike a blow! We'll see tomorrow. By the way, Dr. Goldry telephoned me this morning to say that he's expecting a visit from the dancer Nora—I have a strong desire to go to the refuge to see her. She's adorable, you know, that child!"

"All I can say is: see Voronoff!"

"You're intolerable, Jacquot. One would think, to listen to you, that I'm completely finished."

"Hmm! With a great deal of experience...of the Virmile genre..."

"Wicked boy! I shan't tell you anything else..."

"And you'll let me divine even more. Nevertheless, I agree with you, that kid Nora is truly charming—and if she wanted, it wouldn't cost her anything..."

"A fine example you're setting me there, Monsieur Moralist. I resent that!"

Jacquot laughed, and said: "Yes my child, listen to my advice, and don't do what your papa does..."

"Jacquot, you're going to end up annoying me. Really, you too often forget who you're talking to."

"No, Master, I don't forget, but you know that there's no genius for the person who lives closely with the man."

"That's true; it's necessary only to judge a man by his work. The work can be sublime, whereas the man is nothing but a dirty pig."

"He will forgive you a great deal, because...you know how it goes, Master."[23]

"And I have no desire to retire to the desert. So, you're saying that in Paris, this little Nora talked to you about me?"

"Who doesn't talk about you? Anyway she had a motive; she was planning to come to Eze to see Voronoff's apes..."

"Wretch! And she's at Voronoff's at present. What time is it, Jacquot?"

"Not yet ten o'clock."

"Good! We have time to telephone Eze to say that I desire to see Romeo again, and that we're leaving straight away. Inform the chauffeur."

"Who's this Romeo?" asked the secretary, intrigued.

"A magnificent chimpanzee that Voronoff will sacrifice for me, if...you understand?"

"Oh la la!" cried the secretary. "May all the gods of Olympus come to our aid! My venerable master is going mad!"

Ernest Paris stamped his foot angrily. "But it's you, poor idiot, who doesn't understand life. What use are all the vanities in the world to me, if I can't f..."—he made use of an unreproducible expression. "Oh, youth, youth! If you only knew!"

"That's all right!" Jacquot muttered. "The man will prevent me from growing old." In a louder voice, he

---

[23] The quotation, here translated literally (the standard English version is differently phrased), is from the French Bible's version of *Luke* 7:47. It goes on: "because He loves you a great deal." Jesus is speaking to the female sinner who washes his feet with her hair.

said: "Is there any point, Master, in me going with you? I don't want to poach on your preserves."

"Hark at the fellow! What—the lovely Nora doubtless doesn't displease you?"

"Don't be annoyed with me. You know full well that my means don't allow me to pay for a luxury whore."

"At your age, my friend, one doesn't need to pay; sometimes, it's the other way around. Come on then—one never knows with women, and I'm not jealous!"

"What about that fatigue, then? Disappeared?"

"Alas, my friend, it's only to rinse my eyes. Then too, I can chat with Doctors Fortin and Voronoff. With those two fellows, there's always something interesting to learn."

IX. Apes Face to Face

In the Paradise of Apes, the four doctors—for Voronoff had been at the refuge for a week—were very excited. Nora had telephoned the day before, asking to visit the famous establishment with her friend Cécile Borel.

At Nora's name, Dr. Goldry had jumped with delight; he was going to see his adopted daughter again. The other three were equally curious to examine the results of their work at close range.

"At the same time," Marc Vanel had said, "it's an opportunity to produce Narcisse before two pretty women. People often talk about "atavism"—we'll see whether our daughter will have another reminiscence of her former existence on finding one of the brothers of her race. I'll get my airplane ready and fly to Paris. Until tomorrow."

At that moment the telephone rang, and Goldry picked up the receiver.

"But of course, Monsieur," he said into the apparatus. "It's a great honor for us. Understood, Our homages, my dear Master."

As he hung up, he said to his friends: "It's going to be a day of sensational visits, then. That was Ernest Paris, asking to visit the establishment. Very flattering for us."

"Pooh! He's a bore," said Voronoff. "Ernest Paris is burning to be rejuvenated, but can't make up his mind, even though I've reserved Romeo for him. He's a high-status client, and I intend to get some good publicity out of him, in spite of the utmost discretion."

"He'd be furious about that—and I'm convinced that that's the only motive that's holding him back," Dr. Fortin replied.

Two days later,[24] at about nine o'clock in the morning, the throb of an aircraft engine was heard in the avenue leading to the refuge, and a few minutes later, the apparatus came to a halt at the door. Three women got down: Cécile Borel, Nora and Maud.

"You see, Doctor," said Nora, "that I haven't forgotten your kind invitation, and that I'm abusing it to bring curiosity-seekers."

"I'm grateful to you for it. A little publicity never hurts, and there's none better than that provided by three pretty women."

"This is my friend Nora, who can compete in agility with your boarders. You must have heard mention of her; for four months she's been the biggest attraction in Paris."

"Won't you come some day to dance in Nice, Cannes or Monte Carlo?"

"Of course, when the Folies Bergère will allow me to do so."

"Would you like to commence the visit right away or rest for a moment? Dr. Voronoff is with us at present; he'll be pleased to accompany you. You'll see this paradise, my beauties; it's enough to make one want to be an ape."

---

[24] The timing of this introduction, in which three days seem to be entangled, has become somewhat confused by this point, as well as inconsistent with the implications previous chapter. The text also seems confused with regard to who has already met whom, probably as a result of its episodes having been composed out of the order in which they appear in the text.

Guided by Dr. Voronoff, they were about to head for the reception room when an auto stopped in front of the house.

"An expected visit, Mesdames: the illustrious Ernest Paris."

"What! We're going to have the good fortune to meet that dear Master!" exclaimed Cécile Borel—and, hastily reversing direction, she drew her companions along with her.

"Ah! Dear *illustrissimo* Master!"—the superlative communicated an impression of the proximity of Italy—"how delighted I am to encounter you here!"

"The pleasure is all mine, my dear friend. Always fresh and lovely—you doubtless posses the secret of the elixir of youth!"

"Alas, no!" simpered the Célimène.[25] "Do you know, Master, that I've discovered a white hair!"

"Impossible! But don't let that warning frighten you—you still look twenty. But tell me... Mademoiselle?"

"Oh, you recognize her? That's flattering for you, Nora. But yes, my dear Master, it's our star of the music hall. Having left yesterday evening in Marc Vanel's superplane, she'll have to return this evening in time to dance at the Folies Bergère. Permit me, Master, to introduce you to Maud Macfield, the most vagabond of Americans."

"My compliments, Miss. What a pity I'm not of an age for vagabondage; I'd gladly do it in your company."

---

[25] Célimène is one of the principal characters in Molière's *Le Misanthrope*—an incorrigible flirt who talks about everyone maliciously behind their backs.

"I'm not a pedestrian vagabond, Master—my Ford and my yacht are at your disposal."

"Ha ha! I won't say no," said Ernest Paris flirtatiously.

Serge Voronoff, Jean Fortin and Marc Vanel appeared on the perron. "You've done well to come today," said Dr. Fortin, after the customary salutations, "for our friend Serge is returning to Paris during the week."

"But I wouldn't have left before your visit, Master, since you had promised me."

"And you can see that I keep my word. What's more, see how lucky I am: I'm encountering three goddesses in your house!"

"Let's go in," said Voronoff. "We'll chat for a moment, and then I'll introduce you to someone."

When the visitors came into the drawing-room, Narcisse, the orangutan, in an impeccable gentleman's visiting suit, was sitting in an armchair reading a scientific journal. He stood up briskly and bowed.

Marc Vanel introduced him. "Monsieur Narcisse Goldry; Madame Cécile Borel of the Comédie-Française, Mesdemoiselles Nora and Maud Macfield."

At the name of Goldry, Nora, who had taken a step backwards, like the other three visitors, at the sight of the orangutan, shivered and looked at Narcisse with a terrified expression.

"That's good, that one!" exclaimed Ernest Paris. "You give a civil estate to your boarders! My compliments, Messieurs! This one's better dressed than the famous Consul."[26]

---

[26] "Consul the Man Chimp" was actually a series of chimpanzees, all with the same stage name, exhibited around the world

"You really think so, Master? In that case, I'm delighted to have that advantage over my compatriot."

A thunderbolt falling in their midst could not have been any more petrifying than those simple words falling from the mouth of the great ape. He continued: "What a happy day for me, to make the acquaintance of three of the prettiest women in Paris and the most distinguished of our literary glories."

"The farce is delightful, but let's not prolong it any further," the novelist relied. "Take off your mask."

"But it's not a mask, it's a face," Marc Vanel interjected. "Beauty is relative, according to the region in which it's found. An Eskimo or a Hottentot would certainly think themselves more beautiful than we would."

"And does Monsieur enjoy the same privilege, and consider himself a type of beauty?" asked Cécile Borel.

"Yes, of course, Madame," Narcisse replied. "True beauty isn't necessarily a form agreeable to the eye; it also consists in intellectual beauty, and from that point of view, I don't consider myself inferior to anyone."

"This is a house of miracles, then!" exclaimed Ernest Paris. "Well, Jacquot, who are threatening to leave me—here's your replacement, readymade."

"I would be sorry to replace you, Monsieur Jacquot. However, if I were in your position, I would consider it a veritable honor to be living with the foremost of our men of letters."

"I sincerely advise you not to envy my secretary, for I'm a very disagreeable individual."

"Master!" said Jacquot. "I can't let you say that."

---

by the American animal trainer Frank Bostock between 1896 and 1910, including a stint at the Folies Bergère.

"I have my excuse: the platitude of the crowd that makes a kind of demigod of an artist of letters, as if a few rungs more on the gradation of intelligences merited the abasement of the mass. Don't take this as a paradox, but I believe that there wouldn't be any intellectual superiorities if there were fewer personal vanities. I recall two engravings that had a certain success in my youth: Molière and his maidservant, and Boileau and his gardener. Can you believe that if Molière and Boileau hadn't judged those two individuals of inferior class capable of understanding and appreciating them, they would have taken the trouble to read their works to them? Those great minds recognized in those humble ones an intelligence that was not inferior but merely different from theirs. We writers only have one veritable talent: that of mirroring, of reflecting what we see, storing the work of our predecessors, and drawing therefrom by combining it with our own observations—or what we take to be such, for, as soon as one puts black on white, who will dare affirm that what he thinks original is not simply the reflection of another thought?"

"That might be, Master, but there's the style. Those whose at consists of lining words up one after another inevitably encounter the reef of which you speak, but they present the thought in a clearer, more familiar fashion and more harmonious fashion; that is the art in which you excel, and which constitutes the mark of your genius."

"If there were not ladies here, before whom I have the conceit of dissimulating my age, I would ask you, Monsieur Narcisse, what yours is, for you have a maturity of thought that seems to equal mine."

Narcisse looked at Marc Vanel in an interrogative fashion that signified: *Ought I to reply truthfully?*

It was Vanel who replied for him: "Narcisse is thirteen years old."

There was a murmur of general amazement. Then Ernest Paris addressed Marc Vanel.

"My dear friend, you and your collaborators have become used to being considered as sorcerers—no, the word isn't improper, since everyone knows that you're uniquely scientists, since science has no secrets from you. At this moment, I have before my eyes an individual who has the appearance of an ape, and who seems to me to possess knowledge that not many people have, If it's an indiscretion on my part, don't answer, but if you can do so, I'd be infinitely grateful to you for satisfying our curiosity—for I assume these ladies are as intrigued as I am."

"Oh, Monsieur Vanel," exclaimed Cécile Borel, "tell us the truth—it's so exciting."

"And you, Mesdemoiselles, what do you think of it?" asked Dr. Goldry, looking at Nora in particular.

The dancer did not reply, but Maud said: "I think that no one had ever seen anything like it."

"Well, it's Narcisse himself who will reply to us, for he's not only our creature—he's become our collaborator. Speak, my son."

Amiably, Narcisse turned toward the ladies and, in spite of the strangeness of the scene and the monstrous face of the orator, none of them dared smile, even though everything about the orangutan's pose made an extravagant contrast with the physiognomy of his auditors: the elegantly-tailored garments, bringing out his formidable stature; his powerful limbs, the hands double the size of human hands, and the enormous feet, buried in patent leather shoes that could have served as violin-cases; above all that, the frightful mask with the flamboyant eyes, the fleshy lips, revealing teeth that could crush iron; and, crowning that apocalyptic head magnificently, a vast forehead shaded by splendid black hair, supple and undulating, like the mane of a lion.

"I consider, Mesdames," Narcisse began, "that your curiosity is very legitimate, since I too felt it when I was able to compare myself with human beings. As Monsieur Vanel said just now, beauty is relative; my first impression was that humans were ugly. I had not yet seen you, Mesdames, for you alone would have modified that judgment. But I only saw men, and I thought them all the uglier because I saw that they were weak, and the sentiment of strength is, among primitives, the true sentiment of beauty.

"I was three years old when those Messieurs, after having modified the form of my cranium, as you can see, and grafted me two pineal glands and two thyroid glands, set about, once the grafts were making good progress—which took nearly a year—commencing my education. They did not stuff my head, as the vulgar expression has it, but they populated it precisely with a judiciously chosen documentation, which they fixed in successive stages, in an indelible fashion.

"Have you ever reflected on the singular phenomenon of memory—the faculty of accumulating facts that we can renew and revive at will within our thoughts? Among other members of my species and the majority of animals, memory is more or less short; among many it is unknown. Those individuals accomplish actions that are always the same, because memory is limited in them to the repetition of the same gestures—those which relate to nutrition and reproduction. In humans, memory has become its own reason for being, since it is by courtesy of it that mentality develops.

"The glory of Monsieur Voronoff will be that of having discovered the enormous role that the glands play in the economy of the human body: a vivifying and reconstituting property, when one can activate its functioning by grafting. That is what has been carried out within me with a maximum of intensity, since the pineal and thyroid glands, the ones that vivify the brain, have been grafted into me in duplicate. If the experiment justifies the attempt, nothing prevents its repetition, on another subject, in triplicate or quadruplicate, and we shall obtain by that method individuals of a mentality triple or quadruple the norm—and, in consequence, superhuman."

At that point Narcisse sketched a smile, which resulted in an abominable grimace, and he continued: "I shall put myself back on the operating table and continue to extend myself before you. The quality of my instruction was not to cram me with all the old texts that repeat themselves through the ages, but a selection that gave me, if I might qualify it thus, a cervical library as complete as possible, on the philosophical side as well as the scientific. Presently, I have perhaps attained the intellectual level of my masters. That has been my goal and I shall limit my ambition to it. That, Mesdames, is all that you desired to know about your very enthusiastic admirer."

The same agreeable smile-cum-grimace underlined that final compliment.

Ernest Paris looked successively at the four fantastic doctors; they had satisfied expressions, and the novelist, nonplussed by what he had just heard, only found the same word as Clemenceau: "Marvelous! Truly, it's marvelous!"

Narcisse, the knowledgeable ape, continued: "Why be astonished that I talk like a doctor? The ape is the animal that resembles humans most extraordinarily; for the master of the earth, he is something akin to a living store of interchangeable pieces. Because one component does not work in an automobile, one does not put the vehicle on the scrap-heap; one examines it, and, if there is reason, one rectifies it, one exchanges the part that does not work. And your automobile works again, very well. Much the same thing was done to me. The glands, in the simian and human mechanism, are essential; Dr. Voronoff has utilized one category for the grafting of sexual organs and the reconstitution of life, but that is only one point and a limited application of the science. My cerebral humanity is proof of that; I am the simple result, which nature alone took centuries to accomplish, of the magnificent effort realized in a few years by four scientists, and solely by virtue of the antithetical will of these Messieurs, I have retained a primitive and hairy form."

Voronoff leaned toward Ernest Paris' ear. "Well, my dear friend, does Narcisse give you enough confidence?"

"Confidence? Hmm. You're damnably dangerous, you lot! You've made this fellow a man—what if you had a whim to make me an ape? Shh! We'll talk about that in private."

Turning toward Cécile Borel, Maud and Nora, Ernest Paris said: "Well, Mesdames, shall we begin the visit to the establishment? Would Mademoiselle Nora care to accept my arm? But you seem troubled, my dear child. Is it listening to the transcendental history of the ape that has confused you a little?—as it did me, I confess. One finds oneself in a fantastic atmosphere here, and if it weren't in bad taste to believe in God and the Devil, one might think that one were in their laboratories."

"Indeed," stammered the blue dancer. "I no longer know whether I'm dreaming or awake."

"If all of this phantasmagoria is rather unreal, believe that I, at least, am not one of theirs, but simply a humble mortal dazzled by your grace and beauty."

Nora looked at the novelist in astonishment. "You deploy mockery very well, Master, so far as I can see."

"Sometimes, but not at the moment. I swear to you that I'm saying what I think; no woman has ever impressed me as you do. I dare not say that it's amour—I can no longer play the Don Juan, alas—but it's a violent desire, and what is desire if not the veritable, the only justiciable amour?"

"You have an admirable way with words. You must demonstrate that to me at my home in Paris."

"You'd deign to receive me?"

"Yes, certainly—with pleasure."

Ernest Paris clapped his secretary on the back, very cheerfully: "Ha ha, Jacquot!"

The latter shrugged his shoulders. "See Voronoff."

"In God's name Monsieur, you're becoming very disagreeable!"

Nora had moved closer to her friend Maud, who was dragging her to one side. "Did you notice, my dear, that the doctor called the ape Narcisse Goldry?"

"Yes, that's true."

"Might he be your brother?"

"Stupid girl! But that doctor might be my father; personally, I daren't interrogate him. But you could ask him whether he has a daughter—without naming me, of course."

"Mesdames," said Marc Vanel, at that moment, "It's decidedly our friend Narcisse who should do you the honors of the establishment, and it will be interesting to compare the civilized ape with his brethren, who have remained as nature created them."

"When I find myself among them again," Narcisse replied, "I don't experience any shame, but, on the contrary, a sentiment of pride—and what my friends have done for me, I might perhaps be able to do for them one day."

"That's a noble altruistic thought," Jacquot muttered in Cécile Borel's ear, "but tell me, does that avalanche of superhumans not seem a little too simian?"

"That depends," smiled the Célimène, "on whether they're superhuman in all respects..."

Jacquot drew away from her, muttering curtly: "She-ape!"

Meanwhile, the little troop had moved into the forest, Narcisse in the lead with Maud; Ernest Paris came next with Nora, and the others followed behind.

Maud thought the moment propitious for undertaking the enquiry that might satisfy Nora's curiosity. Overcoming the fear caused by her strange companion, she said to him: "Do you know my friend Nora's family name?"

"I only know your friend via the articles in the newspapers, Madame, where she is only designated by her forename."

"My friend's name is Goldry, like you, and, I believe, one of the doctors."

"I don't think that Dr. Abraham Goldry, my adoptive father, has ever had a daughter, or even a child. As for me, in giving me his name, it was merely an amicable recognition, for he could not recognize an orangutan legally as his son. I remain grateful for that confidence in my morality, but it's necessary not to draw any conjecture offensive to him. As for your friend it might be that she's related to the doctor's family; there's no shortage of Goldrys in America, or even elsewhere. Is Mademoiselle Goldry American?"

"No, French—at least according to the extract of her birth certificate necessary for her entry to the convent."

"Well, doesn't that birth-certificate inform you of the name and origin of her father?"

"That's exactly what she lacks, for my friend has never been able to recall the name or the address of the convent."

"I'll be very happy to be useful to her, and I'll talk to my father about that similarity of names."

"It would be very kind of you to do that. I'll tell Nora to leave you her address in Paris. I don't know whether you're aware of it or not, but we're leaving the Riviera in two hours."

"Oh! I regret that; we rarely have such charming ladies visit us."

"You'll doubtless find my question very indiscreet and very bold, but you seem to me so devoid of vanity that I'll dare to risk it. Have you been frequenting society for very long?"

The orangutan smiled—which caused the American to shiver.

"Today is the first time that I've had the pleasure to talking to a woman," he replied, simply. "Until today I've only known my four doctors and the establishment's Malay servants. Don't be astonished. My reading has taught me a great deal, and I believe that I could present myself appropriately in any civilized society."

"Much better than many others—and I can predict a social success for you."

"Oh, a success of curiosity, which I wouldn't abuse. We've arrived...excuse me, but the instruments of torture that I have on my feet make it difficult for me to climb this ladder."

Astounded, the American woman saw him remove his shoes and deposit the immense objects at the foot of the ladder.

"Permit me to precede you..."

And Narcisse, taking hold of the ladder, was on the landing of the cage within a matter of seconds. Nora, on seeing the ape's action, felt a rush of blood rising to her face. She too could have taken off her shoes and climbed up four-handed. What relationship was there, then, between her and those monstrous animals?

"Would you like to take the trouble of going up, Mesdames," said Vanel.

"Oh, I'll never manage it," simpered Cécile Borel. "It must be very difficult..."

But Nora had already rejoined Narcisse.

While pulling faces like a fearful child, the Célimène imitated her with sufficient skill.

"Aging doll!" muttered Jean Fortin.

X. Nora Among Her Relatives

The orangutans were not accustomed to seeing so many people at the same time; they made their anxiety manifest, but Narcisse calmed them down by explaining, in the orangutan language, that the phenomena he was bringing them were the females of the human race. In spite of the fashionable garments, the orangutans had immediately recognized their brother Narcisse, whom they saw frequently. As for the visitors, they provoked a curiosity in the orangutans that soon became embarrassing for them.

Having retired to a corner of the cage, the doctors, Ernest Paris and Jacquot, his secretary, watched to see whether the great apes were behaving appropriately, ready to intervene. The novelist and Jacquot could not help feeling the sensation of sadness that humans experience in the presence of an anthropoid—a sensation similar to that provoked by a degenerate, an idiot or a cretin.

"It's singular, said Ernest Paris to Dr. Voronoff. "I've already been subject to that impression when you put me in the presence of Philemon and Baucis, and it is, I believe, the best proof of our simian origin. It's like the specter of the past looming up before us."

"And the past is not so far away, not so extinct that we can't still feel it's influence," Voronoff replied. "The spirit of imitation subsists in us even more so than in the apes. We substitute mimicry by speech, but how many grimaces, how many repetitions! The need to escape heredity has created the schools of artistic decay that have led to the retrograde movement of cubism, Dadaism, impressionism and all the other isms produced, in countless clans, by individuals drunk on novelty. They don't perceive that, instead of going forward, they're going backwards, and are inferior to the artists of the Magdalenian era. Humans have remained more apelike than they should, you see. Their 'new' is diluvian art, and their ideal is inferior to that of the Stone Age."

"Perfectly true," Marc Vanel put in. "We're still apes, and it will require a veritable scientific effort for us to become something else. The further we go, the more humans lost their sense of collective life, in order to concern themselves with the self alone: everything for me, nothing but that which is advantageous to me! They're detaching themselves from everything that might elevate human mentality: devotion, love, friendship, emulation. What is today called socialism or communism was, in the minds of our forefathers, synonymous with human progress. Today, there's nothing but little chapels ending in the satisfaction of the individual self, infinitely, bringing us inevitably back to animality, to life for life's sake: to eat well and fornicate, but with the difference that humans aren't aiming for the continuation of the species and, on the contrary, are doing everything they can to destroy it. Are humans apes? No, less than apes, and much more maleficent."

"Discouraging!" said Ernest Paris nonchalantly. "But what can one do?"

"Renew humankind by growth, by grafting, by a rejuvenation of the organs, by the development of the brain, by means of an education that doesn't clutter up the memory with obsolete and useless documents—in sum, by gaining time on the future. What wouldn't you have been able to produce if, instead of repeating the Greek and Roman authors, you had simply been yourself—rather than an ape remaking the grimaces of yore?"

This time, Ernest Paris was vexed. Not daring to take on the doctor, however, it was his secretary at whom he directed an irritated glance.

"Do you hear, Jacquot? You're the secretary of an ape, and you're stupid enough not to notice!"

"Oh, I've known it for a long time," replied the other, waspishly, "but I didn't have any way to tell you."

The great writer stamped his foot angrily. "There's no means of having the last word, even with that accursed fellow!"

"Messieurs," intervened Dr. Goldry, you're missing a curious sight. "Look at our boarders..."

In fact, as the American said, the mute scene of the orangutans merited attention.

After the initial effusions, when the two orangutans had greeted Narcisse, who returned their caresses without any arrogance, the she-ape had begun to palpate the talking ape, seeking to rediscover, beneath his garments, their friend's hidden form—and her gestures sometimes assumed a liberty that scandalized the three female visitors. Narcisse undoubtedly understood that, for he gently pushed the unthinking female to one side and resumed his role as a cicerone.

"Don't be offended," he said, "by the slightly free manners of my brethren the apes; they're still unaware of the hypocrisy of civilized mores. Natural laws are the basis of their intellect. What you call modesty, decency and morality can have no existence for them, who only know needs, and don't know how to constrain themselves from their satisfaction."

Cécile Borel did not miss a single detail of the scene, and her expert eye followed a certain rigidity that was designed beneath the orangutan's garment. The other two, doubtless inspired by the presence of three females, had drawn closer together with an unequivocal intention. Narcisse, who understood decorum, seized them by the skin on the back of the neck and pushed them behind a "*buen retiro*" forming a kind of tent.

Very excited, the three women almost made a gesture of protest. As for Narcisse, taking hold of a branch above his head, he disappeared into the foliage.

"Hmm!" said Maud. "I believe we're missing the most interesting part. What do you think, dear?"

"I think that I regret having come," said Nora. "Everything that happens in this place takes on a fantastic character, and strangely, enough, it seems to me...that...I've lived similar events in another life."

"In dreams, that's not uncommon," said Cécile Borel. "For instance, I once dreamed that I was Pasiphaë.[27] Unfortunately, it was only a dream—but just now, looking at Narcisse..."

"Well?"

"Well...I remembered my dream. But where has Narcisse gone? Ah! Here are our lovers coming out of their bedroom. They don't scare me as much now; I understand them better."

The two orangutans approached hesitantly; the female was carrying her nursling, whom she showed off proudly. She came toward the three women, and sudden-

---

[27] Pasiphaë, the wife of King Minos of Crete, was cursed by Poseidon, and thus caused to lust after a white bull; as a result of the consummation of her passion, she gave birth to the Minotaur. Champsaur had never seen an actual orang-utan, and was thus unaware that their reproductive apparatus is by no means taurean in its dimensions.

ly placed her baby in Nora's arms—who instinctively hugged her to her bosom, to Maud's great alarm.

"Give that horror back!" she exclaimed. "How can you touch it?"

"But it's a baby! I find it much less ugly than its parents."

The she-ape had drawn closer; leaning on one of her long arms, she stood upright in front of Nora, and seemed to be saying to her: "Isn't my son beautiful?" She did say so, grunting softly.

Nora, with the little ape in the crook of her arm, stroked his head. The infant rolled his eyes, and gave voice to the singular vibration that is the purring of orangutans. The male had drawn closer too, and was gazing slyly at the Célimène and the American woman, seemingly making comparisons between them.

Gently, and hesitantly, the she-ape stretched out her free hand and touched Nora's dress. She must have thought that the fabric was the white beast's skin, because, when she felt the soft silk give way beneath her fingers, she snatched the hand away immediately and seemed puzzled. The baby became bolder, however; he put his arm around the young woman's neck, and suddenly, with a long thrust of the neck, he licked her,

That was a true *coup de théâtre!* The orangutan's tongue had, with a single stroke, removed the rice-powder and make-up covering Nora's face. Her pale, slightly blue-tinted face appeared, making a contrast with her other cheek, where the make-up remained.

"Oh, the dirty beast!" cried the dancer. "Take her back," she said to the mother, who was looking at her in bewilderment—but the little ape was comfortable, and did not let go, in spite of the efforts of the young woman, who rolled her eyes with sudden ferocity. Her lips drew back in a savage rictus, showing her teeth, and her jaw made a terrible grating noise. The little one, frightened, leapt away, reaching his mother's neck with a single bound. The latter, irritated, growled dully.

It was at that moment that Dr. Goldry, who had been following all the actions of the ape and the visitor, drew the attention of his companions to them.

Nora had turned toward the she-ape; their eyes met. The same growl escaped the dancer's throat, and Maud and Cécile Borel watched the scene uncomprehendingly. The male, however, profiting from the general inattention, lifted up the hem of the dress that the actress from the Comédie-Française was wearing and rummaged underneath. Frightened, the Célimène would have fallen backwards if Maud had not caught her in her arms.

"Damn!" said Fortin, running forward. "That's torn it."

He did not have time to intervene though. By the same route along which he had disappeared, Narcisse let himself fall. Grabbing the male by the hips, he sent him sprawling; then, seizing the female by the hair, he dragged her backwards.

"Quickly!" shouted Vanel. "Get back. Narcisse—protect us!"

They were just in time. Furious, the two orangutans bounded toward them. Narcisse absorbed the impact, while the doctors rapidly drew the three women away. Only Nora had a vague desire to stand her ground, but she renounced it and followed the others, growling.

On seeing their visitors outside the cage and out of reach, the great apes gradually calmed down, the conciliating Narcisse probably having convinced them that they were in the wrong. They parted as good friends, but the future superhuman's clothes were in a pitiful state;

his trousers only had one leg and his jacket one sleeve. Seeing that his attire was no longer impeccable, he judged it unnecessary to put his shoes on again, and without further ado he launched himself into the trees, preceding the group by leaping from branch to branch.

"Well," conserved Ernest Paris, "your superhuman seems to me to enjoying himself."

"What do you expect?" replied Jean Fortin. "He needs to relax a little. Even God rested on the seventh day."

"He might as well have done the same on the other six, the poser of enigmas!"

"Are we going to see Romeo?" asked Voronoff.

"Oh no!" replied the Célimène, swiftly. "I'm too frightened."

"I'm going back to Paris tomorrow," said the celebrated practitioner. "Will you do me the honor of coming to see me at my clinic? I'm having a few operations filmed—it's very interesting, as you'll see."

"Gladly," replied Cécile Borel. "The Master will come and pick me up in his auto."

"And Mademoiselle too, if the spectacle interests her," added the doctor.

"A great deal," Maud replied.

"She would much rather have seen what was happening behind the orangutans' tent," Jacquot whispered in the ears of the proprietors.

"Me too!" replied the academician, naively.

"I thought there was a mirror at the back of your alcove?"

Ernest Paris only replied to that gibe with a punch in his facetious secretary's back.

"Still apes, you see!" said Dr. Goldry to Marc Vanel, who was following the two companions.

After a few circuits of the garden, where flowers were picked for the ladies, they went back into the drawing room. A lunch had been prepared, and Narcisse, who had put on a smoking jacket, served it gracefully. He had resumed all his gravity, and the poise of a man of the world.

Nora was thoughtful. In her mind, she reviewed the morning's tumultuous events, and the strange sensation that the sight of the great apes had caused her. As they returned, when she had seen Narcisse bounding through the trees, she had felt a crazy desire to imitate him, and if he had not been aware of being watched by the four physicians, perhaps she would have committed that folly. As soon as she had come into the house she had noticed that she was the focus of the attention of the marvelous scientists. Why? That was what she would have liked to know.

"They're not always easy-going, your boarders," said Ernest Paris, sprawled in his armchair drinking a glass of champagne. "Do you know that I was seriously scared. Brrr! They're nasty when they're angry."

"That doesn't happen often. They're usually very gentle."

"If you saw them in the free state, as I've seen them in Borneo," said Goldry, "there would be reason to be afraid—especially of their defunct chief, King Ouha, a superb beast, who was my close friend for six months."

"Truly?" asked the Célimène. "Is that the one we've seen in the cinema?"

"The very same—but the role was played by our friend Narcisse."

"Impossible! So, you've made a film, Monsieur?"

"I've done a little of everything," the ape replied, modestly. "I saw that it gave pleasure to these Messieurs, and it didn't disturb my studies at all, since it was filmed in our establishment."

"So that's why people were ecstatic about the strength and agility of the actor who was believed to be an acrobat in disguise. And the plot, Monsieur Goldry— was that the product of a romantic imagination?"[28]

"No, Madame; unfortunately, it's rigorously true; I lost my dear friends that way."

"How exciting all that must have been!" exclaimed the American woman. "Don't you think so, my dear?"

"What? Yes…gripping, even."

"All my life as a scholar," Dr. Goldry went on, "has been devoted to the study of the precursors of humankind. Cheerfully, he added, pointing at Narcisse: "And you can see the result."

"Will Monsieur Narcisse be coming to Paris?" asked Cécile Borel.

"Certainly! Paris is the only place where the completion of our work can take place, but he'll only go when he'll be able to demonstrate his superiority in everything."

"It's fortunate, then, that my work is finished!" said Ernest Paris, fearfully.

"Pardon me, Master," said Jacquot, "but your masterpiece, *Le Vrai Jésus*, isn't finished."

---

[28] Champsaur could not have been aware in 1929 of the fact that Edgar Wallace would write the script that eventually became the basis for the movie *King Kong* in 1931, but he had probably seen the silent movies based on Edgar Rice Burroughs' Tarzan books, which might have helped to prompt him to write *Ouha*.

"I don't believe that it ever will be; it's not progressing, as you know very well."

"Doubtless because you lack documents."

"On the contrary, I have too many of them. They all contradict one another—and they call that history! Oh, my friends, what a cacophony historical documents make! One flounders trying to determine what happened fifteen years ago, and I had the stupid idea of wanting to revive a man dead for nineteen centuries! I have a strong desire to abandon that great agitator, whom I was perhaps wrong to consider as the precursor of democracy, and content myself with living on my laurels."

"And what if I were able to revive that singular prophet just for you?" said Marc Vanel. "If you could follow him, step by step, through his singular existence?"

"Then I'd believe that you really are a sorcerer, and I'd demand a pyre for you!"

"Thank you! But you'd regret it. In all times, people have wanted to see everyone bringing a new idea as a sorcerer. I'm not talking, of course, about those who only find a new way of exploiting human credulity—I'm talking about those who were the actual precursors of present day science, the likes of Flamel, Paracelsus, Van Helmont and many others. They committed errors, were imbued with the prejudices of their time, and believed in God and the Devil, but they were seekers nonetheless, and sometimes they found. What are we, the scientists of today? Seekers like them, but better equipped, and, informed by the very errors of our forerunners, more suspicious, rid of the lumber of superstitions, we have more elbow room. In science, as in literature, my dear Master, the blossoming of our discoveries only takes place of the dung-hill of our predecessors. The very word sorcerer indicates *sourcer*—which is to say the source of the stream, the river of science, which flows into the ocean of human knowledge."

"Perfect deduction," said Ernest Paris, "and I offer you my humblest apologies. Instead of burning you I'll surround you with the burning incense of my admiration."

Dr. Fortin did not blink. In his usual bantering tone the replied: "Be careful that I don't punish you for your incredulous smile."

"Punish me? How?"

"By causing your self to pass into the brain of Narcisse."

"My God!" And, putting down his glass, the Academician fled as fast as he could.

"Oh, Monsieur Fortin, what have you done?" Jacquot pretended to moan. "My poor Master!"

The doctor writhed with laughter. "No! Did you see him run, the old ape!"

"You were wrong, Fortin," said Serge Voronoff. "He won't come back."

"Excuse me," said Jacquot, "but I can't let my employer leave alone."

"But I haven't gone," said Paris, "showing his mocking face at the door. I had a fright, it's true, but on reflection…and with apologies to Fortin…"

"Indeed!" said the latter. "And to Vanel—after all, he started it."

"Messieurs, you're stronger than me. So, I can abase myself without shame. Against strength…"

"All the fantasies of the mind are authorized," said Marc Vanel. "From one spark a conflagration can bring, and a great discovery from the most puerile thing. So, I was telling you that I can revive for you the epoch and the person of Jesus. Do you know how? By cinematography."

"Films before our era? You're going to recommence your phantasmagorias?"

"Have you heard mention of photography at a distance, and its results?"

"Of course," said Ernest Paris. "My portrait was made, from Vaugirard, at Saint-Raphael."

"Well, what can be done over distance it's sufficient to do over time. It's quite simple, you see."

"Especially in words. But in fact?"

"It's quite simple. A luminous ray propagates through space like a wave in the immensity of the ocean, a wave in the atmosphere and, we now have the proof, a sidereal wave in the ether. Thus, a continuous ray is made of an object struck by light, and propagates to infinity; thus, the ray that, in the year 33, illuminated the death of Jesus, will soon have been in progress for two thousand years, and can be recovered at the corresponding distance with the speed of light."[29]

"Good, good! Fine, in theory. But if you think that I can follow you at that speed...! So you, Marc Vanel, will be at the end of that ray with a cinephotographic apparatus, to capture the agony and the death of Jesus?"

"Certainly I shall be there! And with an apparatus more accurate and more rapid than photography, which requires several fractions of a second. Mine will be instantaneous."

---

[29] This notion, first popularized by Camille Flammarion in the classic *Lumen* (1872), had already been the subject of a speculative novel written in English, *Around a Distant Star* (1904) by "Jean Delaire" (the French-born Pauline Touchemoulin, later Mrs. Muirson Blake, 1868-1950).

"What do you call this trick?"

"It doesn't have a name yet."

"In that case, my dear Jacquot, we can let Jesus sleep until then. We'll be able to remain unable to do anything... What, Mesdames, you haven't gone to sleep during that conversation?"

"I wouldn't have wanted to," Maud replied. "It's too exciting. Will you let me see the film of the Messiah, Monsieur Vanel?"

"Whatever you wish, Mademoiselle. I have no secrets for a pretty woman."

"Oho!" said Cécile Borel. "You see the boldness of these scientists! Well, personally, I'm not like Miss Maud. All these hypotheses—or realities, since it's necessary to believe in them—scare me. I'd rather remain in the ignorance and credulity of the good old times than compromise my salvation with the Devil."

"A good Devil, at any rate," said Nora, "and not frightening at all. Where are the scholars of legend, white haired, with massively long beards? Our modern scientists aren't yet sixty, and as solid as oak trees. And the acorn is still growing, I think. How much science it has been possible to acquire in so few years—especially in your case, Monsieur Vanel, still so young and so..."

"Go on, Mademoiselle, finish. So...?"

Nora hesitated momentarily, and then, bravely, admitted: "So visibly handsome."

"Really? I might please you?"

"Although the scientist frightens me a little, the man seems very agreeable to me."

"Will you permit me to come and hear you repeat that at your home, Mademoiselle?"

"I'll be as flattered by that as the visit of Master Ernest Paris, who solicited the same favor just now."

"In that case, my first visit in Paris will be to you, I assure you."

"I have many friends—but I prefer quality to quantity."

"You're exquisite, Mademoiselle Nora."

Cécile Borel stood up. "One doesn't get bored with you, Messieurs, but time's passing, and the moment has come to fly back to Paris. I hope that we'll see one another again in Paris. My box will always be open to you, and my drawing room too." Turning to the celebrated writer, she added: "And you, dear Master and bad lot, also know that I live near the Académie."

"Oh, the Académie—I don't got there very often. On the other hand, I adore the quais. I shall therefore come to ask for shelter on rainy days or when the sun is too hot."

"You'll always find a good welcome."

"*In Paris*," sang Ernest Paris, "*there are roses...* That's the influence of the environment! You see, Voronoff, I feel quite sprightly. You're going back too, then?"

"It's necessary. Business, my dear. The vacation is over. Shall I take Romeo?"

"What a demon tempter! Let's see, my friend, I still have a little left...that little Nora, you know—I only have to look at her...but yes, it's just as I say!"

"Shut up, you old ape—as if I didn't know you! Be very prudent."

"Let's go then. All the same, I'll come to see you...I'm not promising anything...but take Romeo anyway."

When the visitors had gone, the four augurs looked at one another, laughing.

"Where the Devil are you trying to lead him with your story of Jesus?" asked Jean Fortin. "The poor fellow's almost convinced that you stroll among the stars."

"Who knows? Perhaps it will come."

"And our daughter?" said Dr. Goldry. "She pretended not to know us, the silly girl. Did you see her in the cage? There are reminiscences, though. There's still a little atavism in her."

"It will be better next time. So, Voronoff, he seems to have made up his mind, the Immortal?"

"He'll have to if he wants to offer himself to Nora. She's not an ape for nothing, and won't always be content with the *bagatelles de la porte*."[30]

"It's singular, all the same, that a man of that intelligence can become so lubricious with age. In him, it's becoming a monomania—because he can't do it anymore he thinks about it incessantly."

"Who knows what the future has in reserve for us? It would be a pity—such a waste of time! What are you thinking about, Homo-Deus?"

"I'm thinking about Nora, our daughter. She's terribly inebriating."

"You're thinking about that too? After all, it's your age…what about you, Narcisse?"

---

[30] I have left this expression untranslated because of its subsequent involvement in wordplay that would be lost if it were merely rendered as "preliminaries." It's literal significance is "the trivialities of the door", and it originally referred to the patter employed by fairground showmen trying to entice clients into their booths; as early as the 1820s, however, it became one of the most commonplace literary euphemisms for sexual foreplay, verbal or physical.

"Me?" replied the orangutan. "To possess her would be heaven...the rainbow...she's so beautiful!"

"Him too! Hang on, I've got an idea!" exclaimed the facetious Fortin. "Narcisse, you'll be the rival of Ernest Paris, and, I'll wager, the preferred rival. By the sacred backside of the Pope, there'll be a few days of jolly fun for us yet!"

XI. The Invisible Satyr

Nora had been back in Paris for ten days. She had retained a certain impression from her excursion to Eze, but her versatile mind had not sought to delve into its cause; she continued her music hall life and fleeting adventures without worrying unduly about the past. Nevertheless, she had taken a certain interest in the existence of her quartet of fathers. That pleased her by virtue of its very strangeness; furthermore, she had sensed that the four fantastic doctors were not men to neglect, and that they might once again have a great influence over her life. So, from time to time, she visited the Voronoff Institute in order to meet one of her fathers there, and to see her goddaughter Nora, in whom she was increasingly interested.

Another motive for distraction for her was Ernest Paris, who was paying assiduous court to her, bringing, at every visit, a rich volume or one of the art-works with which his town house, in the Villa Saïd on the Avenue Foch, was overflowing. Jules Ducon took great pride in the Academician's visits to his mistress, taking in good part, for the benefit of his vanity, the luster that that glorious presence gave his relationship with the dancer. She was much less interested, being entirely indifferent to matters of literature. But as, on several occasions, Cécile Borel and Ernest Paris had run into one another in her drawing room, with Maud and other people better informed than she was, she had observed the servility of those visitors before the illustrious writer, and had concluded in consequence that she ought to welcome the Master with consideration and amiability.

The reputation as a fine talker that surrounded Ernest Paris was not, in any case, superficial, and, ignorant as the dancer was, she ended up finding a considerable charm in his reiterated visits. As for the Master, who desired Nora ardently, he took full account of the fact that he was in no state to satisfy her, for he divined that she was very voluptuous, and thought it wiser, while awaiting the favorable moment, to limit himself to the *bagatelles de la porte*—certain that both battens of the door in question would open easily on the day that he felt the strength to penetrate it.

On the day in question, Ernest Paris had just left, after having tried to awaken a certain virility by means of lewd talk and tentative caresses. Although he had made transparent allusions to it, he had not dared to ask the young woman squarely for what he obtained so benevolently and actively from the Marquise de Virmile, and Nora, left alone and slightly excited, was rather nonplussed by that unexpected retreat. Having not thus far frequented old men, she had not taken account of the frustrations of senility. Why, she wondered, awaken her sensuality only to retire before the decisive gesture? Was it disdain on the novelist's part? Did he judge her unworthy of his love? She remained somewhat irritated by the adventure, and went back into her drawing room shrugging her shoulders. Decidedly, she did not understand.

She stood in front of the mantelpiece and looked at herself complaisantly in the mirror above it. From her face, her gaze descended to her shoulders, her arms, slender but not thin, and parted her dress in order to free her firm, small breasts, whose tips suddenly became firm under the caress of her hands.

A whim came into her head then. She was quite alone; the chambermaid, Berthe, was not due to return, and the cook never emerged from her domain. The desire to see herself naked and admire herself in lascivious poses, to dance for herself alone, for her own pleasure, caused her to undress herself in a trice and to display herself, a splendid statuette of blue-tinted marble, in the middle of the room. With her arms gracefully curved above her head, she admired herself at length.

Then, slowly, with the suppleness of a cat stretching, her entire body entered into a dance, without her quitting her sculptural pose, and every part of her began to move. By turns, her breasts, her shoulders, her abdomen and her hips made particular graces, gyrations, slow or rapid comings and goings. It was like a symphony of flesh animated by a voluptuousness that did not depart from the dancer. Nora was dancing for herself; her entire body and al her senses participated therein, and she enjoyed herself fully—more, even than if she had had a male partner.

Suddenly, she stopped, staring into the large mirror. Two luminous points were scintillating there, like a vague green reflection of emerald or beryl issuing from an unknown source.

That's odd, she said to herself. *One might think that the eyes of a god or a genie were looking at me...*

And that thought reminded her of her childish dreams, of enchantresses, genies and Prince Charming. She smiled, blew a kiss to her dream, and resumed her dance, which suddenly became wilder.

Was it an atavistic memory of past times? She bounded, ran on all fours, leapt, spun, and, as in the theater, stopped a vertical leap and remained as motionless as a Tanagra statuette, a marble of quivering flesh, in front of the mirror, where, naively and bestially, she admired herself, detailing all her perfections, and caressing her belay and loins with her hands.

And another fantasy surged forth: that of getting to know that Flower of voluptuousness better. She went to fetch a hand-mirror from the sideboard, and, bending over, contorting herself in order to see more clearly, she examined that delicate organ attentively, which plays such a large role in the life of a woman.

In the depilation of her ape's body, the physicians had contrived a silky black triangle of public hair, and Nora, amused, caressed it softly, while bending over further and further in order not to miss any detail of the voluptuous contractions of that orchid.

Suddenly, she felt two caressant hands seize her by the hips, and an ardent breath burning the nape of her neck. Frightened, she pulled away and paraded a bewildered glance around her. There was no one there, and yet, the same expert hands recommenced running everywhere; a mouth glided, searching for hers; she felt herself pushed and pulled toward the divan.

A convulsive tremor gripped her and, as she finally found herself laid down on the cushions, as she felt a body extend over her, she made a supreme effort, and escaped once again.

A burst of laughter rang out.

Then, terror took possession of her; her bestial nature got the upper hand. With savage howls she bounded over the walls, the paintings, the tapestries, the curtains, which tore and collapsed with her on to the carpet. Frantically, she leapt, bounding over the furniture, running on all fours, panting, her eyes bulging, her jaw menacing, her mouth foaming. In that disorder, to be sure, the beauty became the beast again—but even so, she remained graceful, desirable.

But the pursuit did not cease. Finally, blocked in a corner, she was seized, dominated and carried to the divan, where more exact caresses recommenced.

Exhausted, Nora submitted.

Then, under the kisses, her nature gained the upper hand again, and, wildly, with frenetic ardor, she gave herself.

For the first time, she sensed that she was in that fantastic domain for which she had searched so ardently and so vainly. It could only be a genie, one of those marvelous beings that had the gift of invisibility, and which would soon reveal itself to her with all the prestige of its omnipotence! And she was the foremost lover of that god of fantasy, the Danaë of that new Jupiter, with the sexual rain that was inundating her with its fecund semen. She waited for the shower of gold and precious gems, and once again, savant caresses made her entire being vibrate.

Then the orangutan purr of pleasure raged within her throat, she felt herself penetrated to the very depths of her being, and, drunk on voluptuousness, she gave herself again, frenziedly.

She was obliged to remain there for a long time, as if overwhelmed by a sweet fatigue, sleeping off, so to speak, an orgy of lustful stupor.

She came to her senses again when she heard the door open, and the chambermaid came in.

At the sight of the devastated room, she took a step back; then she perceived her mistress, naked, looking at her with a wild expression.

"Good God!" cried Berthe, alarmed. "Help! Someone has tried to murder Madame! Help! Murder!"

"Shut up, Berthe! Since no harm has come to me, there's no point rousing the whole house."

"But Madame..." With a gesture, the chambermaid indicated the chaos. Precipitate footsteps sounded, and Jules Ducon appeared on the threshold.

"Nora! Nora! What's wrong? What's been done to you?"

Nora passed her hands over her face. *Did I dream that adventure*, she thought, *or am I mad?*

Jules Ducon had picked up one of the lacerated curtains. Already, he was wrapping the young dancer in it.

"I don't know," she said, by way of apology and explanation. "I was alone, tranquil...suddenly...I don't know any more...I must have had a moment of dementia...I no longer remember anything..."

"Are you subject to such fits?" the millionaire asked, suddenly anxious.

"No, it's the first time. It's frightful! I had the sensation that a man was here, that he tried to grab me...I struggled, I fought, and then..."

She had slid a hand beneath the curtain that veiled her. *And yet*, she said to herself, feeling an abnormal dampness beneath her fingers, *it wasn't entirely a dream, but a reality...*

"But Monsieur, Madame," said Berthe, "you're not alone here! There...there's a...a...kind of man!"

Ducon turned round, suffocating.

"What! In the name of God, what's that?"

The individual he had addressed took two paces forward. "Excuse me. I was just coming to your house when cries of 'Help!' caused me to hurry, and I came in behind Monsieur. That's how I got this far." He added: "I came to give you this on behalf of Master Ernest Paris, whose secretary I am."

And Narcisse held out a long, flat package.

Ducon could not say anything more. He was petrified.

Nora, meanwhile, had recognized the orangutan, and was studying him with an increasing anxiety.

What if it were him? she thought, still haunted by the idea of enchantment. *He ought, therefore, to resume his appearance as a young and handsome lord.*

But the thick stature of the great ape, his long arms and short legs reassured her. No, it wasn't him. But in that case, who was it?

She reached out and took the package. "Thank you, Monsieur," she said. "Please express my thanks to the dear Master, but don't tell him in what state you've discovered me. I've just had a nervous crisis that I can't yet explain; I hope that it won't have any consequences—I feel much better already."

"Will you permit me to return to obtain news of your health, on the Master's behalf?"

"Yes, if you wish," Nora replied, indifferently, "but for the moment, what I need above all is rest."

Narcisse bowed profoundly and withdrew.

"But...but...that's an ape!" stammered Jules Ducon.

"Yes, I know him—I saw him at Eze, in the home of Doctor..." She was about to add Goldry, but remembered that that name was also her own and said instead: "Jean Fortin. He's an ape who can talk."

"And you seem to find that quite natural. However..."

"The ape is the work of four scientists, who seem to me to be four rather fantastic individuals. I'll tell you the whole story another time."

"And that orangutan is Ernest Paris's secretary? At least he's not risking going unperceived. So, our national genius is continuing to pay court to you?"

"Yes, he's come three times since my return. You know that I met him at Eze?"

"Yes, I know, and I even approve of your receiving him; it will make the reputation of your salon. What's that he's sent you?"

"Doubtless the inscribed book he promised me—a luxury specimen,[31] probably. Open the package."

"Damn!" said Jules Ducon. "It's one of his master-pieces, *Phryné*.[32] On Japanese paper, three states and an

---

[31] It was conventional for Parisian publishers of the era to produce a number of special copies of their books, usually large-sized and cloth-bound, printed on high quality "Japanese paper," which would be signed by the author. The preliminary material of *Nora* states that ten such copies were produced of that book.

[32] *Phryné* was a famous Greek courtesan. As the book is ficti-tious, we can only guess at its contents, but it doubtless made use of the legends stating that she was the model for at least two famous statues of Aphrodite by Praxiteles, that she fi-nanced the rebuilding of the walls of Thebes, and that when she was put on trial (on an unspecified charge), the tide was turned in her favor when her defender—one of her many lov-ers—removed her robe in order to display her breasts to the judges, who were so impressed that they acquitted her. The courtroom scene was featured in a famous painting by Jean-Léon Gêrome, *Phryné devant l'Areopage* (1861) and she was the subject of an 1893 opera by Camille Saint-Saëns. Anatole France wrote a novel about another famous courtesan, *Thaïs* (1890), which some consider to be his masterpiece. It was not illustrated by Édouard Chimot, although a reprint of the novel would have fitted very well into the series of high-quality il-

original drawing by Chimot. Let's see the dedication: '*To the loveliest of beauties from the most fervent of her admirers, Ernest Paris.*' This is a regal gift, you know, my love?" I have a great many things to tell you, but I can see that you're extremely tired. Lie down... Until tomorrow..."

lustrated editions the artist produced in the 1920s under the rubric of Les Éditions d'Art Devambez.

XII. Homo-Deus, the Invisible Satyr

1. Animal Triste, Post-Coïtum[33]

On emerging from the dancer's house, the orangutan had leapt into a superb limousine that was parked outside the front door.

"Ah, there you are! Good!" said the voice of Marc Vanel, Homo-Deus. Addressing his chauffeur, he added: "Home, Mardruk."

Narcisse was doubtless accustomed to the doctor's invisibility, for he did not manifest any astonishment

"You gave the book, *Phryné*, to Nora, then?" the voice continued.

"You made a fine mess in the drawing room! The poor girl!"

"Excuse me, my friend—I'd forgotten that Nora pleases you."

"I can't be jealous of you—but I love her!"

"Let's see! Let's explain ourselves. You love her, you say. Is that with your senses or with your brain?"

"In two fashions: as an ape and as a human. Like much else, I'm trying to understand amour more fully."

"You won't understand anything at all. A lot of white paper has been dirtied on that subject. There are as many different amours as there are human mentalities.

---

[33] This chapter title adapts the famous Latin proverb, the source of the phrase "post-coital triste," attributed (apocryphally) to the physician Galen: *post coïtum omne animal triste est, sive gallus et mulier* [all animals are sad after sex, except for cocks and women].

Thus, I'm a sensualist, a satyr, seeing nothing in women but the personal pleasure I can extract from them. I have, however, known true love."

"And how did you experience it?"

"In a totally unexpected fashion. I could easily have possessed the woman I loved, but I respected her, because it was necessary for me to wait until she gave herself to me, under pain of being an object of scorn for her."

"And Mademoiselle Jeanne Fortin loved you?"

Marc Vanel smiled in a strange fashion that the orangutan could not appreciate—and with reason—but when the invisible man resumed speaking, the orangutan sensed, in the sound of his voice, that he had touched a sensitive fiber, ever ready to vibrate in Homo-Deus' heart.

"She's never ceased to love me, Narcisse. Although our bodies remained estranged, our souls have melted into one another, and that's the most sublime sentiment that the human beast can know."

"I don't understand you very well, but it's thus that I love—that I'd like to love—Nora."

"Your Nora can't be compared to Jeanne Fortin."

"You're a man of the same race as her; why haven't you sought to make yourself cherished by her?"

"Because I don't have the time, and because Nora..."

"What about Nora? Finish your thought."

"I'll tell you that, one day...the day when Nora loves you."

"That dancer will never love me; I'm only an ape," said Narcisse, bitterly.

"Patience, my friend. Trust me when I tell you that she'll love you—perhaps precisely because you're an ape."

"Oh, I beg you, tell me how I can win that woman. Tell me how you, Homo-Deus, have experienced love. Was the woman who triumphed over a genius such as you as beautiful as Nora?"

"You're burning to know how Marc Vanel could allow himself, like an ordinary man, to be influence by that sentiment... Listen, then, and may you obtain some profit from my story."

It was an exceedingly strange spectacle: the ape attentive to the voice of an invisible being.

"Love," Marc Vanel went on, "can't really be defined, because it's as various as individuality, and everyone has his own way of comprehending it. For some it's simply called pleasure. In that case, it's renewed with every woman possessed, and the sensation is so brief that, in order to prolong it, the man uses artifices into which he puts all his senses, but always coming back, in the end, to the primal act: copulation.

"Others create for themselves an artificial love, by the force of the imagination; they ought to be the most favored individuals, because for them, the image of the beloved individual, being in the mind, can be varied at will. The woman is no longer a female animal but an idea being, whom they decorate will all graces and all beauties. They're the Pygmalions of love; they've created a magnificent statue, which they strive to animate. But disappointment follows: the statue, idol, angel, divinity—the designation varies—can't compete with the unbreakable laws of nature, and the seeker of the ideal is annihilated in sexual intercourse. For all the amorous imaginations of poets, all the heroines of amour, garlanded with the roses of passion, the Laures, the Béatrices, the Dona Sols, the Mireilles, the Marquisettes and so many others, end up with an ignoble act...

"Oh well, in spite of my cognizance of defects and virtues, I once fell in love like the common run of mortals—which is to say, stupidly, and without knowing why, and I've suffered all the more for it because I'm intelligent. That amour, in which I, handsome, ardent and poetic, invested all my life, was odiously betrayed by a hussy. I suffered from it, it's true, but today I rejoice in it, since it's to that unfortunate passion that I owe being what I am today. If that adored woman had responded to what she inspired in me, I would have married her, I would have striven, in order that she wouldn't suffer in life, to make a great deal of money, and I would have become a physician like the rest, making rich men endure, and not caring much about the poor.

"That chagrin deflected me from a deplorable goal and caused me to flee society. I traveled; I acquired extraordinary knowledge; I sought and I found invisibility; and then I returned to France. It was in Paris, at the Red Nest, that I encountered love—the only veritable love, the one I desire—but which could never be the desire to have a Nora!"

"But the one that haunted you at twenty…?"

"My first romance was merely the effect of an exuberant youth, something instinctive, the first appeal of nature to the great law of the conversation of the species. Humans, in their vanity of believing that everything belongs to them, wanted that law—which all beings obey—to be an exceptional law for them, and they invented amour, which is a word that makes no sense if one tries to define it, but which has its justification if one abandons on abandons oneself to it stupidly, animalistically, and takes it for what it ought to be…for what it is, however one tries to disguise it. Thus, that kind of amour I've known, and like the common run of mortals, I've suffered from it, because, by virtue of a false education, I too had wanted to create an amour in accordance with my fantasy.

"What I felt for Jeanne Fortin, however, was of another essence altogether—which is to say that I loved her with my senses and my brain as well. If Jeanne had responded to the appeal of my senses, perhaps I would have cherished her less, for a man has the peculiarity that nothing ever satisfies him. Only that which is refused him has attraction for him; in reality, one submits to the present, but only loves the future. The past lives on in memory, but, as one is bound to pass judgment on it, one finds flaws in that which, from our viewpoint, was not lived as it ought to have been. In sum, the present doesn't exist, since, from one moment to the next, it has changed.

"You want a woman for a week; during that lapse of time, she is for you the most beautiful and the most perfect being. The present arrives, the moment when you possess her—it would be more accurate to say 'when she possesses you' because it's the man who gives and the woman who receives, but let's allow the convention to stand—and the man, satisfied if he doesn't have the hypocrisy of vanity, turns his back on his ideal, like any animal in creation. The act accomplished, nature demands no more. But a man, out of laziness, contents himself with the same female, with whom he finds his pleasure without fatigue and carelessly—unless he makes the further illusion—and that's the basis of marriage. But I'm straying from what's truly interesting, the story of my true my unique amour. I'll get back to it…"

"I'm listening, Master."

"I had exhausted all the genres of amour, and at first I desired Jeanne Fortin as I'd desired all the pretty or beautiful women I'd met. Thanks to invisibility, which spared me time needlessly wasted in more or less long flirtation, I really was the invisible satyr, who can satisfy all his desires without fear of being driven away. But with Jeanne Fortin I understood that, this time, the satyr couldn't meet his expenses. With any other, I wouldn't have cared whether I was loved or not; the habitual coitus satisfied me—but I wanted Jeanne to love me; and, in fact, she did love me. But Jeanne, Jean Fortin's daughter, was above humanity...

"One night, being invisible, I got into the bathroom where she was naked; she told me, frankly, without blushing, that on the day she surrendered to a man, it would be uniquely for the sake of curiosity for the sensation to be experienced, not to yield to a sentiment that she didn't understand. And the admirable virgin didn't understand amour, because she had studied it and dissected it, and knew all its defects, and was scornful of the act as a mere satisfaction of the senses. She judged it indecent, and a sensation too brief to be worth the trouble of desiring it."

"So, Monsieur Vanel?"

"I spoke to Jeanne Fortin eloquently. I strove to awaken desire in her; I described the pleasures of the flesh, reinforced by imagination and fantasy. She laughed in my face, patronizingly, and said to me: 'Marc, you're wasting time here that you could use more pleasurably. I'm a virgin bodily, but not mentally. You believe that you love me; you don't love me—you want me, and that's all. By contrast, I love you, and my love is the height of my intelligence. You could be a frightful

135

monster that I would love just as much, because what I love in you isn't the conjunction of our sexual organs, it's your mind, your intelligence; and if I resist that attraction of bodies, it's because I have the certainty that the sexual act would kill the love. I love you ardently for your mind, but I disdain your body. If, one day, having nothing to do, or—one never knows what natural law will impose upon us—I feel the need to be a mother, I swear that I won't seek out any other man than you...'"

Marc Vanel, invisible, remained silent for a few moments. Then his voice resumed, but the habitually mocking voice became majestically grave:

"What do you think of that love, Narcisse? You see, *She* didn't have any of the weaknesses and hypocrisies of her sex. So I understood, and inclined before her will. We continued to live side by side in a sublime communion, that of science, and desire never—never, you hear—came between us. But a fatal day came, and Jeanne Fortin, expiring in my arms, told me again that she loved me, with a love more human, since, having refused me her body, a transmutable form, she gave me her soul, an immortal fluid. Thanks to her father, Jean Fortin, that transmission of the soul was accomplished. Is not that magnificent gift, that union of two elite intelligences, the most beautiful amour that can exist?"

Another pause; after a few moments, Marc Vanel's voice recommenced its speech, but in a tone of ironic gaiety: "The beast isn't dead; the invisible satyr obeys the appeals of the flesh, all the more so as all our sensations report to the brain. I can say that I live, now, the sensations of both sexes, masculine and feminine, and that I experience a double sensual pleasure in the act of amour."

"I understand, Master," said the ape, pensively. If, one day—and the day will surely come, since my intelligence has not yet reached its apogee—it's necessary for me, too, to double my soul with its sister soul...but where shall I find a second Jeanne Fortin?"

"There is none. I'll give you my own double mentality, when I judge that the moment has come."

"Oh, Master—you'd do that for me...an ape?"

"Not for the ape, Narcisse, but for the superhuman. In any case, isn't that, for me, the sole means of not dying?"

2. The Man in the God

In the portrait that Marc Vanel had made of himself for Narcisse, he had not completely dissected—if one might put it thus—his amorous mentality. Not only was the man, as he had said, multiple in his amours but materially, he was submissive to a slavery from which, in spite of his intelligence, he could not abstract himself: a slavery of instinct, a kind of irresistible physical flaw that overcame his reason.

Thus, accomplished and apparently normal married men can be seen devoting themselves to onanism in spite of the fact that they have alongside them the means of satisfying the natural desire to copulate. Others indulge in acts contrary to nature, and what might be called veritable tortures. Certainly, degenerates are more inclined to that than others, but great intellectuals are not excluded from it; it is, above all, in remarkable intelligences that sensual exasperation shows itself most actively, for in them, the imagination leads all passions and all vices to exaggeration. A certain elite is subject to the law that Edgar Poe called "the imp of the perverse." For want of finding a justification for the accomplished act, the intellectual knows perfectly well that he is committing a stupidity, but he gives in to it anyway, because it is independent of his will. Perhaps it is madness, since reason cannot dominate it; if so, there must be a seed of madness on everyone, which only requires to germinate and bloom.

Homo-Deus, more than anyone else, was able to analyze his own impressions, but however great the strength of his domination over others might be, he had not been able to vanquish a need within him that, for his physical organization, had the same force as thirst and hunger. That need, that passion, was woman, and, in reality, he had never tried to resist its influence. If fable is not entirely a lie, Marc Vanel would have been, in fabulous times, a veritable satyr.

As he had told Narcisse, he had experienced in his early youth an amour of the imagination, an amour inspired by reading exalted by the first awakening of the senses, Having passed that crisis, he no longer had any other needs than sensual amour—the best understood, in any case, in the Orient, where he had spent ten years of his life. Having returned to Europe, he had had no difficulty, being handsome and well-built, in finding female partners; he had used them abundantly—but, once his senses were satisfied, he regretted the time wasted in flirtation that could have been better employed in his scientific work.

When he discovered invisibility, Marc Vanel became veritably worthy of the name of Homo-Deus. Like the master of Olympus, he had only to set his designs upon the beauty that attracted his attention in order to satisfy his desire, without wasting precious time in grimaces that were henceforth unnecessary.

He had gone to Nora's house without having made a preconceived decision to posses the she-ape, to whose metamorphosis into a woman he had contributed, but he had been curious to know how far Ernest Paris had got with the dancer. He knew from Narcisse that the writer had inscribed a book to Nora, which the secretary was to take to her. Thus far, the orangutan had only gone out in Marc Vanel's car, in order to avoid the curiosity of idlers. His entry into Ernest Paris' home was recent; few people were aware of it, and hardly anyone knew that Jacquot Blakson had been replaced.

Marc Vanel, invisible, went to find Narcisse as soon as the Academician had left the house in the Avenue Foch, and had reached the Rue Spontini ahead of him. By that means, he had witnessed the amorous old man's visit, and had become increasingly convinced that Ernest Paris was ripe for the sexual graft. He contemplated making his exit behind the Academician, but, as chance would have it, Nora and the chambermaid blocked the door, in such a way that he would have been forced to jostle them in order to get out, and he had gone back into the drawing room with Nora, who, believing herself to be alone, had started dancing for herself, completely naked. It did not require as much as that to awaken the sensuality of the invisible satyr, and, without premeditation on his part, he had surrendered to his dominant passion.

No one is unaware that the human brain is merely a reservoir of energy, in which each faculty is localized in a particular place; but the individual self is not localized, it is the ensemble of all those different faculties. The mystery is still ill-defined, since the suppression or amnesia of some parts of the brain leads to the death of certain faculties. The self seems to be a subtle fluid animating the whole, and yet, a part can be suppressed with a certain area of the brain. In the course of Marc Vanel's studies with Jean Fortin, the two scientists had tried many times to elucidate the bizarre circumstance, but had never been able to resolve it. And Marc, in his mental duality, felt that a part of his self escaped him, and subjugated his entire self to lustful acts that Homo-Deus, in the state of mental repose considered unworthy of him.

"What do you expect?" Jean Fortin said to him. "Fornication is, for you, an imperious need. It's necessary to support that vice as the outlet of your intelligence, the waste-disposal of your brain. Its excrement is sperm; let it out and don't worry about the rest. The subtle sadnesses aren't yours but those of my daughter Jeanne, who has passed her soul into you, and has always been scornful of the gestures of the loins. I find it very interesting, that struggle between your two temperaments, but thus far, I've merely observed it. It's you, my son, the male, who holds sway."

"You must be right; our intellectual fusion is tending more and more to complete the sensual fusion. Our mingled sexes caused a perturbation at first to which Jeanne's senses have finally awakened, thus doubling the voluptuous sensation, but as you say, the struggle continues—which is to say that Jeanne is still struggling."

"It's difficult, isn't it, to explain and analyze your miserable sensations? Jeanne, my daughter, that duality of thought...in you, Homo-Deus, the man too often commands the god."

XIII. The Conquest of Life

Ernest Paris rarely went out alone, but since he had taken Narcisse on as his secretary, he could not show himself arm in arm with an ape without giving rise to equivocal comment. The Master therefore went out to stroll alone or in the company of a friend. That day, the weather was mild and dry, and, in spite of the injunctions of Pédauque,[34] the Academician had gone out alone with the intention of taking a turn around the Bois de Boulogne. With a newspaper in his hands, he was walking slowly, reading bits here and there and commenting aloud on the articles. Among the papers he had bought was *L'Humanité*, a daily to which he occasionally submitted reports of public meetings.[35]

The article that he was reading concerned a strike in the metallurgical industry, which was seeking support

---

[34] Pédauque was a mythical queen of the Visigothic kingdom centered on Toulouse in the fifth and sixth centuries, who was supposed to have had (as her name signifies in Occitan) the feet of a goose. Anatole France summarized her legend and many historical variants thereof in his Voltairean comic novel *La Rôtisserie de la Reine Pédauque* (1893). The Pédauque whose injunctions Ernest Paris is ignoring, however, will subsequently be revealed to be his maidservant.

[35] *L'Humanité*, founded by Jean Jaurès in 1904, was the newspaper of the French Communist Party for many years (it still exists but has long been independent). As an enthusiastic member of the party, which he had joined during his angry participation in the Dreyfus Affair, Anatole France assisted in the founding of the paper and was a frequent contributor until his death.

from all the trades unions in order to bring about a general strike.

Again! Ernest Paris thought. *The workers must be mad to allow themselves to be led by these pamphleteers. A strike! Don't these imbeciles see that a strike always coincides with a lack or orders or an overabundance of stock? Truly, I was wrong to associate myself with those people. To anticipate the future—what a joke! All this is the fault of the Dreyfus Affair. I thought then that there was a popular consciousness. But it's beginning again and it's always the same: they demolish, they rebuild, and it's still the same. Men can't liberate themselves from their passions; nothing will change. We play with our passions, but the greatest events don't change anything at all.*

A general strike to do what? To jabber, to idle, to get drunk, and then to shoulder the yoke of misery again. After all, perhaps it's not so stupid. During those few days, the workers will live like the directors; they'll even imagine that they amount to something. Idiots! Puppets, whose strings are being pulled by a few disaffected bourgeois! And they believe that I too am one of theirs, because, disgusted with the conservative regime, I fell back one day on anarchism. An anarchist, a smasher of everything, so be it—but a socialist, a mumbler and tower of the line? No, my lads!

Why am I mixed up in all that? And no means of getting out! The brothers have me and brandish me; I'm one of their flags—red, naturally. And they don't sense that I'm a bourgeois, a dirty bourgeois, like Jaurès, like Karl Marx, whom they've never read, any more that they've read me. What, then? The people make gods with legends, phantoms of men that they take for realities. In sum, theoretically, underneath these strikes, there's

nothing but the instinct of the capitalist presented decep-
tively to the mass of the credulous.

Bah! Let's resign ourselves to it; we don't know, we
don't understand, we're no different from the men of all
ages. But practically, what remains to us is the game of
appearances, the graceful movement of the body, and the
illusions of thought. That's enough for me...but for them,
poor devils? Egotism! Divine egotism! It's You who di-
rect and lead everything, and that ideal suffices to fill
our existence... Apart from that, I don't believe there's
anything at all!

"But it's the dear Master!" cried a joyful voice.
"How glad I am to run into you!"

Ernest Paris opened his arms and pressed the man
who had interrupted his reverie to his heart.

"What a pleasure, my dear friend! Such a long time!
Let's see, since...since...?"

"Since the Dufusne sale, which you bid against me
for the *Elegies de Jean Second*.[36] Do you remember? It
was the Tissot edition with the subtitle: *suivies de*
quelques baisers inédits par P.-F. Tissot. Ha ha! I even
had the advantage of stealing that curious volume from
you."

"It was the subtitle that made me let it go. One
would have to be from his village to imagine that there
was anything unpublished in that material. The unpublished kisses of Monsieur Tissot! Where could he
find unpublished kisses? In the first days of creation?
Adam and Eve, after a few weeks, certainly knew as

---

[36] A famous collection of Latin love poems by "Janus
Secundus", which went through numerous French versions in
the 18th and 19th centuries. The edition cited was published in
1826.

much as Second and Tissot. Those patented kisses have mouths full of Greek and Latin, and he must have slobbered them all over the cheeks of his darling when they passed from theory to practice. In brief, that theft wouldn't tarnish our old friendship, my dear Jacques."

"Ha ha! I've stolen many other things since, my dear Master!"

"La la! Not so much of the 'dear Master,' Lemay—it ages me too much. The wind of the century must have stolen from your memory the passage from the gospel: 'Do not allow yourselves to be called Rabbi, for one alone is your master, and you are all Brothers.'[37] I too, in my youth, called people 'dear Master,' but that word signifies, etymologically, Magister—which is to say 'you are three times greater than me three times greater than anyone...' It translates intimately as: 'Poor old pedant, you drivel and drool and wobble your head—don't linger in this world; you've lasted long enough; it's time to make way for the young.' Yes, my friend, that's what those who butter up their old idols at arm's length think. Where has the time gone when I gave them the 'dear master'? I was an adolescent then. Don't age me, Lemay, my friend!"

"Ha ha! I'm one of the young ones, myself...and so..."

"No! If I'm not mistaken, you're a year older than me...you've seen more than eighty springs."

"Yes, if you trust chronologies—but look at me!"

And Lemay stood up straight, fine and sprightly, before his friend Ernest Paris.

---

[37] I have translated this quotation from the French Bible literally, although the standard English rendering of *Matthew* 23:8 is not much different.

Jacques Lemay, the son of Pierre Lemay, the founder of the Bars Lemay, a chain of coffee-houses, was not just anyone. The Bars Lemay had more than a hundred branches on Paris: *Gourmets go to Lemay's*. Jacques was a very Parisian specimen, a socialite, a great lover of women, and also of the arts and letters. There was not a salon, theater or music hall where Jacques Lemay was not welcome, and where he was not the king by virtue of his bonhomie, his amiable criticism and his large fortune. Physically he was short and plump, with a doll-like face under an impeccably shiny silk hat. The Lemay hat had its celebrity, akin to that of the old Sardou beret. The friendship of Ernest Paris and Jacques Lemay dated from their adolescence; they were always happy to bump into one another. Their "do you remembers?" had the joy of only evoking pleasant memories.

Lemay had good reason to strike a pose in front of his friend, because, in spite of his gray and slightly thinning hair, he was astonishingly young and lively, shorter than Ernest Paris but well-balanced and looking very well. The writer studied him with an affection mingled with envy.

"Do you know, Lemay, that you look marvelous! My word—you're rejuvenated! You're *le May*—the jolly month of May!"

"Ha ha!" said the other, shifting his weight from one foot to the other. "You never spoke a truer word." He passed his arm under the Academician's, and drew him away. "Do you know, my dear, what I'm doing here?"

"Here? What I'm doing myself, of course—talking a walk."

"Phooey! I live in Passy; I don't come to stroll in the Avenue Foch, do I? No, my dear, I've simply had a stroke of luck. Don't roll your eyes like that, can't you see that I still have a little in the locker? And women have always been my little weakness. Ha ha! Yours too, eh? Come on, don't deny it—your reputation's made, my friend. But there you go! You daren't risk it, for fear of a breakdown, whereas I...ha ha! I tell you, my dear, I still have a little put by! A little girl, a jewel! Sixteen—that's fresh—a little flower, what? Ha ha!"

"Get away, joker! You're older than I am."

"One year more, but thirty less. Look at me, old man."

And, pivoting on his heel, Jacques Lemay sketched a few steps of the Charleston.

"Eh? There! Eh? There!"

"You're going to get us noticed, my lad. At our age..."

"At my age? But I'm twenty years old, my dear, and at that age, one has fun. My little friend is sixteen, I tell you; she's a rosebud...phooey! Phooey!"

And the little man leapt into the air.

"What's got into that fellow?" muttered Paris. Aloud, he said: "Are you mad or in your second childhood?"

"The latter; I'm getting younger every day. If the nurse is pretty, I come back..."

"Come on, Lemay, this isn't natural. Sixteen? And you can?"

"And how!" He started singing: "*She's sixteen! I'm sixteen! The age of amour! It's the age of amour!*"

"Ta ta ta! You're intoxicated—are you full of spanish fly?"

"Better than that old man. Lean over." He whispered into the other's ear: "I've had a graft!"

"Ah!" said Paris, open-mouthed. "You…you've dared…?"

"I've dared! I confess that I was anxious about the result, because it's been long enough coming, but now…here!" He indicated a dimension on the Academician's cane.

"Damn!" said the latter, dazzled. "And it holds up?"

"Does it hold up? Come in, come in, Monsieur…as soon as one finishes, one recommences!"

"I'm salivating," said Ernest Paris—and it was true. "Good God—how stupid I've been!"

"Just between us, no?" said Jacques Lemay. "It isn't to be shouted from the rooftops, and you need, my dear Master…"

"You can be sure of my discretion—all the more so because I'm hesitating…groping…myself."

"You're groping yourself? Limp, is it?"

"Don't be silly. I mean that that I'm hesitating over the sacrifice of Romeo, or Philemon…"

"What are you telling me? Philemon? A model of conjugal fidelity. Oh, no, no conjugo! The crazy nights of intoxication for us! Plurality! Boom boom boom!"

"He's mad, I swear! Damn! I want to be rejuvenated, but what will people say if I rejuvenate myself too much?"

"What does it matter? Oh, my old friend, I don't give a damn what anyone says. Those who purse their lips, it's because they can't do it anymore. Sixteen! Blonde…a jewel…!"

"And you've arranged to meet this blonde spring in the Avenue?"

"Yes," said Lemay, suddenly anxious. "At the Metro station. I'm taking her to the Pavillion Dauphine, or the Pré Catelan."

147

"But we're at the Porte Dauphine. What if you've been stood up, Lemay?"

"What an idea! No, she loves me, my dear—she told me so."

"And what did that cost you?"

"Thus far, nothing at all. It's new, since a week ago. A shopgirl at Chez Pateret. Sixteen years old!"

Yes, I know, since you keep on repeating it. But what if the jewel, the flower, the rosebud, doesn't come?"

"I'll die of it, old man! I told you: I'm twenty. I'm palpitating as at my first rendezvous." He broke into song again: "I'm Cherubini…*Marraine, chère marraine*…but no, the Comtesse was thirty…Angèle, my Angèle is only sixteen…a jewel… a fl…ah, there she is!"

In fact, a very pretty girl had surged forth from the stairway of the Metro. Lemay ran forward and kissed the hand that the lovely girl held out; she blushed—but very slightly, playing to the gallery.

"Well, Paris, what do you think? A jewel…a rose-bud…"

"Introduce me," said the Academician, majestically.

"Oh yes! Mademoiselle, my best friend: Ernest Paris of the Académie Française, the famous author…"

"Bonjour, Monsieur," said Angèle. "How are you?"

"Very well, Mademoiselle, thank you!" Paris replied, vexed by the slight effect that his name had produced on the shopgirl.

"You're high up, Monsieur Jacques says—in fact, you're taller that he is."[38]

---

[38] The girl has mistaken Lemay's *auteur* [author] for *hauteur* [height], perhaps deliberately.

Lemay guffawed, delighted with his young friend's wit. "No, my child, he's an author, a novelist…a man of letters, in sum."

"Oh, I understand—you write feuilletons in the newspapers. Do you know where I read them? In the W.C."

"She's amusing, the child, eh? What did I tell you, Paris? Oh, I'm certainly not stupid. So, Angèle, let's go. Shall we have lunch at the Pavillion Dauphine…no? Armenonville, then? Will you join us, my dear Master…pardon me, *my dear friend?*"

"No thank you. I'd hinder you in your effusions."

"Oh, I only invited you out of politeness!"

"Decidedly, Lemay, you're becoming too young for me. Adieu, children—enjoy yourselves!"

"If you're not coming, we'll have fun by ourselves," said the shopgirl, taking Jacques arm. "*Au revoir*, grandfather!"

Furious, Ernest Paris stood there watching the couple climb into Lemay's auto.

"Grandfather! Grandfather! What an insolent hussy! To compare me to a feuilletoniste that she reads in the W.C. Oh, glory, what nonsense!"

At a slow pace, somewhat downcast, and somewhat weary, having walked for more than an hour, the illustrious Academician headed for home, thoughtfully.

XIV. The Call of the Forest and Amour

The old master Ernest Paris was increasingly infatuated with the blue-tinted dancer, and Narcisse had taken Jacques Blakson's place in the Academician's house, while the latter was attempting to carve out a place in the literary world by writing for the new periodicals. Ernest Paris had had several reasons for taking on the orangutan: originality, the chic of the unique, as well as a warm recommendation from Georges Clemenceau, and the amusement of having an ape-man as an *alter ego*. In addition, the orangutan brought an efficacious collaboration to the eccentric book, *Le Vrai Jésus*, in which, thanks to an adroitly modified compilation and his own imagination, he was setting the prophet on his feet, very much alive. The extraordinary intelligence of Narcisse, and his surprising gift of adaptation to all ideas, supplemented and rejuvenated the qualities of his employer, whom age and habitual idleness sometimes paralyzed. He felt that the presence of the orangutan was for his mind what Voronoff's graft promised to be for his matter.

In the latter regard, he had not yet made up his mind, experiencing a kind of shame in confessing his physical debility. Furthermore, the generative act no longer seemed to offer him the same attraction as of old. He found as much pleasure, so to speak, in what might very justly be called the *bagatelles de la porte*; all the more so because he was perfectly well aware that his octogenarian carcass, although half-conserved, was somewhat ridiculous beside the body, so supple and so beautiful, of a child of less than twenty. Even rejuvenated by the method of the celebrated surgeon, he would not be in physical rapport with his partner, and that dread troubled his natural conceit; whereas he had the advantage, in badinage that was half-paternal and half-gallant, of preparing the courteous liberties that excite women, and cause them to accomplish acts in which senility finds its count without compromising male pride too much.

Ernest Paris thus enjoyed that role with Nora, the star of the Folies Bergère, and did not find it too bad. Without engaging the future, he had arrived at certain familiarities that almost put him in the position of an *ami de coeur*. Let us say, in passing, that the libertinage in question cost him very dear, even though he did not spend a sou. An erudite art-lover and collector, Paris had artistic treasures and curiosities in his home. Under the pretext of forming the young woman's taste, and in order to have the possibility of a caress, a friction by means of a bold touch, or even a gallant phrase, carefully researched and generously spiced, he brought Nora an eighteenth-century fan, marvelously constructed, of inestimable value, a lace collar of royal provenance, antique embroidery, a rare trinket, a marquetry glove-box, miniatures, and once, he gave her a wax sculpture attributed to Raphael, with was pure beauty. The least of those gifts represented a considerable fortune; each was a pretext for a caress or a comparison: small, discreet, but precise acts.

In sum, he was no longer a visitor but a kind of spoiled grandfather—spoiled in more ways than one—whom Nora welcomed without ennui.

In any case, Ernest Paris was an admirable talker when he was possessed of verve, and he always was in Nora's presence. That quality made him the most agreeable of pastimes. At first, the young artiste, who knew very few people in Paris, only gave audiences to Cécile Borel and her intimate comrade Maud Macfield, and a few people of no interest; but the news spread rapidly of the Master's assiduity at the house in the Rue Spontini, and that caused the members of Parisian literary high society to do the impossible to be received in the house of the blue dancer Nora Goldry.

Very flattered, Jules Ducon attracted flies by that means, whom the financier made his victims, and that success gave Nora a position, almost transforming her into a socialite. Besides which, a mutual sympathy brought the two men together: their love for Nora. There was no jealousy between them, but a cordial understanding for the happiness of the beloved women.

Occasionally, the great man brought Narcisse with him—when Nora asked him to do so, either to cause a sensation or to please a desire to have a new guest in the house. The orangutan understood that perfectly; he knew that he was only there in the capacity of an astonishing animal, and yet, he welcomed those occasions with joy, since it was the only way that he could see Nora, with whom he was increasingly smitten.

To facilitate those excursions, it was indispensable that Narcisse had an automobile at his disposal—Paris's, Jean Fortin's or Marc Vanel's; an ape, even dressed as a city-dweller, could not risk his large feet in the streets without provoking regrettable incidents. Having noticed that, in the young woman's drawing room, the venerable Academician always held forth, he employed a trick in order to go there with him more frequently; he played the humble admirer, aiding him in his difficult phases—for the Master was beginning to lose his memory, and sometimes stopped short, searching for a recalcitrant word—guiding him toward piquant anecdotes and facilitating his speech. That stratagem succeeded marvelously; Ernest Paris took his orangutan secretary with him increasingly frequently.

Sometimes, taking advantage of the invitation offered at Eze, one of the four extraordinary doctors, Fortin, Vanel, Goldry or Voronoff, appeared at Nora's home, in order not to lose contact with her, rather than with the goal of joining the number of the intimates of the house.

One day, Ernest Paris, having decided to separate himself from a fourteenth century reliquary with shutters that formed a triptych, asked Narcisse to take it to the Rue Spontini. In accordance with its destination, he had allocated it a place in her drawing room. The object was heavy and precious, and Paris did not want to entrust it to just anyone.

The orangutan installed himself in the Master's auto with the trinket; then he took it up to Nora's apartment personally and installed it on its pedestal in the agreed location. He then found himself alone with the young woman for the first time. He felt very emotional, all the more so as he realized that the opportunity to talk to the fashionable dancer in private might be unique. Suddenly, however, he caught a glimpse of himself in a mirror and could not suppress a dolorous groan.

Nora looked at the model and his image: that face, habitually impassive, which emotion caused to grimace, was so comically intense in the mirror that the young woman, in spite of everything, burst out laughing.

The orangutan had a sudden inspiration. He moved swiftly behind the armchair in which Nora was sitting, and said: "Laugh, Madame, laugh! Gaiety suits you so well. Laugh, in order not to hear the one who weeps! But no—I don't even have that relief; my tears are internal and fall back upon my heart. Laugh, for the thought could never cross your mind that a miserable ape might dream of rising up as far as you. And yet, it's the truth. Yes, I love you, with an amour all the more insensate because it is devoid of hope, for, beneath this grotesque envelope, burns a heart capable of understanding the most delicate sentiments. You know the fable, as old as the world, of Beauty and the Beast. The greatest of poets, Victor Hugo, sensed its justice in creating Quasimodo and Gwynplaine, the Man who Laughs: immortal types of dolor, and sadness via amour, but also of absolute devotion to the object of their love—their adoration!"

Nora, the ape-woman, was frightened. The ape, who had fallen silent for a few seconds, continued: "That amour, that devotion, I also feel, Madame, and I would have kept the secretly jealously if I had not had a moment of weakness, if my lacerated heat had not allowed that groan to escape that caused you joy. Oh, believe me, that's not a reproach. If each of my hours of pain could cause you the same hours of merriment, of pleasure, it would be a double joy for me to endure them. My love for you is so exclusive that I wonder whether, if, by some miracle, my adoration for you were not rejected, I might regret that intense dolor, which is for me a kind of voluptuousness..."

Nora was no longer laughing. She listened to that soft and captivating voice, to which the tone of suffering communicated a very particular charm; she listened to its tone, which, veritably emerging from the heart, was a beautiful epithalamium addressed to her beauty, to her sensibility. Breathless, she was still listening.

"You're not laughing any more, Nora? You sense that your beauty can excuse all follies, even the most implausible! If only you were blind, like the poet's Déa, who could not see the face but sensed the love, and loved![39] A monster can have a heart, a thought, a dream as well as the most magnificent of men, you see. But I don't even have the consolation that is hope...

"Who knows, if I had hope, whether I would not see, in the penchant that you were beginning to show for me, a kind of sadism, of depravity, a perverse quest for unknown, unprecedented sensations? An ape of my stature might have physical resources that men do not possess, and lubricity sometimes communicates bizarre inspirations..."

Narcisse was showing himself to be clever, for he was speaking to the senses of the former she-ape, and Nora was not a vestal. Thus, the thought having been evoked, she suddenly sensed a voluptuous frisson spring up in her loins, which caused her entire being to palpitate.

"But no," the orangutan went on. "I will not appeal to sensuality; my love is too pure; it has put you on such a pedestal; it has dressed an altar to you in my soul, and sees you as a divinity, a creature above humanity. My love for you is more akin to a divine worship than a terrestrial passion. It is necessary for me to spread at your feet the overflow of my heart; it is necessary that you know that one being in the world adores you as no woman has ever been adored, until the detachment of everything, until death itself."

---

[39] Déa is the object of the affections of the surgically-deformed Gwynplaine in Victor Hugo's novel *L'Homme qui rit* [The Man Who Laughs].

Nora, moved, stood up, pushing back the armchair that masked the orangutan. The latter prostrated himself before her. At the sight of the enormous monster, grotesque in his fashionable clothing, ridiculous in his pose, she felt a surge of indignation and anger. What! That formidable caricature, that animal mutated into a human being by speech, dared to love her, perhaps to desire her? And as he approached his horrible mouth to kiss her feet, she shoved him away, and showed him the door with an imperious gesture, shouting: "Get out, insolent! Get out, filthy beast!"

The orangutan uttered a terrible growl. That was too much! That she disdained him, that she felt for him the repugnance of a woman for a creature who had nothing human about him but intelligence and speech, was understandable—but that she did not understand that an ape, moved by intelligence to her level, and even, from that point of view, far above her, deserved better than to be considered as a vulgar animal, a stupid beast, he could not tolerate. Anger vibrated within him; the civilized ape disappeared, to give way to the ape outraged in his pride.

"Well, yes, I'm only an ape," he said to her, with a formidable expression, "but you're wrong to remind me of it so harshly, when you're in my power, and no human power could extract you from my arms...."

Horrified, Nora recoiled, her gaze not missing a single expression of that horrible visage—and by a singular affinity of atavism, the anxious eyes of the dancer rolled in their sunken orbits; her forehead wrinkled; her hair, usually flat on her cranium, bristled; her lips curled back, revealing the terrible jaw; and a dull growl emerged from her contracted throat.

Astounded, the orangutan looked at her, and suddenly, he recalled phrases pronounced by one or other of the four doctors, here and there, on the Riviera, at Beaulieu, in the place known s Little Borneo, the paradise of apes. He had the intuition, or the memory, that this seductive doll was a member of his race; he divined that her gracious envelope hid a soul similar to his own, and morally inferior, for he sensed singing within him, in addition to love for the woman, all the poetry of his natal forests.

Throwing his jacket and waistcoat rapidly to the ground, displaying all of his powerful hairy body, and extending his immense arms toward Nora, he cried: "Come to me, Nora! To me, your brother and your equal! Four doctors have made of an orangutan the cerebral human that I have become, as they have made of a little she-ape, by means of esthetic surgery, the pretty dancer that you are. Wake up, Nora! Wake up! Listen to the appeal of our ancestral forests singing in your heart!

"Yes, I am the Beast, but I have the superiority over human beings that the harmony of primitive nature vibrates in me! Listen to me, for I am the soul of the world! Yes, I am the Beast, but also the ancestor and the precursor! I am the Beast, here—but in the lands of the sun, I am the uncontested master, being the strongest and most intelligent of animals.

"Do you remember, Nora, our forests, our mountains, our rivers and our sunlight? Our forest, so vast, so profound, of a thousand tree-species, a thousand flowers, drowned in shadow and terror at the base, but resplendent at the summit beneath the blaze of our incomparable sun! Do you remember our mountains, with bizarrely jagged profiles, outlined against improbably colored skies? Do you remember Borneo—our rivers, our impetuous torrents rolling their hasty and foaming waters through a chaos of rocks; elsewhere, as calm and restful as a lake? Irradiating all of that, the tropical Sun! Compared with that Sun of ours, the pale sun of Europe resembles one of our full moons...

"Tell me, Nora, do you remember? And our brethren, the real masters of that land of dreams, the apes, the orangutans—can you see them, bounding through the high branches, in vertiginous leaps, living in habitations suspended like nests, and living free, untamed, innocent and simple, ignorant of hypocrisy and modesty? The Beast, they will say—so be it, but the Beast triumphant, because it is strength, and because it is instinct, that intelligence of primitives, the instinct to which all the pretended civilized revert at every convulsion of their so-called progress...

"Wake up, Nora, to the appeal of the Beast, to the appeal of amour, the only amour truly worthy of you, worthy of us—for you are of my race! Let the soul of the ancestral forests sing within you; let the entire scale of the sounds and colors of our fatherland of light sing within you! Remember Borneo, our great natal island, Nora! Remember, Nora!"

Bewildered and hypnotized, the young woman seemed to see the magical tableau of her homeland, evoked by the orangutan's cantilena, unfold before her. No, all of that was not dead in her memory; from the faded past, a half-effaced dream surged for from the utmost depths of her self. She abolished the milieu in which she found herself; the sumptuous apartment disappeared in the mirage of mysterious virgin forests. Humans no longer existed for her; the orangutan who evoked her land of yore was the simian lover that she would have been obliged to take in the décor of her infancy.

Then, with the cry of a wild beast, the cry of war and amour of her former brethren, she fell into the great extended arms of the orangutan, and embraced him frenziedly.

The she-ape had finally found her male!

And strangely enough, that simian embrace was mingled with cries, stutterings, bizarre articulations, guttural onomatopoeias that had a precise meaning, baroque vowels, mingled with cavernous or nasal sounds that constituted words; and the two apes understood one another, for they were gesticulating without modesty and speaking orangutan.

Oh, if Dr. Goldry had been present, what a lesson he would have obtained! At that moment, the air of the virgin forest was caressing the couple in folly.

XV. The True Jesus, *by Ernest Paris*

In Ernest Paris's study, the Master, buried in his high-backed chair, sitting before a sumptuous blotter fabricated with one of those superb morocco bindings decorated with coats-of-arms and dating from the beginning of the eighteenth century, was perorating, as was his habit. He was clad in dressing-gown like a pilgrim's robe, and simply coiffed in a cardinalesque skullcap.

Narcisse, sitting a short distance away at a small table, was sorting out notes and pads of paper, which he was taking from his immense sack, made from an old bed-sheet.

"I agree," said Ernest Paris, "that this preliminary work is rather tiresome, but think, my dear boy, that it's more than twenty years that this book, *Le Vrai Jésus*, has been in progress, abandoned, then taken up again, dropped, and picked up again. That's because, you see, I've always striven to believe in the existence of the man, Instead of making, like Renan,[40] a work of the imagination, I was obstinate in ferreting through texts in order to base myself on something solid—which won't prevent me from being accused of similarly making a Messiah to my own whim. Certain pages are very good, and, if they become harmful to the unity of the book, I'll

---

[40] The historian Ernest Renan (1823-1892)—from whom Champsaur might have borrowed his hypothetical author's forename—published a classic speculative *Vie de Jésus* (1863; tr. as *The Life of Jesus*) treating the account given by the gospels with a conscientious scholarly skepticism, which scandalized the devout.

be able to utilize them in the form of tales—which I've already done, on occasion. So, it's necessary for you to carry out a triage of all that rubbish, classifying the different documents in folders, according to their genre, and their religious or historical scope. You can already find the folders in…in…oh, where the devil are they? Damn! It's always the same; here, under the pretext of arranging things, everything gets turned upside down. Pédauque! Pédauque!" Ernest Paris rang his hand-bell frantically. "See how wretchedly I'm served! And that wretched Paphnuce,[41] who's still God knows where… Pédauque! Ah, finally!"

"What is it? No need to make such a racket. What's the matter now?"

"My folders! There were a whole lot of them. What have you done with them?"

Pédauque started laughing—which always exasperated her master.

"Well? Don't stand there laughing like an idiot. Where have you put them, the folders?"

"Monsieur is sitting on them. You put them there yourself, when you found that you were too low down to look in the big book of pictures that…"

"That's right…that's right! Indeed. My apologies, Pédauque. Go."

The good woman went, shrugging her shoulders. Ernest Paris stood up, lifted up the cushion, and took out thirty red cardboard folders.

"It did seem that the seat had something abnormal about it, but I thought my stature was growing along with my reputation. Oh, vanity! Perhaps I'd do better to

---

[41] Paphnuce is the name of the central character of Anatole France's *Thaïs*.

abandon the book. I'll have all the Christians on my back, Catholic or Protestant. And you know, Narcisse, that I value my repose above all else..."

"Did you hesitate for a moment over the Dreyfus Affair? For Jesus too, it's a matter of the triumph of Truth."

"Possibly—but people don't like anyone to prove to them that they're idiots. Bah! After all, the book, *Le Vrai Jésus*, will only be published after I'm dead. By then, I'll have nothing to fear from anyone."

"Are you yielding to Monsieur Vanel's arguments then, Master?"

"It's necessary. St. Paul, the true founder of Christianity, didn't know Jesus. And obviously, neither did the Apostles; otherwise, they wouldn't have waited so long before spreading their doctrine, forty years after its original composition—and there are also serious discrepancies between their texts. I except Saint John, whose amphigoric caprices in the Apocalypse have nothing to do with the existence of the Messiah."

"So you're writing the life of a human Jesus, who didn't exist anymore gloriously than his contemporaries, except that he died crucified."

"No, that's not entirely exact. I'm writing the history of a mythology based on the possible existence of a man that the Apostles created to form the basis of the new church. There was among the prophets who were abroad in Judea at the time—who were numerous—one who really was crucified as an agitator, in a political context, evidently, for the Romans were very tolerant in religious matters. That man was not called Jesus, or Christ, since those names have a significance other than a proper name. Jesus was a myth, but a real individual served as a basis for him. By substituting an annunciator, invented for the needs of the cause, for the crucified individual—evidently an adversary of the government, a kind of Ravachol[42] of the era—Mark, Luke and Matthew were as malign as the simple folk they were...

"By the way, Narcisse, since we need a name to substitute for that of Jesus—which signifies something like 'Savior'—what if we were to take the letters of the name of that anarchist, Ravachol, to make that of the revolutionary Jew. Cholavar, or Colvarah, that doesn't sound out of place as a Jewish name, does it?[43] Then again, the fellow couldn't have been of any great importance, since no one mentions him, Romans any more than Jews, although there were already famous soilers of papyrus at the time."

"Why preoccupy yourself with these details? In sum, Master, what you want to do is to write the fictionalized life of a Judean prophet, leaving him among the ranks of human beings—to which he belonged, in any case, even if his father was God. Although a legend, consecrated by twenty centuries of success, has made a

---

[42] "Ravachol" (Francis Koenigstein, 1859-1892) became the archetypal anarchist bomber of legend when he was guillotined for having carried out dynamite attacks against two magistrates, although his responsibility for those crimes remains highly dubious; the one murder to which he actually confessed had no political significance whatsoever, and was seemingly motivated by desperation. He was, however, glorified by real anarchists as a hero and a martyr, and it was in protest against his judicial murder that Auguste Vaillant threw a firework into to the Chambre des Députés in 1893, which was also described as a "bomb" by his prosecutors, and cemented the scarecrow image of the bomb-throwing anarchist.
[43] The central character of Le Crucifié is simply named Jesus, in spite of this argument.

minor agitator unknown in his own time except in the petty land of Judea, into an exceptional being, God himself, glorified in thousands of churches and cathedrals, all you have to do, in sum, is to return him to his original plane, and simply show a poor dreamer and speaker of twenty centuries ago to whom women of ill repute lent their assistance."

"Here, Narcisse, make a note on a piece of paper of all the names that we can indicate as founders or detractors of that legend. Firstly, all seniority and honor to Saint Paul, who utilized the three evangelists and was the true founder of Christianity; secondly, the Apostles Mark, Luke and Matthew, who only preached the Gospel, each in his own manner, with serious variations, well after the death of Jesus, and seventy years before there as a definitive version...

"Also remark that the historians of the reign of Tiberius make no mention of him, and that Pontius Pilate ignores him.[44] Pliny mentions him, in the year 111 or 112, but after the Christian versions, hence without any historical value. Tacitus says very little about him, and the text is probably apocryphal. The Jewish authors, Philo of Alexandria, Justin of Tiberias and Josephus don't breathe a word about Jesus. As an involuntary hero of the independence, they ought to have mentioned him, but in fact, they said nothing."

---

[44] Pontius Pilate never published anything, and thus cannot be held to have ignored Jesus, but Anatole France's most famous short story, "Le Procurateur de Judée" (1893; tr. as "The Procurator of Judea"), in which a retired Pilate reminisces about old times, reveals in its punch-line that although he can remember Mary Magdalen very well, he has no memory at all of Jesus.

"The consequence of all that, Master, brings us back to a non-violent Israelite revolutionary whom the Apostles deified."

"Yes, by imposing upon him the life of the Hindu Krishna, the son of Mahia or Mahria. There's a comparison to be made there, for there's a singular similarity in the two names that form the divinity of Christianity: Christ and Krishna, Jesus and Hésus—the war-god of the Gauls. Within that mythological gibberish, we need to make our symbolic speaker move, and strip him of that divine vestment, which stifles him like a veritable shirt of Nessus. What a task to disentangle the truth from that thicket of errors! What consoles me and encourages me is that our modern history is scarcely any clearer; today's Truth is tomorrow's Lie."

"That's why, my dear Master, the history of humankind, with regard to physical evolution, is more interesting than the political history of peoples."

"You're preaching for your saints, my dear orangutan, and damn it, you're right—there, at least, we don't have to struggle against interests and passions. Damn! There's a fortunate diversion, which brings me closer to people who interest me far more than this book, *Le Vrai Jésus*. Have you seen Voronoff lately?"

"Yes, I saw him yesterday, and he's hoping to see you before his departure."

"What! He's leaving? When?"

"In ten days or so. A congress in Geneva."

"Damn! I need to make up my mind, though. That swine Lemay has influenced me strangely. Let's see, my friend—frankly, what would you advise me to do?"

"Am I not the best of responses myself?"

"That's true…but…let's go! The die is cast; I shall cross the Rubicon. Telephone Voronoff, please."

Narcisse went to the apparatus and asked for the requested connection.

"Do you know, Narcisse, how long it takes to recover fully from this kind of operation?"

"It depends, Master; there are some who leave the Institute the same day, but it's more prudent to stay there for a week."

"And how long does it take for the effect of the renovation to become manifest?"

"That also depends on temperament. Two or three months."

"How long that interval will seem to me! By the way, Narcisse, did you know that I'm a candidate for the Nobel Prize?"

The orangutan made an interrogative gesture.

"Nobel was a Swedish chemist, born in Stockholm, the inventor of dynamite. In 1896, to his credit, he founded the Nobel prizes, to the profit of literary, scientific and philanthropic endeavors throughout the world. Was the suggestion of that candidacy an assurance of success? Oh well, I'll profit from my convalescence to undertake a trip to Sweden."

"And what shall I do in the meantime?"

"You'll replace me here. From the day of my departure, you'll be my other self—try, however, not to make the same grimaces. As for occupation, there'll be no lack of work: all of Jesus to disentangle. Then, you can commence a kind of sketch of him; when I return, we can establish the definitive text."

"I'm grateful to you for that confidence, Master."

"No false modesty, my boy. I assure you that you're entirely worthy to replace me...especially at the Académie."

"You aren't flattering your colleagues, the Immortals. As it happens, the regulations haven't anticipated the candidature of an ape."

"Too bad! The sessions would be no less grimacing, but more interesting. Do you believe, then, that Voronoff has made you a very valuable gift in giving you speech and intelligence?"

"I can foresee one of your paradoxes. Go on, Master, it's always profitable to listen to you."

"How human you are already! You capture me by vanity. So be it; it's the weakness of humankind, and I'm not exempt from it. I'll tell you, then, that intelligence is, in sum, a paltry gift that the demiurge has made to human beings. Intelligence, take note, doesn't only serve to make us suffer; it has limits that it cannot surpass; it is only able to awaken our curiosity, our desire to know, and leaves us in an indecision of which ignorance is unaware. As it isn't spread universally, it only excites envy and scorn.

"The dream, the good dream, is not only to be ignorant but to be stupid, which doesn't exclude the means of success—one can be stupid, but very clever in organizing one's life. For example, our legislators, our judges, our physicians, our advocates and many other people are certainly not idiots—they've received an adequate education—but all the same, it's sufficient to chat with them for an hour, as Lefèvre says, to comprehend that they're perfect imbeciles. One can be very stupid, and enjoy the consideration of one's peers.

"Undoubtedly, you prefer to be intelligent—in which case, you're mad! Think about it: we aggravate our chagrins and our dolors by meditating and reflecting on them; we then suffer twice, from the dolor in its reality and the image that our intelligence gives us of it. I've spent a large part of my life doubling my ennuis, but since a certain experience has come to me with age, I now content myself with suffering once. After that, I don't care!"

"And do you think, my dear Master, that you would have been happier if you hadn't used your intelligence for the work, for the worldwide expansion of your genius?"

"I don't know—but I know that there are publishers who would have lost by it!"

Art any rate, the day after that conversation, Ernest Paris went to see Dr. Serge Voronoff, in order to reconquer his youth.

XVI. The Nobel Prize

This time, Ernest Paris was firmly decided. In his imagination, he already saw himself competing with his friend Jacques Lemay; his mind fully preoccupied with the enigmatic Nora, he was only envisaging the green fruits for what they would become.

Nora did more than excite his desires; she impressed him with something unexpected that he could not explain, but to which he submitted. He sensed that she was, at the same time, something more and less than a woman, something akin to a personification of sex, in the lustful sense of the word, a marvelous instrument of pleasure. That imagination came to him from the facility with which the young woman played with all her organs, making herself into an astonishing plaything of love. Only one thing disturbed that comprehension slightly: the blue dancer's intelligence. He would have preferred her to be very stupid, like a hortensia,[45] judging that intelligence was somehow anachronistic with her nature.

Moreover, the petty liberties that he had permitted himself with the young woman, while putting intimacy into their relationship, were a trifle vexing for him; he

---

[45] I have left this noun in lower case, as the author does, evidently referring to a plant of the hydrangea variety. If it were a proper name it would refer to a female Roman orator famous for making a speech opposing the taxation of women, on grounds similar to the slogan adopted by the American Revolutionaries—no taxation without representation—but that would make a paradox of the employment of the word as an emblem of stupidity.

was well aware that Nora expected a more precise manifestation, and that the role of flirtatious suitor could not last indefinitely. The fashionable woman might become smitten with a young and vigorous man—her official protector, Jules Ducon, did not count in Paris's mind—and then, he would no longer play any role with regard to her but that of an old minor character, retained for his prestige, but nevertheless somewhat ridiculous.

Ernest Paris did not want—and with good reason—to look stupid.

The day was not too far advanced, and Ernest Paris resolved, before going to see the illustrious surgeon, to render one last visit to Nora, leaving Narcisse plunged in piles of paper.

Already buoyed up by hope, he went to the Rue Spontini. However, when he went into the drawing room to whose ornamentation he had contributed so many works of art, a disappointment awaited him; Nora was not alone. Her friends, Cécile Borel and Maud, were sitting beside her on the divan.

Given what I'm going to do, he thought, *perhaps that's better, in order to leave her a good impression of myself. The essential thing is to explain my long absence in her eyes.* Even so, he contrived a slight movement of chagrin—just enough to make the young blue star understand that he would have preferred to find her alone.

"My dear Master!" exclaimed Cécile Borel, hurrying to meet him. "How glad I am to run into you!"

"Less than me, beauty among beauties, certainly less than me."

Hand-kisses, reciprocal congratulations—and, as usual, Ernest Paris found himself the center and unique attraction of the place.

"I didn't hope to find myself in such brilliant company," the Master said, negligently. "I've come to take my leave of my incomparable young friend, being on the eve of a rather long voyage."

"I can guess," said Cécile Borel. "You're going to Sweden to collect the Nobel Prize, which had just been awarded to you."

"You're better informed than I am, for I don't yet know..."

"We dramatic artistes know everything before everyone else. It's therefore a joy for me to be able to give you good news."

"I thank you. I consider the good fortune of the Nobel Prize, awarded to France, less as an unexpected satisfaction for my vanity as a man of letters, or as a source of personal gain, than as a consecration of the superiority of French literature. Nevertheless, I see employment in it, for some time to come." The victor addressed a rapid wink to Nora.

"Money is still money," Maud put in. "It's necessary not to consider it with disdain."

"No one appreciated money for its true value as much as I do, Miss Macfield. Money dominates and crushes everything, as you know better than I do. It's Capital that rules the world, laughing at the bloodshed, the human lives sacrificed! Money, alone, is the universally-worshipped god, the uncontested master of the world. It's what makes wars and profits from them, which makes peace and extracts even more from it than from war. Long live money!

"Thanks to money, anger and disgust reawaken the stomach overcharged with humanity, and make it vomit forth all the filth that it has been made to absorb for centuries. They smile, the Messieurs of Finance, because they say to themselves that everything will last as long as them, and that they are the kings of the world. Wrong, Messieurs! Your money, which you consider as a force, you are in the process of destroying yourselves, by replacing it with paper. As long as the old world lived by the exchange of metallic value, it was maintained, come what may. On the day when the Bank valorized it all with paper, the decadence of public life commenced.

"How long will your reign last, Messieurs of Finance? I cannot say, but I believe its end to be imminent. Let humanity understand that, and money will no longer have any but its exchange value between direct consumers."

"Humanity will be what we make of it," said the American woman, harshly.

"You're mistaken. Humanity is not made; you will submit to it, and it will drive you to suicide."

"The theory of a litterateur. Money has always been the supreme Master, and it always will be."

"Then why has the Nobel Prize been given to the litterateur whose theories you scorn? There is a force above money, a force to which humans cling as the sole reason for their existence: it is confidence in themselves, in an ideal of beauty, justice and love."

Maud Macfield shrugged her shoulders. "Beauty! Justice! Love! All that can be bought with money—even paper money."

"Oh, my dear, you can speak ill of everything, except amour," simpered the Célimène.

"Amour, my dear Master," said Maud, "is a subject more exciting for you and for us than all your nonsensical theories about money, and you ought to have interesting things to say to us about it, being so expert in that chapter!"

"How wrong you are! Everything has been said about that subject, and I don't feel that I have the courage of a Michelet, to try to write a book about it.[46] All that one can say, without the risk of being mistaken, is that each individual has his own way of comprehending love, and that the best is the one that one feels oneself—and above all, it's the manner in which one submits to the influence of beauty, or of sex.

"Obviously, beauty is only one of the innumerable traps of which nature makes use to constrain us to her obscure will. It constitutes the supreme artifice of the marvelous and essential mirage that is amour. But truly, we ought not to be suspicious of it, for then, to what would we entrust ourselves? On the contrary, it's necessary to abandon ourselves to amour, to beauty, to find a religion therein, a recipe for happiness. There is salvation, for there, also, is forgetfulness! Certainly, it's not easy to emerge from oneself, but if one ever hopes to succeed in that, it's only with the aid of the beautiful.

"And it's you, Mesdames, who conceal the formula. In contemplating you, we escape from life, from its ennuis, its struggles, and its servitudes. It seems that we are savoring a magical beverage, as if we are transporting ourselves to another element, where all sadness and dolor are forgotten. Supreme opium! Source of arts, letters and everything of which humanity can be proud, beauty is the ransom of the universe. The demiurge who created the illusion of the world and imprisoned us within it was—for I believe it to be dead—a malevolent demiurge, to judge by its work, but it has ceded us beauty as a privilege Thus, it has permitted man to dream, to love,

---

[46] *L'Amour* (1859; tr. as *Love*) was one of the historian Jules Michelet's most popular books.

to glimpse an ideal of sorts—and for that, if only for that, much can be forgiven it..."

A new visitor had come in, but, in order not to interrupt the Academician's speech, the chambermaid had not introduced him. After a mute salutation, he approached the group formed by the three pretty women.

"Perfect!" said Dr. Jean Fortin. "I've arrived just in time to applaud you, Ernest Paris, for I strongly approve of your theory of amour via the fascination of beauty." He turned to Nora and continued: "You see, Mademoiselle, that I'm abusing your permission, and that I'm glad to be able, like your friends, to bring you the testimony of my profound admiration."

"What, my dear friend," said the sempiternal speech-maker, "is it possible that your labor of genius leaves you the leisure to think about beauty?"

"Why not? The work is, in itself, a manifestation of beauty; and do you not know, Mesdames, that everything men do on earth has no other objective than the adoration of your sex?"

"In the strict sense of the word?" asked the American.

"Yes, my dear Mademoiselle. We can surround the idol with all kinds of tinsel, but the true goal, the true alliance, is sex. Three quarters of human copulations are practiced in the dark; what, then, is the role of beauty? Certainly, celestial mechanics are well regulated, but amour is also an ingenious mechanism."

"You've done well, Doctor," exclaimed the Célimène, "but you haven't proved that amour, in its ideality, in its sentiment, is possible. It has been made into a god; it's necessary to consider it as such, and worship it."

174

"Are you forgetting, then," Ernest Paris put in, "that our great scientist is the bitter adversary of all gods?"

"That depends; I'm only the enemy of religions that I consider as a hindrance to intellectual progress. Think of the time that people have wasted in the dissection of theologies and their schisms! But as for amour, I bow down before it respectfully, for it's the great animator of the human species and the immense whole of animality."

"Yes, my friend, but isn't what these ladies are demanding of your science the proof of the ideality of amour—or, if you prefer, its spiritual relationship with the curt brutality of the act?"

"Evidently; while other creatures accomplish the act in accordance with the invariable ritual imposed on them by the great law of the conservation of the species, and such as primitive humans must have accomplished it, outside what we call morality and modesty, as humans have become more refined, more intellectual, they have sought to spiritualize the sexual act, garlanding it with all the flowers of dream and poetry, just as they have sought by any means possible to prolong its brevity by means of various refinements. Futile efforts; the effects continue, but the end is still the same, and if the denouement is postponed, it merely out of politeness, of the male for his partner. Otherwise, the act accomplished, he would turn his back and ask for nothing except to sleep..."

"Well, what do you think of this fellow, Mesdames? He accords very little importance to our little naked god."

"Oh, these scientists," sighed the Célimène. "They're atrocious destroyers of illusions; they have to submit everything to their need for analysis." She turned to the Academician. "How preferable I find your delicate speech, my dear Master, always so full of unexpected charms, to that glacial anatomy of our passions!"

"But I share your taste, Mesdames!" replied Jean Fortin. "If the illustrious Master Ernest Paris had not, so to speak, forced me to do it, I would have carefully refrained from removing the rose petals with which you ornament the sex organ of our god."

As was his habit, Ernest Paris launched forth on another theme: "The concrete form of beauty is a beautiful woman's body. All poets of all times have celebrated it, we vary the formulae to infinity, with disconcerting fantasy. What is eulogized in one country seems monstrous in another. We adopt similes that are sometimes ludicrous, saying of a woman that she has the eyes of a gazelle, the neck of a swan, shoulders of marble, pearly teeth and I don't know how many stupidities of that sort, realizing, in thought, how ridiculous that ensemble is.

"On the other hand, an Arab says, in forging a gallantry, that a woman has a cow's eyes. Make that compliment among us and you'd pass for a fool. So goes the world. The terms of praise with which we surround beauty prove that it is only a sort of ideal that we associate with our individual taste. We have adopted, as the most perfect feminine form, the antique Venus. Well, clothe the Venus de Milo in one of your dresses, and see whether she corresponds to the slim tomboy fashionable today...

"At any rate, the type-specimen of beauty varies according to fashion, and, amazingly, the female body models itself in accordance with the multiple variations of that fashion; the breasts stand out or don't; the waist, once as narrow as the neck, no longer exists; the hips become slim or prominent; even the color of the skin is modified; have you not seen, in the summer months, the youngest and prettiest girls resembling redskins? The eyes are made up, the lips rouged, the jaws ornamented with gold, and even diamonds; where, then, in all that, is true beauty? Conclusion: it's conventional.

"Phidias and Praxiteles, in sculpting their master-pieces, probably followed the fashion of their time; the sole fault of ours is that artists, by virtue of an excess of modesty, dare not paint the contemporary nude as they see it, and continue to obey tradition. It's true that there are others who, by virtue of a horror of convention, fall into the contrary excess, and paint or sculpt feminine figures for us that one would only take hold of with tongs. Among painters, there's only one that I admire: Prud'hon.[47] No one has penetrated female charm be-tween than him. There's nothing as pretty as a woman's derrière; it's the most essential and charming part of the feminine body.

"In that it's where the wastes are expelled," said Fortin, brutally.

Ernest Paris detested anyone undermining his ora-torical effects; he pretended not to have heard the doc-tor's remark and continued his speech:

"I've always loved women greatly, and I confess that, in my youth, I preferred quantity to quality; all women made me desirous. But I had a preference for shopgirls, because those young persons are almost al-ways fresh and pretty, and have the habit of smiling and being amiable. I loved them, similarly, because of their

---

[47] The Romantic painter Pierre-Paul Prud'hon (1758-1823) was not very exceptional; it is not obvious why Ernest Paris would prefer him to all others, but Anatole France wrote a biography of him for a book of his paintings and drawing is-sued in connection with the centenary of his death.

attire, very tasteful, because they have the sense of being 'well-dressed,' of what harmonizes best with their type of beauty. I also loved them for the ingenuity of their little hearts. And I was full of fire... God, how good it was!"

"Is it no longer as good, dear Master?" asked Nora. "Do our contemporaries not measure up to them?"

"Aah! Prettiest of the pretty, you touch a delicate point there. Yes, certainly, you're all as desirable, but it me who can no longer, as you put it, *measure up*. Fortunately, science"—he tapped Jean Fortin on the shoulder—"promises us a new Youth. Progress marches forward, and humanity follows it, singing. And yet, I have sometimes railed against that unfortunate progress!"

"Why, Master, you who are one of its torches?"

"Because, in progressing, we have become less resigned, more apt to suffer. Civilization has not aided us to tolerate, nor to hope, because it shows us the reality in all its hideousness. Reflection causes me to regret the past, because the past was youth, and because your progress, in spite of its inventions, acquisitions and multiplied knowledge, in spite of the telephone, aviation, wireless telegraphy, etc., reminds me that I am of a time when all that does not exist, and when no one any longer thinks it bad, and I cannot see that we have replaced, in the moral domain, that which sustained our ancestors..."

"Excuse me," said Doctor Fortin, but I've lingered longer in your agreeable company than I should, and I'm expected..."

And after the final handshake, the scientist made his exit.

In his turn, Ernest Paris took his leave. Nora escorted him to the door.

"How long the time will seem to me, Master, without seeing you."

"Be certain, young friend, that I shall come back as soon as possible, but the ceremony in Stockholm might retain me for some time. I can't decently pocket a rather large sum and run away like a thief. I anticipate a series of galas that I would have preferred to avoid."

He put his arm around the young woman and felt her small breasts.

"And you know, Nora, this Nobel Prize, or at least the sum it represents, will be for you, even though I know that, probably, the communist comrades are already counting on it. Better that it should be you, so dainty, so genteel, who will profit from it. Oh, Nora, delicious idol, you will be my last and dearest amour!"

And that was said in good faith, without any thought of a double meaning.

After a warm kiss, the illustrious man drew away, with a lively hope in his white head, of April youth and new sap.

XVII. The Inferno of Apes

At the Voronoff Institute, the personnel and chiefs of service were all exhausted. They had been forewarned of the visit of Ernest Paris, and from the first to the last, from the director of the hospital to the humblest orderly, they all wanted to be noticed by the celebrated writer, sensing that a little of his glory might be reflected on them.

There was, however, one place in the establishment where the general enthusiasm had no echo; that was in the hall of Dr. Voronoff's simian inmates. Was it instinct, or a veritable consciousness of what lay in store for them? Either way, a somber anxiety weighed upon the souls of the great apes.

A great deal has been written about the words *instinct* and *intelligence*. Some, in that problem of ideas, leave intelligence to humans and instinct to the other animals. More noble in essence, intelligence is the aristocracy of souls; instinct is the proletariat—but in the same way that every aristocracy has its source in the people, instinct has its own in nature; hence the supremacy of instinct over certain phenomena that intelligence cannot foresee, but which instinct perceives, and which certain minds still primitive call presentiment.

Examining the matter carefully, there are few people who have not felt, at least once in their life, that impression of anguish at the approach of an ominous event, or when a beloved individual is in danger. Women, it is affirmed, are more subject to such phenomena than men, and the closer a soul is to a simplistic condition, the more occult intuitions it receives. Thus, the animal that is the most simplistic of creatures is the best prepared for prescience of what is about to happen to it. That is why rats are seen to quit a vessel bound for shipwreck, or a house doomed to a conflagration. The sensibility of insects is even greater, since it enables them to anticipate, not merely danger, but the phases of their metamorphosis

Thus, anxiety reigned among the apes, all the more so because, in them, instinct is combined with the gift of observation. They arrived from Little Borneo, the Paradise of Apes on the Riviera, in a narrow and low cage adapted to their size: a "clog." That was the name given to the boxes in which, for the necessities of the journey, the apes were imprisoned. From the clog the apes passed, in Paris, into the cages of the Institute. Alas, they were no longer the green prisons lost in foliage beneath the warm sun of the Midi. At Auteuil there were comfortable cells, but they were devoid of verdure, and they were warmed by central heating. There was no longer a disguise of liberty, but naked slavery, the hand of force overcoming weakness.

That change in their existence was combined with observation. Simians are close enough to human for their minds to be capable of a certain measure of comparison. In the interval of their fairly extensive growth, they had seen many of their fellows leave the refuge and come back. Having left in good health, joyful, and above all amorous, they returned sad, and torpid, gazing with a kind of tragic melancholy at the gallant exploits of their fellow. Sometimes, reminiscences seemed to inspire them, but without any appreciable result. Thus, those unfortunates returned as creatures disappointed in life, for whom existence had no other objective than death; while the others bounded, intoxicated by joy and erotic folly, they contemplated them, seeming to say: *brother it's necessary to die!*

Well, Voronoff's boarders had the instinct, the presentiment, that they were destined for a mysterious operation, which would make them invalids of amour, like those who returned to the Paradise of Apes, which had become their Purgatory.

Dr. Goldry had sensed that impression in his pupils, and that is why he had, after a time, had a new building constructed, named the Invalids' Hospital. It was in the laboratory of that building than Jean Fortin worked on his renovation of the sexes—which is to say, the artificial culture of different organs. We know already that the scientific genius in question—aided by Marc Vanel, Homo-Deus—had realized the culture of arterial blood, and then that of the creative molecule. Now, they were studying the strange properties of glands, suspecting that the predominant force in all creatures resided therein.

Among the animals destined for the work of rejuvenation by grafting were two chimpanzees already seen at Eze during Georges Clemenceau's visit to the Paradise of Apes: Romeo and Juliet.

The situation had changed considerably for them. The two apes, since their arrival at the Voronoff Institute in Auteuil, had been living in an indefinable anguish. What was about to happen? They could not define it, but they sensed that they were on the eve of a catastrophe. So, the cheerfulness of old had been succeeded by a kind of bewilderment. They spent the day in one another's arms, huddling together in terror, but without any attempt at love-making—and yet, as Fortin had said, Romeo was an "ace" among chimpanzees.

At nine o'clock an hour before the arrival of Ernest Paris, who had announced his visit for ten o'clock, the preparations for the operation began. Dr. Fortin and four orderlies came into the cage, after having brought the clog, with its door open, to transport the ape. At the sight of the five men, the two chimpanzees, horrified, hugged one another frantically.

"Don't be afraid, my old Romeo," said Fortin, stroking the animal's head gently. "There's a bad moment to get through, but you, at least, won't have the fate of your old pals. You're going to become a man again, and you'll be able to embrace your Juliet. Come on! Courage and patience! Be reasonable, then, Juliet, since I'm going to return your Romeo to you in good condition."

But the two spouses seemed disinclined to yield to the doctor's arguments, and when hands were laid upon them in order to separate them, they started howling and opening their mouths menacingly. Then, at a sign from Fortin, the orderlies threw thick woolen covers over the heads of the two apes, and while the doctor and one of the orderlies held Juliet back, the other three tore Romeo from her arms—which was not done without difficulty, as Romeo fought with his four hands. Victory went with strength, however, and the poor chimpanzee was stuffed into the clog, thus reduced to impotence.

When the great ape had been picked up and taken to the operating theater, the doctor and his aide released Juliet and beat a rapid retreat. When the she-ape had got rid of the hood that was stifling her, she remained immobile for a moment, looking around the cage anxiously. Then, when she saw that she was alone, there was a terrible despair. She circled her prison, uttering frightful cries, to which all the residents of the menagerie responded. Then she leapt at the bars, biting them with rage, until, exhausted, she let herself fall on the floor, rolled herself up into a ball, and did not budge again. But her piteous eyes, fixed on the doctor—safely out of reach beyond the bars—seemed to be addressing a mute reproach to him.

"Patience, patience, my girl! Your Romeo will be back, in as good a state as when I took him away, and perhaps...well, one day, we'll see..."

And Fortin rejoined his aides in the operating theater. At a sign from him, the clog was placed in the inhalation chamber, where an anesthetic would put the victim to sleep; it was a square box with a grille on one of its faces; the chloroform was introduced into it through a tube that terminated in a funnel inside the box. A mobile panel slid behind the grille and the narcotic took effect; the operator followed the progress of the drug from behind a small square window, and when the patient was sufficiently paralyzed, the box was opened and the animal taken out of his clog.

That was what was done for Romeo, and a few minutes later, he was solidly attached to the operating table. Immediately, the practitioners took possession of the subject; from that moment on, the chimpanzee was nothing more than inert matter in the hands of the operators, who devoted themselves to all the necessary manipulations, painlessly.

First the ape was carefully shaved from the navel to the middle of his thighs, washed and rubbed with the greatest care, initially with a mixture of soap and carbonate, rinsed and washed again with alcohol.

Toward the end of these operations Romeo had woken up, but, still numbed by the narcotic, he looked around unconsciously.

The parts on which the operation was to take place were anesthetized by injections. Then, the animal was ready; the man could take his spoils from the ape.

Dr. Fortin cast a last glance over the final preparations, rectified a few details, and then, certain that everything was perfect, he went out to receive Ernest Paris, accompanied by Dr. Voronoff.

Romeo remained alone, delivered to vague and sad obscure meditations.

XVIII. Ernest Paris's Graft

That morning Ernest Paris, who had slept badly, preoccupied as he was with his operation, had gone back to sleep again. Pédauque came to wake him up, accompanied by Narcisse, who, in accordance with the agreements made the day before, was to reside in the Villa Saïd until the Master's return.

"Well." said the orangutan, "how do you feel today?"

"Hmm! I don't really know. What time is it, then?"

"Nine o'clock, Master, and you need to be at Voronoff's clinic by ten."

"Yes, yes, I know. Damn! It's just that I don't feel very well, my friend. If you were to telephone…to say that I'm ill…and..."

No, my dear Master. Since yesterday, it's been decided. You can't back out now. I've just left the Institute. Everything is ready to receive you. Romeo is waiting for you!"

"Oh, the poor fellow! Tell me, Narcisse, do I really have the right to deprive one of my fellows of that which is dearest to his heart?"

"You need have no remorse; it's only a loan that you're accepting from him. Doctor Fortin is almost certain that he can restore, with interest, that which he's lending to you."

Fortin's name reminded Ernest Paris of the conversation of the day before, at Nora's, and a slight frisson ran down his spine.

"Ah, that damned Dr. Fortin! I wouldn't like to have him for an enemy. I've known him for a long time, and I've always thought him somewhat diabolical."

"And yet, you don't believe in God or the Devil."

"But when one sees types like him and that Marc Vanel, one is very tempted to believe..."

"Oh, with Dr. Fortin anything is possible. Am I not the proof of it? But my dear Master, it's necessary to hurry; time's passing..."

"Time's passing! Isn't that its métier, to pass! That's all it's made for!"

"Come on, Master, be brave! It would be shameful to back out now. Think about your friend Lemay. He didn't hesitate, and he's congratulating himself for it every day."

"Lemay! That's true. He was less windy than me. To us the crazy nights of intoxication...a jewel...sixteen years old...a flower... I'm getting up, Narcisse, I'm getting up! Hand me my trousers, please."

And, indeed, Ernest Paris arrived at Serge Voronoff's clinic at half past ten; he was only half an hour late.

The illustrious surgeon, flanked by Fortin and Vanel, was waiting for him on the threshold of the vestibule. All the medical students and employees surrounded the Maters, which gave an air of regality to the reception, by which the Academician was flattered. Ernest Paris drew himself up to his full height, and bowed gracefully to the right and the left.

"Slightly late," he said, shaking the hands of the three doctors, "but I had so much to do..." With a hint of anxiety, he added: "Is everything ready?"

"Everything. A cordial, my dear Master, before the operation, in order to drink to your rejuvenation?"

187

They went into a small drawing room, were glasses and a glass of Mariani wine awaited them. Paris felt a trifle weak; he stiffened himself, and seized his full glass bravely.

"To your amours, Master!" said Fortin.

"I accept the augury," Paris replied, and emptied his glass in a single draught.

"Would you like to go into the study now? You'll find one of my pupils there, who will help you to undress."

Ernest Paris still had a glimmer of indecision, but he sensed that it was impossible to flinch now. He uttered a sigh, and went into the study.

The three scientists exchanged a triumphant glance.

"Oof!" said Voronoff. "I have a subject who will shine the light on my work that it deserves. To work, my friends, to work!"

"It's understood that Romeo belongs to us, after the operation?" said Vanel.

"Yes, of course—for if you succeed, it will put the crown on the edifice; we'll possess grafts at will, and after what I've seen, I have the greatest confidence in your success."

"Without the slightest doubt, we'll obtain the culture and rejuvenation of glands at will, since we'll be able to synthesize them."

While talking, they had gone into the operating theater.

It was a large rectangular room, lit from above, the ceiling being replaced by glass. Above the individuals, a bright white sheet of velum filtered the light, spreading an even glow everywhere. At the four corners of the room, projectors could illuminate the operating table at will. A kind of cabin rose up to the glass, enclosing an apparatus for filming, when the professor thought it appropriate.

The operators, wearing rubber gloves, had prepared forceps, hemostats and scalpels.

Ernst Paris came in, supported by the pupil who had helped him to undress. At the sight of the operators clad in their long white smocks and gloved to the elbows, the poor Academician went pale. At a sign from Voronoff, however, four pupils lifted the patient up and gently deposited him on the table.

"Would you rather be asleep, my dear Master, or anesthetized locally? Either way, you'll feel absolutely nothing. If you prefer magnetic trance, Dr. Fortin can put you to sleep."

"Oh no, not Fortin! Do what you think is best."

"I'll opt for the local anesthetic, then, because chloroform can cause post-operative malaise. Don't worry about anything. Chat, Master, about whatever you like."

A few adroitly disposed injections, and Paris thought he had been cut in two; the inferior part of his trunk no longer existed, so far as he was concerned.

The operation began as for the ape, with shaving and washing with alcohol. An employee held a mirror inclined so that the operatee could follow all the phases of the work.

"Very curious," said Paris. "I can't feel anything at all. That's what we are! To think that a few drops of anesthetic abolishes our will. What use is our intelligence, then? Tell me, Fortin, you who've scrutinized, so to speak the slightest creases of mental function, is it possible for a brain like ours to resist chloroform? Can our mind, our self, be annihilated by that small measure of material essence?"

"Alas, yes. The most subtle mind can't resist it. That, for materialists, is one of the proofs of the impossibility of intellectual survival. In sleep, that false death, our brain can wander, but it conserves its activity; anesthesia is a fall into absolute blackness, devoid of dreams. The mind is abolished; however, it's still there; it's like a suspension, an interval, a hole in life. I've had myself put to sleep in various fashions, and magnetic trance is the only one that doesn't suspend thought."

While the two men were talking, Voronoff and his aides worked on Ernest Paris. For his part, Vanel was working on Romeo.

While speaking, Paris followed the operation in the mirror, without noticing that the mirror hid the photographic operator's cabin from him. He could hear the motor of the cinema camera, like a coffee-grinder, but he attributed the sound to some other cause.

In reality, he did not see much of what was happening, for the sheets and the hands of the operators masked the flesh. Now and again, he perceived a detail that did not give him any idea of the ensemble, all the more so because the operators were doing their best not to hinder the work of the cinematographer.

"Truly," said Ernest Paris, "if I couldn't see this environment, so new to me, I could believe that I were lying tranquilly in my bed. It's marvelous, and that gives me a confidence that, I'm ashamed to admit, I was lacking. Tell me, Fortin, how is Romeo doing?"

"Romeo? We've anesthetized him completely, because we haven't finished with him. As the fellow was amply provided, we've left him a piece of the seminal gland, and on that strip, we'll heap up, not a graft, but a molecular culture that ought to—that will—reconstitute the organ."

"What! You're not grafting all of it? What if there's insufficient for me?"

"Don't worry about that. You too will be an ace. Do you know the story *Deus vobiscum?*"

"No, but I scent some lewdness. Go on, then—tell me a dirty story."

"Once upon a time—it's always in an indecisive era that these things happen—there was a village curé who, like you, felt more desires than effects. One day, by the roadside, he saw a poor devil who seemed to be in a bad way. As our curé was compassionate, he took the mendicant home with him, did his best to restore him, gave him a few clothes, and finally permitted him to sleep there. The next day, the pauper took his leave of the curé and asked whether, in recognition of his hospitality there was anything he could do for him."

"'Alas, my friend,' the curé replied, 'I don't lack anything, for the locality is good. I'd be very happy here if...'

"'If what, Monsieur le Curé? Speak...one never knows...'

"'Well, if the women weren't so pretty and the temptation stronger than my means of satisfying it. But, there...no longer than that.' And the worthy curé showed the last phalanx of his little finger.

"'Monsieur le Curé,' the poor man replied. 'God will provide. Every time you say *Deus vobiscum*, the thing you're talking about will grow by an inch...'

"Wings suddenly sprouted on the shoulders of the mendicant, who was an angel, and he flew away.

"Now, as our curé had a great many occasions to pronounce the fateful phrase,[48] our man, who had initially seen his...hope growing, was soon obliged to wrap it around his waist like a rope, and in the end, was only able to make contact with a beauty at improbable distances. He was obliged by that fact to hand in his resignation as a curé, and his sole resource became exhibiting himself as a phenomenon, a living greasy pole...

"Which old story, my dear Paris, should serve you as a lesson, to be content with a *juste milieu* and not to desire the superfluous."

"You're a wise man, Fortin, because science raises you above our petty sentimental miseries. But we men of letters put our passions under a microscope, so to speak; in order to amuse our readers we're obliged to mask our desires, so as not to resemble the common run of mortals. If, like you, I'd been able to detach myself from society, I would have been able to abandon myself without remorse to my instincts—but no, our epoch and our mores oppose that. The *belle époque* for a builder of voluptuous dreams was that of Olympic Greece! How I admire it, for having created those immoral, impulsive, unjust gods, so similar to humans! In acting thus, what logic it displayed! While our just God, who created this enraged, cruel universe in which we live, appears to me too absurd, too malevolent in his consciousness, his omnipotence and his perfection...."

Dr. Fortin glanced sideways; the operation was progressing. He had brought Paris to the peak of his inex-

---

[48] The story is, of course, implausible, because the formula used in the Latin mass is *Dominus vobiscum* [The Lord be with you], which could just as easily be employed on any other occasion...

haustible loquacity; the Immortal was following his idea, and, believing himself at home, talking to his admiring public, he went on, untiringly:

"How can we believe him to be god, that God, considering the atrocious way in which he works? He has thrown us on to the earth full of instincts and desires, and he demands that we be moral. Furthermore, he menaces us with Hell and Purgatory if we fall, when he has organized everything around us to trip us up. His malignity and his perversity seem unwarranted, putting as a condition on his grace that we save our souls while he works to doom us!

"The Greeks, by contrast, didn't mingle religion with virtue; they didn't introduce morality into it, that strange attempt to mask the foundation of life, which is amour, amour devoid of restraint and devoid of regulation. For them, Olympus sheltered gods superior to humans in beauty and strength—human attributes—and not by virtue or morality, which are conventional, and what's more, inhuman...

"The creation most contrary to the Greek genius is precisely the Israelite region. Look at petty Yahweh, in his origins: he protects the flocks, he is a patriarch, and placid. Quickly, however, he acquires a taste for blood on contact with other semite religions, and it pleases him to exterminate and put to the sword the followers of Moloch and Chemosh. His is so ferocious that he becomes furious.

"One day, when a polite man approaches, in a procession, the holy ark that is about to fall, with the intention of sustaining it, Yahweh strikes him with a thunderbolt, because he dares to touch it—and he demands thereafter that we become just, as if the condition of creation permitted it, as if injustice were not his signature...

"Then again, what light there is in the religion of the Greeks, what union with nature! Although all beliefs are born in fear, and agitated in the nightmare of superstitions, that of the Hellenes is almost an exception. There is only Saint Francis, in the history of Christianity, who seems to have rediscovered, instinctively, a gleam of the fraternity between the creators that the Greeks knew...

"The Greeks were as pessimistic as we are, since, before us, they had looked into the nature of things, but they didn't make a fuss, they didn't lament, rending their garments, like the Jews. They were good company! Polite and superior people, they knew how to oppose ill fortune with a good heart. Do you remember the captured satyr, from whom the secret of life was demanded? 'The best thing for you humans,' he replied, would be not to have been born, but since you exist, the preferable thing is for you to die soon.'[49] That's how they tried to introduce a smile of beauty into the deplorable promenade that is life!"

"Bravo, Master!" said Voronoff, approaching the litterateur. "The thing wasn't too painful, as you see. A few days rest, in which you'll charm us with your amiable conversation, and you'll only have to wait patiently for the effect of our little operation."

"What!" exclaimed Paris. "Is it done already? I didn't perceive anything. It's true that our friend Fortin, held me constantly under the charm of his conversation."

"Many thanks, Master! It's the first time that anyone has ever paid me such a compliment."

---

[49] The reference, found in Plutarch although nor original to him, is to the god Silenus, a prototype of the satyrs.

Ernest Paris hastened to look down at his lower abdomen and thighs, swathed with bandages, from which a minuscule rosebud emerged.

"What's that?" he asked.

"The indispensable, my dear Master, the principal attribute of the god Priapus. But have no fear; although it's no sword, it will grow..."

"Great God! I've never seen it so small. I confess that I'm anxious, my dear friend, very anxious!"

"Once again have no fear. It's the effect of bleeding...from the nose...."

"Have I lost a great deal of blood, then?"

"No, very little; you won't even notice it. Not the slightest weakness. Now, you're going to be taken to your room, and, since you slept badly last night, you're going to have a little nap until dinner time."

"You're all aces! All the same, though, I saw almost nothing of the operation."

"Although it's not strictly necessary, I want you to stay in bed tomorrow as well, and the day after, we'll let you see every detail the grafting operation, with the aid of the cinema."

"Not mine, I hope?"

"Oh, I wouldn't permit that. No, one that I carried out on an old man hospitalized at..."

"Very good. Truly, I regret not having followed mine more attentively. It's Fortin's fault. By the way, where has he gone? I was in the process of exposing a few ideas to him on the morality of religions."

"Fortin has gone to join Vanel in the laboratory. They're both occupied with Romeo."

"And how did poor Romeo stand up to it?"

"Perfectly—but you'll be in good form before him. In his case, there's the entire organ to reconstitute, and we don't know yet how long it will take."

"The poor friend! I'll send a few flowers to his wife."

"That's a nice thought, but I think she'd appreciate a few fruits more."

"Whatever she desires, poor thing! In the meantime, give her my respectful condolences."

The immortal was delicately lifted up by four orderlies and on that new platform he made an exit every bit as majestic as his entrance to the Voronoff Institute.

In accordance with the anticipations of the celebrated surgeon, Ernest Paris was in a fit state to get up two days after the operation, and Voronoff came in person to invite him to come with him if he wanted to watch the progress of the grafting operation by means of the cinema.

"Gladly," replied the Master. "I'm weary of lying down like this."

"Oh, that's finished now; you can come and go about the house; your condition is satisfactory, as I expected. Your physiological condition, perfectly healthy, dispels any fear of complications. Besides, it's very rare for this sort of graft to have unfortunate consequences."

"It's a fact that although I felt a trifle enervated yesterday, I'm in perfect condition today, mentally and physically."

"We has no more to do, then, Master but await the expected result: a progressive rejuvenation."

"Oh, my dear friend, how I'd like to be a few months older!"

"A nurse attached to the Academician's service gave him an ample brown woolen dressing gown to put on, which gave him the appearance of one of the learned scholars of the Middle Ages, with a fine and elongated face. He looked at himself complaisantly in the large mirror surmounting the dressing-table. He was shod in sandals of light brown leather; then the nurse offered him a supportive arm.

As she was a well-preserved woman, in spite of being over fifty, and astonishingly fresh, the Academician did not fail to rub up against her like an old tom-cat. In that fashion they reached the projection room, lit by a few electric bulbs. At the back there was a canvas sheet over the smooth white wall, forming a screen. An English armchair had been brought for the unique spectator. Voronoff, Fortin and a few senior staff members sat down on chairs.

"As I told you," Dr. Voronoff declared, "this operation was carried out on a hospitalized pauper."

Darkness fell, and the advertised individual appeared on the screen: an old man with a degraded and sickly appearance.

Voronoff then explained, briefly, the physiological condition of the old man, who had almost died in childhood, and was incapable of any manual labor, and, from the mental viewpoint, in a state of complete brutalization.

The scene changes, representing the same individual after the graft: his gaze is keen and interested, the face is firmer; the wasted muscles have recovered their strength and elasticity; he looks at least ten years younger.

Three other individuals were presented thus, before and after the graft. All three presented, before the procedure, the same appearance of physical and mental debility, and showed, after the operation, the same progress in revitalization.

"Now," said the professor, "we're going to pass on to the work of the graft." As the film went on, he explained: "We'll see the two subjects alternately: the donor ape"—the chimpanzee appeared—"and the human recipient. As you can see, the subject is completely hidden by the sheets, which only allow the sight of the organ to be operated on, the hands of the operator and his instruments."

A pause.

"Here, on the other hand, is the donor ape. You can only see the testicle ready to be operated on. With one hand, the operator holds the dissecting forceps, in the other, the straight scissors, with which he cuts the skin, and lays the testicle bare, which will be the graft transferred to the receptive subject."

Another scene:

"The operator splits the testicle, in such a fashion as to make a kind of flower with six petals; it's the petals that are the grafts. The operation is performed on the ape without cutting the testicular cord—which will permit us, we hope, to reconstitute the organ. It's that reconstitution which my friends Fortin and Vanel are carrying out this moment on the chimpanzee Romeo, who served you."

Third scene:

"Here now is the receptive subject: the human, presented in the same fashion. Only the testicles are visible. The scrotum will be cut, as in the ape, but two or three injections of novocaine are made beforehand to render the testicle insensitive. Then the operator takes the testicle between the index and middle fingers, in such a way as to stretch the skin and make the section easier. Then the skin—for the vulgar; the cellulo-crytreo-fibrous envelope, for the surgeon—is pulled back above, below and to the sides. And it's between the leaves of the parietal envelope that the grafts will be placed, one on each side and another on top. The location of the graft is lightly scarified in order to render the cohesion of the graft with the receptive testicle easier, not on the testicle itself but in the internal face of the parietal leaf of the vaginal—or, in common parlance, the ultimate envelopes of the vaginal gland, which is, as I've told you, the organ of revitalization par excellence.[50] We have no more to see than the work of closing the envelopes, which is either done with fasteners known as Michel clamps or with a needle and silk thread. As dressings, compresses, padding and an ordinary bandage."

The film had finished; the lights came on.

"And that, my dear Master, is the operation that you have undergone, with all the more courage because you did not even perceive it."

"I had a very different idea of it. Receive my anticipatory thanks, my dear Voronoff, and the testimony of my profound admiration."

"The interesting point of my discovery is based, above all, on the primordial role played in the ensemble

----

[50] The term "vaginal gland" is nowadays restricted to Bartholin's glands, which secrete mucus into the vagina and are homologous with the bulbourethral glands, or Cowper's glands, in males. The description of the operation is not sufficiently clear to determine whether the latter are the glands to which Voronoff is referring, although they seem unlikely candidates for a crucial source of revivification. He cannot, however, be referring to the prostate gland, which is singular, although its homologue in females is the paired Skene's glands.

of the economy by the glands whose importance, until now, has not been understood. That role seems, in fact, to be the principal one, since they are the vivifying source from which all our organs draw nourishment. The proof is that the suppression or insufficiency of the thyroid gland causes of idiocy or cerebral decay. Similarly, the suppression of one of those little glands situated in the neck, the function of which, as for the pineal gland, we have not yet specified exactly, leads to death in a short time. From that we can conclude that a more profound knowledge of the role of the glands will lead to the reconstitution of organs in a poor state, as I have done for the vagina gland, and to their complete revivification."

"Oh, science, science! It is truly the most beautiful of human conquests! It alone is truly making progress. I regret not being a scientist."

"Each to his profession," concluded Dr. Fortin, "and yours, my dear Ernest Paris, makes many people envious. Every man fills his career as best he can. We combat physical death. Will we be masters one day of intellectual death?"

XIX. Four Times Twenty Years

As soon as he was in a fit state to travel—it was ten days after his entry to the Voronoff Institute—Ernest Paris set out for Sweden. As the distribution of prizes was not to take place for another fortnight, however, he made a detour to Germany, where, like all those who have become pacifists, or who have even conserved their sympathy for the science and literature of the land beyond the Rhine, he was sure of a good welcome, the intellectual party of the post-war period seeking to have the bellicose manifestations of their elders during the hostilities forgotten.

In Berlin, Ernest Paris met Einstein, and strove to comprehend the great revolutionary of old scientific theories. In spite of his genius, however, and perhaps even because of it, Ernest Paris was no mathematician. He listened with respect and patience, but when the physicist tried to convince him that light was material, he could not understand any more, and escaped politely, his head spinning.

By contrast, he found in Professor Nicolai[51] a man after his own heart, not only in scientific terms, but

---

[51] Georg Friedrich Nicolai (1874-1964) was one of the co-signatories in 1914, with Albert Einstein, of an "Appeal to Europeans" opposing Germany's entry into the Great War and invasion of Belgium, and lost his status in consequence, although he was still assigned to military duties until he was court-martialed in 1916, when he escaped to Demark. Briefly rehabilitated by the Weimar Republic, accusations of treason by right-wing groups forced him to emigrate to South America

above all from the viewpoint of humanity. Having entered the German army in 1914 as a physician with the rank of general he had emerged as a second-class orderly; he had been brought before a court martial after pacifist demonstrations, and had only escaped military justice by fleeing in an airplane.

"What a beautiful military career!" Ernest Paris said to him. "How I admire you for having so much courage!"

Nicolai showed him around Berlin, which Paris judged rather severely. In fact, that city, where everything was symmetrical and ordered in a disciplinary fashion, was not calculated to please him, a lover of the picturesque and the beautiful.

"Berlin," Ernest Paris said, "is the triumph of the Potin style!"[52]

In the German capital, even more than in Paris, cosmopolitanism reigns in 1929. Life is localized, so to speak, in bars and restaurants.

"The folly of expenditure and squandering reigns nowadays over the whole world," said Ernest Paris to his

---

in 1922, where he became a professor at the University of Chile, so Ernest Paris could not have met him in Berlin in 1929. Anatole France paid tribute to the Appeal, which was reprinted in Nicolai's book *Die Biologie des Krieges* [The Biology of War] (1917), after receiving the Nobel Prize for literature, and he met Nicolai in Berlin on his way back to France from Stockholm in 1921, in company with Einstein (who was awarded the 1921 Nobel Prize for physics belatedly, the following year.)

[52] The reference is to Félix Potin (1844-1955), a successful grocer who became the proprietor of a chain of department stores, which were at their peak in the 1920s, and were seen by some as an emblem of vulgarity.

new friend. "Money has so little value that everyone hesitates to keep it, so it is transformed instead into immediate pleasure. Doubtless they're right, for tomorrow they might have to pay twice as much. If there's a comparison to be drawn between our two nations, however, it's in the manner of squandering money. In Paris our *nouveau riches* spend a great deal but consume very little; here, I've observed that if the Germans spend as much, they waste less; they empty bottles and clean plates. If the intellect loses, the stomach gains. For my part—I'm saying this in my capacity as a foreigner—I don't like the hotel; there's a lack of linen; for the purposes of toilette, it's smaller than my handkerchief; at table, they use paper napkins. In sum, it's uncomfortable."

The German smiled, and took him to dinner at his home; Ernest Paris was then obliged to recognize that if public life there lacked certain charms, family life in a well-to-do environment was above reproach.

Stockholm, on the other hand, had his full support. The city pleased him by virtue of its cleanliness and the superb orderliness of its monuments. Having arrived five days before the ceremony he had time to explore the city and admire its different aspects. In the capital of Sweden it was the novelist Rolf Torndisson who was his host and guide. With him, he admired the grandiose aspect of the Biddarholm, seen from Lake Maelar, that of the Royal Palace, seen from the Nanho, a bridge of great width garnished with shops even more picturesque than those of the great boulevards of Paris.

What enchanted the Academician, however, was the popular quarter, which, on another arm of the Maelar, behind the Royal Palace, stacked up its picturesquely winding streets, alleyways and cul-de-sacs. Set on the flanks of a high hill, there was, in fact, nothing more curious than those streets, terminating in an arm of the sea or a wall of granite. Then, there was the southern quarter, whose Medieval profile was reflected in the waters of the gulf. That is the industrial quarter, and in consequence the ne where the popular spirit is easiest to study.

"I only know your French life by way of reading," said Torndisson. "What a difference there is between our deeply honest and hospitable people and those depicted by your litterateurs! The difference is so great that, in order to reach your level, our writers are obliged to force the character and mentality of the people they describe in order that you might find them interesting. Here, theft is unknown; you can see the proof of it in our trams without fare-collectors. All travelers put their fares in a money-box placed at the front of the vehicle. There is little crime and, which might astonish you, little adultery.

"With that penury of vices, what can we do? Turn to cerebral phenomena, imagine special and unnatural characters? A literature completely out of tune with our habits and our mores, but which, by its false originality, has been able for half a century to take on the impression of yours, which gives it a lugubrious aspect that, in sum, is neither in your character nor ours."

"I've sensed that, in fact. That's why I've always tried to react against the excessively misty and pessimistic tendency of Nordic literature."

"Our admiration for your work proves that we appreciate you. The literature that you criticize, I do too, since you're not unaware that I belong to the realist school, not as it's understood in France but in the true sense. Life in Sweden, in spite of its long winter, isn't sad, and the character of its inhabitants is rather cheerful.

It's a slow and placid cheerfulness, but which is sometimes as noisy as your southern gaiety."

"I believe you, my dear friend, and I admire your social organization. One thing only—and it's the one that, for me, has the greatest importance in life—seems rather obscure. What are women like here?"

Rolf Torndisson started to laugh. "The same as they are everywhere: amorous and coquettish. They only differ from the women of your homeland by virtue of a fundamental frankness and honesty, which even renders depravity estimable. I could cite the example of a young woman who, in accordance with her temperament, has had numerous lovers, and who, not considering herself worthy to found a family, in spite of numerous offers, because she is beautiful, obstinately refused to marry. Another has run away with a lover but has not, ostensibly, deceived her husband. Here, women love amour, but detest adultery. Hence the bizarre character of our heroines, whose mentality we twist, so to speak, in order to inspire the reader's interest in them. You believe vice to be natural; we know that it is artificial."

"Hmm!" said Ernest Paris. "That's very inconvenient for foreigners."

"What! Are you still thinking about that, then, my dear Master?"

"Am I still thinking about it? But it's my principal concern. You'll know it too, in time, my dear friend. In youth, one is profligate; later, one spends with more profit..."

"Well, Master, if you desire to spend in Stockholm, you have enough admirers here."

"You're a charming fellow, Rolf; you understand the work and the man."

"I can see that you want to spread the reputation of the French! I would have thought, however, that as an Academician, you were a fervent apostle of Monsieur de Montyon?"

"In reality, I'm not overly attached to the Academy. Virtue is so tedious, my dear."

The charm was beginning to take effect, and Ernest often thought about Nora. However, he deemed that he was not bound to conserve the first fruit of the graft for her, and, as Torndisson had told him, admirers were numerous; he was spoiled for choice. And the adventures of Ernest Paris in Stockholm were a pleasant diversion from the distribution of the Nobel Prizes, which was very banal.

This is the description that the French Academician subsequently gave his French friends:

"It's the simplest ceremony in the world, rather reminiscent of a distribution of school prizes, with the difference that in Sweden, the king, who gives the prizes, is down below, and the laureates are on a stage, whereas here, the masters are on high, and the pupils below. That's because we're a democracy! When someone's name is called, he goes to fetch his prize which is handed over by the king. One goes down a little stairway that resembles a ladder. When I was called, colleagues wanted to support me, but I had no need of it, damn it! I went down the ladder with the agility of an ape—yes, an ape, ha ha!

"It wasn't the same for the laureate in chemistry, a far German scientist whose enormous belly prevented him from seeing his feet. He missed a step, stumbled, and fell at the king's feet. There was laughter, almost a scandal! Finally, they picked the professor up and the king handed him his prize: a simple tankard in which there's a check for two hundred thousand francs. In the course of that scene I couldn't help observing how little men are able to vary the recompenses they receive. Although it's permissible for them to vary means of punishment and modify penalties, there's nothing they can do to vary the form of rewards."

"And what do you think of our King Gustave V?" a lady asked.

"He's like his subjects: very benevolent. He invited me to dinner, and we had a long chat. He's simplicity itself, as those who are born on the steps of a throne know how to be. He's much more accessible than a President of the Republic, a Poincaré, a Millerand or a Domergue, who judges it indispensable to surround himself with external pomp because he knows that in himself the represents nothing. The king said some very interesting things to me, imprinted with great common sense and a real knowledge of men. 'The majority of heads of State,' he declared, 'are more afraid of words than things. That's a great error, and is contrary to the truth. It's necessary to grasp the words and let the things go. Thus, I've chosen a socialist minister, Monsieur Branting, and he's abandoned socialism. It's necessary to know how to use men against words.'"

"Don't you do the same in France?" someone asked.

"That's true—but the former comrades of successful revolutionaries treat them as renegades, and in France, words carry weight. Hence, continual changes of Ministry. The pure have long teeth and are in a hurry to dig them into the butter-dish. Party quarrels are less dangerous under a monarchy. In Sweden, one can say that socialism no longer exists."

"That can't be good in your eyes. Aren't you a socialist?"

"No labels, my friend. I don't like labels. An opinion is a question of the moment or of interest, and even of environment, since here, I feel like a royalist. In sum, I'm just a poor man who would like humanity to be les stupid and happier."

"I assume, my dear Master, that the Nobel Prize will be employed for some great social endeavor?"

Ernest Paris adroitly avoided that importunate question, and launched into a grandiose eulogy to Swedish society, its amiability, its honesty and its humanitarian progress.

The Academician was obliged to remain in Sweden for some time to respond to the general enthusiasm and to social invitations in which the celebrated talker did the honors of the drawing rooms. To satisfy the wider public, he was even obliged to give a few lectures. He was unable to quit a country so welcoming, where he had received a large sum of money, without showing himself worthy of that benevolence. Time passed, however, and the desire for Paris was boiling within him when he thought about Nora, the star of the music hall, and the Folies Bergère, a Babel of pleasure.

There was further delay, however: meetings, friendships, and, at the same time, his vanity as a man of letters, and the need to maintain his stardom on the literary stage, obliged him to direct his return via Great Britain, where new triumphs awaited him. It was an epic struggle between amour and pride, a struggle all the more painful because the Academician was visibly rejuvenating. His sprightliness, his sonorous voice, his shining eyes, his casual speech, his firm stride and his precise gestures excited admiration to the point off enthusiasm.

Two months passed in that triumphal march, the echo of which reached Paris, caressing Nora's ears and maintaining her good impression of the Master.

Finally, however, saturated with glory, Ernest Paris embarked for France, no longer aspiring to anything but amour.

XX. An Orgy of Women

One morning, a few days after Ernest Paris's departure for Sweden, Marc Vanel and Jean Fortin were both working in their solitary abode, the Red Nest, when Narcisse came into the laboratory.

"Have you decided?" said Dr. Fortin. "It's not too soon! You know very well that there's work for you here."

"Forgive me, Master, but truly, I can't keep my mind on work at the moment."

"Leave him alone," said Vanel, indulgently. "Our friend is going through an amorous crisis—which is understandable, as he's reached the age of puberty, when the senses command with an indomitable authority. Let him get through this difficult time; he'll come back to us afterwards, calmer and more intelligent than ever. Have a little patience, my boy! As soon as we've had lunch, I'll take you to see your beauty."

"Thank you, Master, but I don't want to go to Nora's until tonight, at half past midnight. I've heard that her friend is traveling, and that she'll be coming home immediately after the performance—and I desire a beautiful night of love-making."

"I don't see any inconvenience in that, my friend," said Marc Vanel. "On the contrary; I'll take advantage of it, having taken you to Nora's, to go to have a joust with a pretty little blonde that I've neglected for some time."

"In that case, I'm content, since everything is for the best, and I'll put myself entirely at your disposal for the work."

"Good!" said Dr. Fortin. "In that case, go down and open the boxes that arrived yesterday, and arrange all the chemical products in their respective places."

As had been agreed, therefore, at about half past midnight, Marc Vanel's automobile—Homo-Deus was in a state of invisibility—deposited him and Narcisse outside the house where Nora lived. To their great surprise, four limousines were already parked outside the door.

"Bad luck for you, Narcisse. There's a reception at your beauty's residence tonight."

"But Master, you can see that there's no light indicative of a celebration; the hall is scarcely illuminated."

At that precise moment, however, another auto drew up outside the gate, Mardruk, on his master's orders, having pulled away, going to park his vehicle on the other side of the street. Four women got out of the car, wrapped in furs up to the eyes, and masked. They went into the house swiftly, chatting and laughing.

"What is this mystery?" the orangutan asked Marc Vanel. "Why this reception in the dark?"

Another auto drew up, and the same scene was enacted, but this time, only two women got out. As the high chinchilla collar in which one of the head was buried was turned over slightly, it was easy to see that she too was masked. That detail intrigued Marc Vanel to the highest degree, and he resolved to discover the key to the enigma. Having left Narcisse in the car, he got out, crossed the street and went in behind the mysterious women.

In the hall, they were received by Berthe, and followed her into Nora's bedroom, transformed into a cloakroom. The large bed, the armchairs and the chairs, were draped with brightly-colored dresses, underskirts that were even shorter, rippling with lace, and sumptuous fur mantles.

"You're the last, Mesdames," said the chambermaid. "Will you please remember where you deposit your things, for there are no numbers by which to recognize them."

"In fact, where shall we put them?" asked the two women, laughing. Are there a lot of people here, Berthe?"

"Twenty guests, exactly. That's the number fixed by Madame and her friends."

"The circle of the vanquished." To her comrade, who looked at her interrogatively, astonished, she added: "Are we not the vanquished of amour? Maud has ideas of a truly disconcerting boldness."

"I hope that we're keeping our masks?" said the other.

"Most certainly. There's no need for these friends of a night to recognize us in broad daylight. Only the President knows who we are."

While talking, the two women had undressed, aided by Berthe. Naked, they admired themselves in the full-length mirror. They were not absolutely beautiful, but young and desirable even so, silhouettes of the fashion of the day: slim and delicate, with small breasts, little in the way of a rump, and arms and shoulders developed by sports.

Berthe opened a door and moved a tapestry aside. Moving rapidly ahead of the two naked women, Homo-Deus slipped into the drawing room, where he had divined an orgy of women.

The drawing room, which was very large, had been cleared of all its furniture except for the piano, which had been pushed into a corner. With her back turned, a woman—this one dressed—was sitting on the stool. Masked like the others, her correct and silvery hair indicated that she was no longer young—doubtless a mercenary, accustomed to these kinds of celebrations.

The electric lamps were dressed with roses, the dainty bulbs artistically veiled in order not to cast harsh light on naked flesh. Rugs, cushions and two large divans replaced the furniture that had been removed. Through a lifted door-curtain, tables laden with a refined supper were visible in an adjacent room.

At the moment when Marc Vanel and the two women came in, the tribades, already coupled, were dancing, tightly enlaced, to the slow and voluptuous rhythm of a tango, while Maud and Nora—whose faces were the only ones uncovered—were sitting on one of the divans, caressing one another gently and chatting.

At the sight of the latecomers, the American woman came to meet them.

"I was beginning to think you weren't coming, my dears, and we weren't going to wait any longer for you."

"Is Brigitte here? You know that it's for her that I've come."

"Yes—she's the blonde dancing with that pretty brunette."

"Oh! Is she in love with her, then?"

"If she is, it's very recent, for they only met ten minutes ago."

"Do me the great favor of separating them my dear?"

"Gladly, if I can thus be agreeable to you."

The invisible satyr had completely forgotten his companion, who was languishing in the auto, waiting for him. The atmosphere of intense voluptuousness, the sight of the naked women, from which a frantic lust emanated, put his scientific philosophy to flight, and he felt himself borne away by a whirlwind of exasperated stupor.

The assembly became more animated. The gestures of the couples became more precise. Through the masks, eyes gleamed, cynical or lascivious; respirations became panting; lust was unchained in brutal and direct gestures; the bouquets of delicate perfumes was fusing now with the inebriating odor of sex organs moist with concupiscence. Sighs could be heard, groans, and even little screams, under overenthusiastic bites.

Moving through that orgy of flesh quivering with desire, the invisible satyr risked a gesture here and there—a kiss, a precise caress—which passed unnoticed in the lubricious desire that was exacerbating the enraged lesbians. For a long time, that apotheosis of feminine lust was unleashed in the drawing room, satisfied without restrained and without modesty. The mask authorized all temptations, all trials, and unusual poses.

Nora had played a good part in that unbridled lust, but her excited senses remained unslaked, lacking the excitement of the dance and, above all, the penetration of the male member. She was thinking about Narcisse, her indefatigable lover, and his hairy might; she almost regretted this neutered and phantasmal bacchanal, these uncertain hallucinations that irritated the senses without giving them the plenitude of the venereal act. She shouted an order to the pianist, suddenly bounded into middle of the drawing room, and began to dance.

She danced a savage and lubricious dance, miming the most suggestive gestures and attitudes of stupor. Then, howling, becoming simian again, she ran on all fours through the crowd of enlacements, rubbing herself against nude bodies, foraging in fleeces, and sex organs, crying unknown sounds: the language of the great apes, her brethren, the anthropoid colossi of Borneo.

Breathless and exhausted, she finally collapsed in the middle of the room. Then, the sensation she had felt once before was repeated; she was seized by the shoulders by invisible hands and tipped backwards.

This time, she knew what to expect, so she did not resist, and abandoned herself to the definitive possession.

Suddenly, a terrible cry rang out:

"Ouha! Ouha!"

Surging through the broken-down door, Narcisse leapt into the drawing room. With one bound, he was upon Nora, for he knew about the presence and the role of the Invisible, and his formidable hands fell upon the god, tearing the semi-conscious blue dancer from his grasp.

"Oh, Master!" he growled. "Not that—oh no, not that! I'll kill you! No more!"

"Hey! Don't squeeze so hard," said a breathless voice. "You must be able to understand that it's not my fault. Even a saint couldn't have resisted..."

Recovering his composure, the orangutan paraded his amazed gaze over the strange spectacle. Frightened by the sight of the great ape, and by hearing the bizarre words, the women were huddled in a corner, like wild beasts in a cage when the tamer comes in with his whip, and the sight of those naked beauties, still vibrant with lust, whom terror had thrown into the most picturesque pell-mell, was not banal.

Narcisse uttered a profound moan. "I understand," he said. "But why has Nora organized this orgy?"

215

"Why are we all dirty pigs? Bah! You'll see many others…look, Nora's bed is there, you know." He pointed at the door. "Hurry up—you'll find me in the auto."

Those few words had been exchanged in low voices. The orangutan understood. He seized the bacchante star in his arms and disappeared, carrying his prey, while the band of crazed tribades howled: "Our clothes are in there! If anything happens to them, what will become of us?"

The chambermaid, brought running by the screams, increased the confusion further. Maud, however, had recognized Narcisse, and gradually calmed things down.

"Shh!" she said. "Shut up! Shut up!"

And, gently, she opened a gap in the bedroom door. It is necessary to believe that what she saw reassured her fully, for she let the door-curtain fall back again, and let herself fall upon a pouffe, in a fit of laughter,

"Don't worry," she said, when she was finally able to speak. "Our friend isn't being badly served."

At the buffet in the next room, now deserted—for the women were mingling to one side—a glass and a bottle were suspended in mid-air; the bottle was emptied into the glass, and the glass into an invisible mouth.

"Ah! That's better. I was thirsty too…but what's that animal doing in the bedroom, where he's taking forever? I've a good mind to leave him here and send Mardruk back to pick him up at dawn…but I'm still thirsty. Let's drink!"

And the airborne bottle resumed its maneuvers.

"To your health, Master!" said Narcisse, returning from the chamber of amour.

"Finally, there you are! Are we going home?"

"Yes," said the orangutan. "Nora's tired. She's asleep. Then again, I'm a trifle disgusted."

216

XXI. The Bankruptcy of Genius

Since Ernest Paris's departure for Germany, Norway and Sweden, the life of Nora, the blue dancer, had continued as usual, with the difference that her possession by the orangutan had thrown her senses into a kind of erotic exasperation almost touching on hysteria. It was, perhaps, that very sensual exaltation before the audience at the Folies Bergère that amplified her success from day to day.

When the erotic fever took possession of her, the beast obtained the upper hand again, and it was necessary to assuage it at any price. Nevertheless, she conserved sufficient presence of mind to save appearances. She succeeded thus in satisfying herself with lovers of fortune, whom she stuffed with sensuality, while reserving for Jules Ducon the part which might be described as the lion's share.

Furthermore, she became suddenly careful to augment her fortune. By giving her the house in the Rue Spontini, her lover had awakened a desire for property in her, for the increase and augmentation of her possessions well beyond her expenditure.

Such was the situation until the day when the awakening of the ancestral beast had thrown her into the hairy arms of the orangutan. Until then, the females and males she had encountered at the hazard of her life had only half-satisfied her. With Narcisse, there was plenitude. For her, the ape was not what he was to others: a monster, an animal. She sensed—she knew, now—that there existed within her an intense rapport of race, an atavism, a heredity that made them very nearly similar.

217

And the orangutan's visits became more frequent. Under the cover of literary reports, Ernest Paris having authorized his secretary to initiate the young woman into the mysteries of the construction of a book, Narcisse had arrived at her home, ostensibly bearing under his arm a briefcase stuffed with papers.

In order to have more liberty, however, and to avoid suspicions on the part of her protector, Jules Ducon, it was decided by Nora that she would go to meet Narcisse at the Academician's house. She found it very original and exciting to make love in that environment, filled with artistic and Medieval treasures.

Pédauque and Paphnuce, who both had a profound horror of the orangutan, were unable to suppose that a young and pretty creature like Nora was infatuated with a frightening and repulsive beast. They therefore left the lovers perfectly free in the Villa Saïd, confining themselves to the servants' parlor. The ape and the she-ape took advantage of that privilege to enjoy themselves to their hearts content.

One day, Narcisse and Nora, liberated from all inconvenient clothing, were frolicking gaily on the majestic bed decorated with ornaments and precious tapestries. Nora's graceful nudity stood out against the massive and hairy corpulence of the ape, and, lost in their voluptuous romp, they were deaf to all exterior noises.

Suddenly, the door opened quietly, and Ernest Paris appeared on the threshold.

On returning from his voyage, the Academician, sprightly and seething with amorous impatience, had first had himself conveyed to the Rue Spontini, where a first deception awaited him. Madame was not at home. But Berthe restored his serenity by giving him the hope that Madame might well be at his house, because she sometimes went there to work with his secretary.

Oh well, I shall surprise them! the great man thought—and, climbing back into his taxi, he had told the driver to take him home.

The two domestics had received him with transports of joy.

"Madame Nora is here!" Paphnuce told him. "I'll go inform to her, as well as Monsieur Narcisse."

"There's no need, Paphnuce, stay here. I'll surprise them while they're working. No one has been informed of my return. Oh, my children, what a heavy burden glory is! I'm positively crushed by the worldwide admiration, so I need a few days' rest. So, not a word about my return to Paris, eh? Pédauque, go pay the taxi. In fact, no; I'll keep it. It can take Narcisse away—I'll give him the day off."

"How well Monsieur looks! He's twenty years younger!"

"Ha ha! You never said a truer word, my dear Pédauque."

And, Earnest Paris went cheerfully upstairs to the first floor.

There was no one in the drawing room...nor in the library...

Coming toward the bedroom, he seemed to perceive a strange purring sound. Intrigued to the highest degree, he turned the door handle, and stood there for a moment, astounded by the sight that met his eyes.

The lovers had not seen or heard him; they bravely continued the inebriation in progress.

Rage and disgust seethed in the brain of Ernest Paris, while the living tableau displayed to him, in its bestial immodesty, excited his virility, already awakened by his imagination, anticipating the joys of his return. With a veritable cry of a beast in rut, he bounded toward the couple, struck the ape in the mouth with all his strength, dragged Nora away from the powerful embrace, and, overexcited by the spectacle and the battle, threw himself upon her with a savage animal sensuality.

The moment was badly chosen. In the three animals, in whom instinct and sexual frenzy were dominant, reason no longer existed. The orangutan, initially surprised, yielded to the instinct of a beast with whom another beast is disputing his female. With one hand, he seized his master, knocked him down, and seized his throat with his foot.

There was a sinister crack; the Academician's tongue sprang out of his mouth, his eyes bulged.

Ernest Paris was dead.

The event had been so rapid that Narcisse's action had preceded thought. He let himself fall on to the limp puppet, and remained motionless, stupid, looking alternately at his victim and Nora, unable to understand as yet.

"Wretch! What have you done?" said the frightened young dancer, eventually.

"I don't know. It was stronger than me. I obeyed a reflex...the struggle for the female. But...is he really dead?"

"Yes, alas, he's dead," Nora replied, having approached the cadaver.

Gradually, the orangutan pulled himself together. He reflected momentarily.

"Only Homo-Deus can save us. I'll telephone him. He'll tell me what it's necessary to do."

Marc Vanel replied, briefly, that he would come right away, because, through Narcisse's mysterious attempted explanations, he had divined something terrible.

Indeed, a few minutes later, Homo-Deus came into the library, where the two accomplices, dressed in haste, were waiting for him anxiously.

"It can be arranged," the fantastic doctor said, tranquilly, having heard the story of the drama. "At Paris's age, an abrupt decease won't surprise anyone. Nora, you're going to leave here, as usual, but to make sure that the domestics don't come to disturb us, tell Pédauque that Monsieur Paris, feeling tired after his long voyage, has gone to bed, and that we're chatting with him for a moment."

Nora immediately made herself scarce, not sorry to be fleeing that ambience of death.

"It's up to us now, Narcisse. Remake the bed while I undress the great man, and make him look presentable."

A quarter of an hour later, the mortal remains of the illustrious man were laid out in his bed. His face was calm and restful. One would have thought that he was asleep.

"Poor old fellow!" said Mar Vanel. "The graft wasn't much use to him."

"Oh, yes, Master! If you had seen..."

"I can still see," said Marc Vanel, lifting up the bedclothes. "All the same, Voronoff will have worked for nothing."

"Look, Master: the beautiful corpse! An imposing statue!"

Indeed, the face of Ernest Paris was growing paler and paler, and taking on the august serenity that the human face only acquires in death.

"In there," said Marc Vanel, striking the forehead of the cadaver with his folded index finger, "was one of the noblest intelligences in the world. Where, now, is the subtle fluid that animated him? Where is his self, Narcisse? I'm not reproaching you for having killed Paris, but what a pity that I wasn't able to do for you what Jeanne Fortin has done for me: I could have given you his soul. If, one day, you make me submit to the same fate to which you've just subjected Ernest Paris—who can ever tell?—at least do so in such a way that I have the time to transmit my mind, my intelligence, my entire soul to you!"

"I would never kill you, Master! But if the opportunity arises, I won't forget that magnificent offer."

Thus spoke those two redoubtable beings, in the presence of the victim of one of them—a victim who was not yet cold.

At that Moment, Marc Vanel scanned the room with an investigative glance. Everything there was in order, and nothing revealed the horrible drama that had just unfolded there.

They went downstairs together.

"The Master isn't feeling very well," said Marc Vanel to the two domestics. "That's why he sent for me. He's resting now. Don't disturb him, but be ready to respond to the first summons. At Monsieur Paris's age, anything is to be feared. So, if our master gives you any anxiety, don't hesitate to telephone me. I'll be here in ten minutes."

Pédauque and Paphnuce nodded their heads as a sign of acquiescence, and Marc Vanel and Narcisse took their places in the auto in which Mardruk had brought the doctor.

"Not a word to Voronoff," said Homo-Deus to his pupil, in the car. "So far as everyone is concerned, Ernest Paris will have succumbed during the night to the rupture of an aneurism, or an embolism." After a brief pause, he added: "Oh sweet philosophy, with an indulgent patience, protect us from all unhealthy emotion!"

XXII. Toward the Panthéon

When, the day after that unfortunate occurrence, the news of the celebrated writer's death was spread by the voices of the press, the emotion was general. Strangely enough, the popular masses were moved by the death of the great skeptic. The people, however, knew very little about the work of Ernest Paris; if, by chance, a few of them had read him, they had certainly not understood him very well.

The celebrity of Ernest Paris was, perhaps, born above all of the need of the multitude to have conquered a patron belonging to the superior bourgeoisie, which the working class combats and, simultaneously, envies. Continually, the prudent writer had eclipsed himself at the precise moment when he would have been able to strike the attitude of a Chief, of a leader of man. The socialists had seen his disdain for all government as an acquiescence with their principles, and because of that scorn for governments they had considered him as one of theirs. It was the same on the part of the communists, and since the Russian Revolution, those who accepted orders and subsidies from Moscow, having received from Rappoport[53] the assurance that the man of letters was a Bolshevist, coupled in their literary references the

---

[53] The reference is to Charles Rappoport (1865-1941), a Russian-born French communist politician, who was a representative of the Comintern throughout the 1920s. His numerous books included *La Philosophie de l'histoire comme science de l'évolution* [The Philosophy of History as Evolutionary Science] (1903).

name of Ernest Paris with those of Lenin and Trotsky. In sum, for the most advanced progressives, the Academician was a "red." Ernest Paris let them believe it.

In reality, he amused himself as a spectator of the human comedy, of its contrasts and its appearances. He did not see, underneath all that formidable racket, anything but the atavistic imitation of the same repeated facts and gestures, throughout the ages, by different races—and since he had had an orangutan for a secretary, he took the tragicomedy back to the primal ancestors, the apes, who made the first social grimaces. Had the great stirrer of thoughts ever worried about the consequences of his inertia? No. He had enjoyed life, playing with it as a dilettante, trying to extract from it ideas or subjects for new novels; and the people, in their naïve confidence, in their need to sense a superior intelligence holding their flag, saw in him a touch destined to set fire to the old world. He knew full well, himself, that he was only a Chinese lantern.

His skill—was it deliberate?—had consisted of maintaining an opinion that served him in all parties, and, as the saying has it, keeping the pot boiling. Thus, for the popular party, Ernest Paris was "red"; for the bourgeois party, of which he was the issue, and which he had never left, he was "good." That bourgeois patrician had never denied his ancestry. The son of a petty bookseller, he hid that so little that he had relived his childhood for his readers, with the numerous qualities and flaws of his milieu. Between the shopkeeper and the bourgeois there is only a difference of accumulated fortune; between the man that is struggling to acquire it and the man that is struggling to conserve it. Ernest Paris had had difficult debuts. Although he had not known poverty, he had, at least, known straitened circumstances—

which, for an intellectual, is often worse. He had remained within his nature, in spite of his apparent prodigality, the economical spirit of his race.

In his home, curious works of art abounded, piled up rather than chosen judiciously. Ernest Paris, the demolisher of beliefs, had, without anyone really knowing why, a mania for religious trinkets, and excused it with a so-called love of beauty—but it was often nothing but the testimony of a grotesque superstition. Again, in that mania, he gave proof of a certain experience; he rarely allowed himself be taken for a ride. In any case, he never surpassed moderation; his expenditure was proportionate to his income.

Fundamentally, Ernest Paris was a great bourgeois; his natural distinction, his inexhaustible and always agreeable loquacity, and the apparent suppleness of his ideas, always ended up with the almost pessimistic conclusion that life is an incomprehensible phenomenon, that is it necessary to extract all possible pleasure from it, and not to attach an importance to human actions that they do not merit. In practice, if not in theory, therefore, he was frankly conservative of his acquired fortune, and he was never prodigal in philanthropic or social endeavors. Ernest Paris remained bourgeois, and, by virtue of that, perfectly "blue."

Apart from his witty religious satires and his whimsical portraits of lewd and riotous monks, the writer never attacked the recognized religions of his homeland head-on; he maintained the tradition of the frivolous storytellers of the eighteenth century, and by means of that adroit method, conserved relations with the Church, whose spirit of tradition he admired, deep down. Perhaps, in fact, if France had possessed a Gallic Church, he would have accommodated himself to it in spite of his mocking and critical mind, not out of belief but for the pleasure of debating texts, priests often possession first-rate erudition. From the Church to monarchy by divine right there is only a single step; each of them only admits one unique leader. That unity of command, of direction, one senses in the majority of his books.

One recalls the indiscreet question that was put to him one day: "Are you a Republican, my dear Master?"

He replied: "Do you take me for an imbecile, Monsieur?"

Ernest Paris was, before anything else, aristocratic, and more so than the nobility itself, for aristocracy in him was natural, not acquired by ancestral heredity. On many occasions, he allowed a glimpse, not of his love, but his marked preference for a regime of unique authority, an authoritarian monarchy in which there would have been only one responsibility. "One can hate a bad king," he said, "so one can detest a thousand idiots." Thus, by taste and by instinct, that ideologue was "white."

And it is, no doubt, that trilogy of opinions, that tricolor mind, which made his success and his glory. The chameleon entered fully into the spirit of his age, in which each political clan adopts labels but no longer has a flag. And it was that diffusion in colors which caused the general emotion, when people learned of his death. Yes, his strength came from the fact that he had laughed at many venerable things, that he had disputed everything without ever constructing anything. In sum, he had not acted. As a man of letters, he had something good to furnish everyone's dream, in accordance with his ideas. He had never exposed himself to bringing the ideal of his books into conflict with the realities of life, making his writings—which anyone could loot according to his

227

temperament—flowers beaten down by the rain, ears of corn battered by the storm: in short, ravaged dreams.

In the world of letters there was a great sigh of relief; that old man, in truth, was becoming inconvenient. He wrote, in a classic French, novels and short stories that were interesting and amusing, and, to complete the horror, sold well, justifying formidable print runs. Why, then, write, in our era, in the language of Racine and Voltaire, combining it with the erudition of Montaigne and the truculence of Rabelais? It was utterly rococo! The human intellect ought to evolve, like everything else.

If, politically, one is cramped by frontiers, the mind surpasses them and goes to eek its nourishment where it finds it. Before the war, it was fashionable to admire the literature of the North-East. The Latin spirit was obscured and intoxicated by beer grain alcohol and vodka; there was a triumph of dense and indigestible German philosophy. Today, it is more cosmopolitan; one mashes up all styles and genres in the wash-tub, and makes literary cocktails to the sound of jazz. Perhaps, eventually, those cocktails will end up becoming sublime, but for the present, they are only ephemeral. All so-called originality is seeking to set fire to a petard that will light a torch.

Thus, in the world of scribblers, there was relief as the disappearance of that old encumbrance Ernest Paris. Since the master was dead, that did not prevent all hypocrisies expanding in elegiac condolences and genuflections of every sort.

In sum, it was not mourning coming from the heart of the nation, but a political dolor made to order, the material of all interests and all opinions.

In those circumstances, on what side ought the government to line up in order to give the funeral celebrations the necessary solemnity, and, at the same time, content everyone? There was a great meeting of the Cabinet in order to resolve that delicate question. Naturally, the Panthéon had to open its doors to the great man, but what attitude ought the central power to strike, to regulate the affair?

It was public opinion that dictated the ordinance. In fact, the great industrial centers, having become since the war the nucleus of workers' demands, gave the signal. Already organized for a long time as free communes of a sort, in a state that had remained conservative, the miners of Carmaux and Anzin, and the factories of the North and the East, sent deputations that positively took possession of the movement, and the government followed them, nervously, but with sufficient skill to reap the benefit. It was sublime stupidity and grandiloquence, but the popular party was flattered by that apparent condescension, and declared itself satisfied.

And, in sum, it had reason to be.

In order to ornament the length of the journey on foot from the Villa Saïd, at the bottom of the very recent Avenue Foch, to the Panthéon, at the top of the Montagne Sante-Geneviève, someone had the idea of transporting the body by night to the statue of Voltaire outside the Institut, whose ever-young smile would look down on the departure of the funeral cortege.

The civil ceremony was combined with a military manifestation; Ernest Paris was a Grand-Croix de la Légion d'honneur, and the holder of numerous other honorific distinctions. Thus, the man who, before his death, had abhorred militarism, was afflicted, after his death, with a military parade. Thus, the individual who had shown himself throughout his life to be indecisive, shifting in all the winds of opinion, had to be accompanied on the final stage of his journey by a funeral as fantastic as himself—for one truly does not know what grotesque decorators preside over the disposition and the staging of funeral pomp.

It was before the façade of the sumptuous and slightly pretentious palace constructed by Le Vau, Lambert and Orbay that the stages and cubic inventions were installed. To tell the truth, they clashed passably well with the sumptuous academicism of the Louvre and the Mazarin chapel, but the spirit of the day most have been satisfied, under the fallacious pretext that it created something new—as if the straight line had not existed forever!

There were, therefore, simple black and red drapes, extended flat and without pleats, from one end to the other of the square where the stature of the Republic, sword in hand, seemed to be the sole protester, by virtue of her presence, against the general bad taste.

At the entrance to the Rue de Seine, which it masked, the official tribune displayed its rigid line extending from the Rue Bonaparte to the Institut. It was in the Rues de Seine and Mazarine that the carriages and automobiles of the guests of note were lined up. Turning its back on the École des Beaux-Arts, a raised platform was set up for the official orators who were to speak in celebration of the illustrious Academician. The habitual plumed carriage of funeral pomp had been set aside, replaced by a brief rectangle forming a platform, supported by long and solid wooden shafts that were to bear the group of miners and metallurgists who had come for the obsequies. That platform, draped in red, hid the cart on which the coffin of Ernest Paris had been placed. The ensemble, aiming at the colossal, had the effect of shrinking the human ants who were swarming in that classic space, too vast for their stature.

Above all that there was, on one side, the ironic mouth of the bronze Voltaire, leaning on his cane, sly and simian, seeming still to be mocking human stupidity, and on the other, Condorcet, disdaining the masquerade, deliberately turning his back on it.

The weather, gray and rainy on that July morning, was punctuated, at moments, by brief rays of sunlight, which came, as if regretfully, to shine their divine light on the assembly of vanities. Would not the great ironist, with a few mordant satires, have flayed that pompous and grotesque ceremony? Once, chatting with one of his colleagues of the Académie, he had pronounced these words, in accordance with his epicurean character:

"Let us spare the living these mortuary allegories in drapes and plumes, all these gross and ridiculous symbols. No speeches in the field of the silent goddess. In my testament I shall say that I want to be buried as simply as possible, without ostentation and above all without speeches, for I have discoursed too much about everything and about nothing, for my soul, if it is immortal—which I strongly doubt—to find pleasure in hearing the lies and the stupidities of official jabbering, in which everyone strives, above, for oratorical effect. No! No noise, no flowers, no speeches: peace silence, repose, dreamless sleep, and then forgetfulness, the great forgetfulness of others and oneself."

But not only did people not want to forget you, Ernest Paris, it was necessary that you serve their purpose. It was necessary that, in your glory, they should could carve out a little morsel, that they should clutch a little of the tinsel of your celebrity, and ornament themselves for a day with a fraction of your radiance.

Now, thousands and thousands of spectators are stifling one another in order to see and hear better, around the official tribunes, and the enormous red and black flags under which the coffin will roll toward the Panthéon.

XII. The Internationale

The Minister of Public Education, Jean Foudre, the député for the Basse-Pyrénées, representing the government, was the first to speak.

"To retrace the life of the illustrious writer would certainly be too easy a task. What always characterized Ernest Paris was his profound love for humanity, for the concord of nations. He would have rejoiced to see his perishable body carried in triumph by these noble representatives of the working class, these artisans of peace, fighting now for peace as they fought during the world war for the cause of right and liberty. In the name of France I deposit on the coffin this olive branch, the symbol of concord."

Discreet applause and flattering murmurs underlined the end of the Minister's speech. Among the members of the Institute, Jean Fortin suddenly looked at his neighbor.

"Damn! Nora, the dancer from the Folies, in full mourning, on that balcony, with her retinue, Borel and Maud—can you see them at that window directly behind the hearse, Monsieur? They've got a fine spot!"

"Are you forgetting that that's our Célimène's house? What is more natural than her inviting her friends to the spectacle?"

Meanwhile, a member of the Académie Française, in a green coat, took up his position at the funeral tribune, coughed, and in a weak but clear voice, said things about Ernest Paris, his talent, his genius—he did not have genius himself—and eventually concluded, in a stormy tone:

"If ever a time comes when poor, weary humanity no longer produces such prodigious educators, it will search in the work of the ancients, in the work of Ernest Paris, the miracle of rejuvenation, for the fortification necessary to its intellectual life; and believe me, it is in his work that it will find the most magnificent cordial of vitality and true good sense. Any litterateur who does not have an education is useless; a way with words has been given to him in order to raise the mentality and intellect of his contemporaries toward the summits. Ernest Paris applied himself to that, and he succeeded, not by example—he was weak and indecisive—but by the magic of his pen, inspired by the most profound love of humanity. Ernest Paris, you who have never doubted the dawn toward which the human ship is bound, in the midst of so much darkness, we shall follow your sacred standard through the tempests of the future..."

At this point, the factory-workers and miners, perhaps thinking that he was making an appeal to their collaboration, unfurled a few red flags and brandished them, shouting: "*Vive l'Internationale!*"

Slightly disconcerted, Foudre beat a hasty retreat, and disappeared among his colleagues, who congratulated him tranquilly.

But the speeches were not finished. After the Minister of Public Education and the Académie, Comrade Rappoport took the podium, paraded an arrogant glance over the ruling class, and cried, in a thunderous voice:

"Comrades! You have just heard marvelous words, which have justly celebrated the great writer Ernest Paris, but that quality was of no importance for us; what is important to us is that alone, among the mass of the ruling class, he turned to us and extended his hand.

"I, who am speaking, have seen him in his home, in an environment that has nothing in common with our tastes and our ideas. We have just been made to sense that: Ernest Paris was a bourgeois, and they would like to make us believe that he was making fun of us. Damn! I know full well that he was a bourgeois, and a very rich well-to-do bourgeois, but I also know that he was a bourgeois whom disgust for his class had brought him closer to ours, and it's for that reason that we loved him and recognized him as one of ours.

"Let them"—he designated the benches where Parisian high society was gathered—"try to pass him off as one of their coterie; we know that it isn't true. Comrade Paris detested the war and militarism that he had seen. He loved peace, because peace alone can bring the triumph of our ideas and the fraternity of peoples—of peoples and the working class, which I represent here, as President of the Internationals of Europe, Messieurs the Bourgeois, Messieurs the War-Profiteers, Messieurs the Exploiters of Peace! And I have come to say to you: 'Ernest Paris was one of us! Whether he was a bourgeois or not, we shall keep him, for today, with his cadaver, the people are entering the Panthéon!'

"Oh, my brave Messieurs, you thought that the brave worker would always yield to the force of money. The hour has finally sounded! We need a pretext for brandishing the standard of our claims. Ernest Paris has given us one. Come on, Comrades, flags in the air! Forwards! The *Internationale!*"

In an instant, hundreds of red flags were fluttering in the wind, and like a storm-wind, thousands of voices thundered:

The final conflict is here,
Come together, and tomorrow
The Internationale
Will be the human race...

The porters of the catafalque took hold of their grips, at arm's length, raised the heavy platform, and began to march while...

XXIV. The Funeral Dance

Marc Vanel had frayed a path through the crowd in order to reach the building in which Cécile Borel lived. The four windows of her drawing room gave access to light first-floor balconies overlooking the quai.

They were filled by the artiste's guests. Marc slid a banknote into the hand of the soubrette, telling her not to disturb anyone, and slipped into the drawing room without being noticed. The mistress of the house had reserved a window that she was occupying with Nora and two friends. All attention being directed outwards, no one paid any heed to Dr. Vanel, who was easily able to slip behind the three women.

The red and black cube on which the cart bearing the coffin of Ernest Paris was then directly under the window from which they were watching the spectacle of saddened France. All three were in full mourning dress, and immense widow's veils in silk muslin formed long harmonious supple pleats around them. Célimène had judged that that set-dressing was strictly necessary and could not fail to attract attention; thus, she was testifying to the late illustrious writer the homage of the Comédie-Française, in her person.

None of the three beauties suspected that Marc Vanel was standing behind them. Then, the doctor extended an imperious hand toward Nora and his eyes, focused at the back of her neck, seemed to radiate magnetic waves that enveloped the young woman and impressed her. She shivered; her eyes, initially staring, slowly closed; an understanding was established between the mind of Marc Vanel and hers; the former gave orders, the latter accepted them meekly.

The spectacle outside, seen from the window, did not lack a certain grandeur; firstly, the staged benches, then the enormous red and black trestle carried by the miners, and also, as far as the eye could see, the thousand faces of the crowd, itself divided into regular sections by the lines of guardsmen whose white harness traced chalky streaks through the black-clad or soberly dressed crowd, further accentuating the cubist harmony of the decoration.

But when, at Comrade Rappoport's appeal, the red flags surged forth, the aspect of the place suddenly changed; the constituent bodies squeezed more tightly behind the guardsmen and policemen, who, alert to the danger, like bulls or turkeys, surged forward toward the seditious emblems. The syndicalist groups moved forward themselves to absorb the shock.

There was a moment of suspense; a conflict seemed imminent. Was the government about to be carried away by that storm? Monsieur Briand,[54] the Minister of Foreign Affairs, calmed for a long time, recalled his youth. Monsieur Barthou,[55] of the Académie Française, the

---

[54] Aristide Briand (1862-1932) was the President of the Council for the eleventh time between July and November 1929, but held the post of Minister of Foreign Affairs continually from 1925 until his death. A co-founder of *L'Humanité*, he is nowadays remembered as the leading pacifist in European politics during the interbellum period, when he put forward a plan for the United Federal States of Europe.

[55] Louis Barthou (1862-1934) had served one brief term as President of the Council before the Great War and held numerous other ministerial posts during his long career, and was appointed Ministry of Justice in 1926. Champsaur loathed

Minister of Justice, making a quip, said to his neighbors: "The fools won't be with us any longer."

But The Prefect of Police, after having exchanged a few words with the President of the Council, Raymond Poincaré,[56] had run forward, and he gave curt orders to which the police had to submit. They arranged themselves so as to double up the hedge of guardsmen.

The prime minister then turned toward the cortege and simply said: "Advance, citizens, advance! The route is clear. Advance, please..."

Everything settled down. Monsieur Barthou said: "The fools will always be with us."

The human flood was about to move of in an orderly manner when a shrill cry caused all heads to turn. On a balcony protruding from Cécile Borel's house, where she had been leaning on the wrought-iron rail, a slender pretty woman in mourning straightened up, extending her arms and her vast black veil. Then a long, heartrending howl escaped from her mouth; she represented an authentic symbol of the statue of despair.

And suddenly, with a formidable leap, she took off like a great nocturnal bird, and came to alight in the middle of the enormous red and black platform.

---

him, not so much for his conservative views as because he considered him to be a model of hypocritical opportunism, and made derogatory remarks about him in many of his novels. The reason why his remark qualifies as a quip is illustrated by the rapid reversal of the commonplace judgment into the conventional form of the common quotation that is being mangled (the word "fools" being substituted for the word "poor").

[56] Raymond Poincaré (1860-1934) served his third term as President of the Council immediately prior to Brian from July 1926 to July 1929, and was presumably still in that post when the author wrote this passage.

An emotional hush had fallen over the immense plaza; all gazes were fixed fearfully on the strange apparition, and only Voltaire, fixed in his bronze mask, seemed amused by the scene. Was his simian mask, with its mocking smile, still laughing across time at modern apishness?

Meanwhile, Nora, upright on the platform, was causing the funeral wings of her great veil to fly around her with her rhythmic movements. Then she became animated, and suddenly, she was dancing!

At first, there was a rapid fluttering around the platform, like some bird of mourning: a bird of eternal regret causing its wings to palpitate above the crowd. Then, returning to the center, she mimed dolor: the eternal dolor weighing upon the human race.

And it was a magnificent poem!

First of all there was the ancestor, the savage cavedweller, struggling against all perils and all dangers, often vanquished, sometimes victorious, and finally, affirming the mastery of the future. Then the first civilizations were sketched: the obelisks, the pyramids, the gigantic profiles of Egypt and Assyria, the dolmens of Gaul, the harmonious and diving temples of Athens and Rome. Then came the invasions, the disasters and the glory, the detail and the ensemble of human glories and miseries. It was the legend of the centuries[57] danced by an artiste of genius, every step of which represented a type, an epoch, a tragic scene; and between each scene of her splendid epic, the dancer paused briefly, and then

---

[57] This reference to *La légende des siècles* [the legend of the centuries] gives the reader a specific clue as to exactly which "poem" Nora is dancing: Victor Hugo's flamboyant epic of progress.

drew herself up to her full height, and uttered her lugubrious and terrifying cry.

The furious dance lasted for a long time, but none of the spectators seemed to perceive that, to such an extent did the fantastic scene exercise a collective fascination. On one side, as on the other, the government and the syndical groups probably attributed that unexpected and captivated intervention to one another.

Nora finished by exhausting that choreographic poem. Then, with one knee on the ground, her head tilted backwards, her arms extended toward the heavens, she mimed dolor turning its hope toward a mysterious dream.

And the cortege set forth, escorting and acclaiming the magnificent statue, while those who had seen nothing came from afar, continuing their song of conquest in muted voices, the red flags fluttering in the faces of the conservatives at the windows, who took fright and stepped back precipitately.

There was a pause in front of the Institut. The large door opened, and the Academicians, costumed in black and green, arranged themselves on the steps in order to send a supreme adieu to one of their own, who was entering into true immortality. Then they fell into step with those marching behind the coffin. The Immortals were groups as advantageously as possible, because all the objective lenses of the photographers and the cinematographers were aimed at them.

Suddenly, abruptly parted, the Immortals, jostled and tottering, nearly fell over. Laughter—formidable, Homeric laughter—burst forth and rolled like a wave.

On the threshold of the temple of glory, an enormous orangutan dressed, like the Academicians, in a suit with green palm-leaves and a tricorn hat, with an épée at his side, had just appeared, and, with a broad gesture, saluted the crowd. He came down the steps and advanced toward the cubic catafalque. And, making his powerful breast resonate like a gong beneath his enormous fists the orangutan uttered his terrible battle-cry:

"Ouha! Ouha!"

The laughter was succeeded by a frisson of terror.

Drawing himself up to the full extent of his powerful stature, Narcisse howled:

"*Vive l'avenir!*"

Then, bounding on to the platform, the simian Immortal lifted Nora up at the arm's length, and held her up toward the heavens, repeating once again his cry:

"*Vive l'avenir!*"

Meanwhile, the cortege had resumed its march, red flags fluttering in the wind; and behind, the song of ten thousand voices repeated:

The final conflict is here,
Come together, and tomorrow
The Internationale
Will be the human race...

In the square empty of people, a bronze statue was still smiling, and the ape himself, Voltaire, seemed to be saying:

"Poor humans! What apes you are!"

But all along the quais, and across the Boulevard Saint-Michel to the Panthéon, the revolutionary song seemed to be prolonged to infinity, and fearful bourgeois shuddered, as if the voice of the earth were singing.

XXV. The Annihilation of Brains

That summer, Dr. Jean Fortin remained in his retreat on the heights of Saint-Cloud, the Red Nest. The habitation was situated in the middle of a heavily wooded garden, which, abandoned to its own devices for more than twenty years, had the aspect of a veritable virgin forest. Only one pathway, wide enough for an automobile, seemed to be extended in order to reach the house; the rest, abandoned to all the exuberance of brambles, clematis and vines, was inextricable.

That night there had been, as the villa's only servant, Frédéric, put it, "an orgy in the tower"—which is to say that the four doctors, Goldry, Voronoff, Vanel and Fortin, had dined there. Now gathered in the laboratory, they were chatting and smoking. A fifth individual, devoid of cigar or pipe, Narcisse, was listening.

Marc Vanel was speaking.

"Last night, I was able to enter into telepathic communication with a Commissar of the people, my friend Selikoff, who is perhaps the only one brave enough to resist his Soviet colleagues. That long-distance telepathy will have no limits, I hope, and one day, will permit us to communicate with the other planets, perhaps with other stars.

"You're dazzling me, Marc," Voronoff interrupted. "I haven't been following your experiments, and nor has Goldry. Your telepathy doesn't tell us anything except its name. One of the inconveniences of science is that the human lifespan is too short to embrace all is branches. You alone, perhaps, thanks to your genius, have been able to reunite the ensemble of knowledge. If you want to be understood, would you care to give us a glimpse of your discovery?"

"You're not unaware of the noise made in the scientific world by the discovery of extraterrestrial waves.[58] That phenomenon, after that of Hertzian waves, and radiography, by virtue of increasingly profound knowledge of the properties of luminous rays, has revealed a new genesis to us. The atom was believed until then to be the constructor of the globe and the principle of life; the study of sidereal waves leads us to consider them as creative of the atom. The question regresses infinitely; fundamentally, it's all the same work. Scientists explain everything by means of atomic progression and religions reply with the word God. Hazard resolves nothing, and the expression 'creative force' nothing more. Our role, therefore, obliges us to limit our studies to what we can see, to utilize our knowledge, and to await from the intelligences of the future, subtler than ours, the key to the enigma."

After a few puffs on his cigarette, Vanel resumed: "That being established, can you not see a correlation

---

[58] The discovery of what Robert Millikan called "cosmic rays"—thought at first to consist entirely of electromagnetic radiation, although they are actually a cocktail whose principal components are now known to be high-energy protons and atomic nuclei—is now dated to 1909 when Theodor Wulf set up his electrometers to demonstrate higher levels of radiation at the top of the Eiffel Tower than at the bottom. The significance of the experiment was not widely accepted or realized at the time, however, and it was not until Victor Hess sent electrometers up to altitudes higher than five thousand meters in 1912 that the phenomenon really began to generate the "noise" that, after an interruption by the Great War, reflected the increasing interest of scientists in the 1920s.

between the extraterrestrial waves and the mysterious fluid that regulates or being—and, in consequence, all living beings? One obtains movement, the will of action, by an entire mechanism of muscles, nerves and various organs, but that movement departs from thought, the center from which the 'waves' that furrow our bodies continuously escape incessantly. That is so true that thought sometimes continues even in sleep, in the form of dreams."

A few more swirls of smoke emerged from Homo-Deus' cigarette, seemingly symbolizing the meanders of what he was saying.

"Let us call that rapport between human thought and the sidereal waves 'universal thought.' From that, a method of communication through space, not by means of the conventional signs of speech or writing, but by the direct communication of minds—or, if you prefer, souls—will be born. Once, the name of telepathy was given to an ensemble of facts that seemed to be abnormal, and which, having not been proven, passed for accidental or shameless charlatanism. Those facts were real, but, as people were ignorant of their causes, they remained in the domain of fable. But almost always, there is a latent verity underlying the fabulous; the discovery of sidereal waves outs us on the right path.

"Thus having observed the correlation that there is between all undulatory phenomena and human thought, we have judged the transmission of that thought to be possible. And that is why an intelligence, prepared beforehand, will be able to receive my thought, sent across space, not by exterior means but by my personal center of undulations, the brain."

"And you believe that you've succeeded?"

"At any rate, Dr. Fortin and I commune in thought with the son of Sun-Yat-Sen, presently in Canton, and, likewise, with Tekewamei in Japan and Selikoff in Moscow."

"How do you receive the response?"

"A thought that isn't mine irrupts in my brain: that's the response."

"Eh? But enlighten me: are the undulatory centers not the glands?"

"No. The glands are organs that only relate to the economy, and thought is fluid."

"We're turning in a vicious circle," Fortin remarked. "You're discussing causes when we ought to limit ourselves to the study and utilization of facts. We've realized one fact, which we've baptized P.T.C.: Psycho-Telegraphic Communication. The results are conclusive; that's the main thing. Your role as a surgeon ought to be limited to the study of the material mechanism, ameliorating its functions, prolonging its duration and, if necessary, modifying a few pieces here and there. We all lack time; let everyone contribute his personal effort to the collectivity—that's our goal."

Dr. Goldry took his pipe out of his mouth. "May I, who limit myself to the study of apes, and providing you with subjects, ask you what we're going to do with Narcisse and Nora?"

The orangutan straightened up. "Stop there Messieurs! By giving me a human brain, you've equipped me with free will."

"You're one of us, Narcisse, taking part in the discussion," Mark Vanel said, "and we're pursuing your intellectual progress with your permission."

"I believe," said the orangutan, the son of Ouha and Dilou, "that it needs to pause. At the moment, I'm experiencing a kind of crisis of puberty, which it would be good to allow to pass."

"Comrade Narcisse," said Fortin, with a brief burst of laughter, "is in love. I told you that you'd be adored. Have you vanquished by eloquence?"

"No, by the appeal of the race. You allowed me to deduce that Nora was a she-ape; I became certain of that in possessing her. The operations you carried out on her in infancy wouldn't succeed in me, as an adult. I shall therefore remain an orangutan. If I'm a monster, relative to human beings, I know that it's relative and that I'm their superior in many ways. I'm nevertheless curious about the role you've reserved for Nora."

"First, how do you love her? With your brain, or the rest?"

"In that woman there's nothing but sensuality—nothing that comes from the intellect. Nora is a magnificent animal of pleasure, no more than that."

"Good!" said Fortin. "We can count on you. As for Nora, shall we let her go on with her life, or recover her for further experiments?"

"What more do you want to do, damn it?" said Voronoff. "She's a woman and must remain one."

"All the more so as Nora, by virtue of her connections, might be useful to me. I'm beginning to lose my taste for politics, though; the people deserve to be exploited."

"There's one interesting one," protested Goldry. "The American people!"

"Oh, no, shut up, old Gold. The United States is an excessively ambitious nation, an unbridled imperialism coupled with religious hypocrisy. We've had a fine specimen of that since the war. Admittedly, fifty thousand soldiers got themselves killed in order to aid the business affairs of the great, clever majority who only saw the general conflagration as a means of making money. Intelligent, courageous, hard-working; I'll grant you that—but do you know where your American people are headed?"

"For the conquest of the globe," said the Yankee, proudly.

"Perhaps—but for the moral death of humanity."

"Get away! We're for progress, above all—above all!"

"We all are, more or less," said Fortin, "to see who can pull the silliest face. Let's see, Narcisse, you who, in your capacity as a new man, who has no atavism of old ideas, how do you see the means of realizing, I won't say the happiness of humankind, but universal peace?"

"Humans are too stupid not to fight one another forever."

"In any case," said the American, "I'm leaving for Eze next week. I don't know whether my apes are missing me, but I'm missing them."

"That's understandable. Who resembles...."

"You're intolerable, Fortin."

"No, my dear, for I'm leaving with you."

"You're leaving too!" exclaimed Narcisse. "What about me?"

"Well, you'll keep this house, the Red Nest."

"And you have Nora," added Marc Vanel, smiling.

What lustful memory passed, suddenly, through the orangutan's mind, and made him angry? He stood up among the four seated doctors and looked down at them, his eyes shining above his broad muzzle, and he uttered a single word, as if it were an insult:

"Brains!"

Then, to the astonishment of them all, he went on: "Nora, whom I love, has remained, in spite of all your practices of esthetic surgery, a she-ape. And I, in spite of all your scientific tampering with my brain, am still no more than a man of the woods: *Ouha! Ouha!*"

His arms raised, the orangutan agitated his powerful hands, cried and yelped, furious and terrible, to such an extent that for a moment, the four doctors, thus set at bay, were afraid of the Beast suddenly revealed in the civilized creature that they had made.

Narcisse, now, was beating his large breast like a drum, and repeating, scornfully:

"Brains! Poor brains! *Ouha! Ouha!*"

SF & FANTASY

Adolphe Alhaiza. *Cybele*

Alphonse Allais. *The Adventures of Captain Cap*

Henri Allorge. *The Great Cataclysm*

Guy d'Armen. *Doc Ardan: The City of Gold and Lepers*

G.-J. Arnaud. *The Ice Company*

Charles Asselineau. *The Double Life*

Henri Austruy. *The Eupantophone; The Olotelepan; The Petitpaon Era*

Barillet-Lagargousse. *The Final War*

Cyprien Bérard. *The Vampire Lord Ruthwen*

S. Henry Berthoud. *Martyrs of Science*

Aloysius Bertrand. *Gaspard de la Nuit*

Richard Bessière. *The Gardens of the Apocalypse; The Masters of Silence*

Albert Bleunard. *Ever SMalher*

Félix Bodin. *The Novel of the Future*

Louis Boussenard. *Monsieur Synthesis*

Alphonse Brown. *City of Glass; The Conquest of the Air*

Emile Calvet. *In a Thousand Years*

André Caroff. *The Terror of Madame Atomos; Miss Atomos; The Return of Madame Atomos; The Mistake of Madame Atomos; The Monsters of Madame Atomos; The Revenge of Madame Atomos; The Resurrection of Madame Atomos; The Mark of Madame Atomos; The Spheres of Madame Atomos; The Wrath of Madame Atomos* (w/M. & Sylvie Stéphan)

Félicien Champsaur. *The Human Arrow; Ouha, King of the Apes; Pharaoh's Wife; Homo-Deus*

Didier de Chousy. *Ignis*

Jules Clarétie. *Obsession*

Michel Corday. *The Eternal Flame*

André Couvreur. *The Necessary Evil*; *Caresco, Superman; The Exploits of Professor Tornada* (3 vols.)

Captain Danrit. *Undersea Odyssey*

C. I. Defontenay. *Star (Psi Cassiopeia)*

Charles Derennes. *The People of the Pole*

Georges Dodds (anthologist). *The Missing Link*

Charles Dodeman. *The Silent Bomb*

Harry Dickson. *The Heir of Dracula; Harry Dickson vs. The Spider*

Jules Dornay. *Lord Ruthven Begins*
Alfred Driou. *The Adventures of a Parisian Aeronaut*
Sâr Dubnotal *vs. Jack the Ripper*
Alexandre Dumas. *The Return of Lord Ruthven*
Renée Dunan. *Baal*
J.-C. Dunyach. *The Night Orchid; The Thieves of Silence*
Henri Duvernois. *The Man Who Found Himself*
Achille Eyraud. *Voyage to Venus*
Henri Falk. *The Age of Lead*
Paul Féval. *Anne of the Isles; Knightshade; Revenants; Vampire City; The Vampire Countess; The Wandering Jew's Daughter*
Paul Féval, *fils. Felifax, the Tiger-Man*
Charles de Fieux. *Lamékis*
Louis Forest. *Someone is Stealing Children in Paris*
Arnould Galopin. *Doctor Omega*; *Doctor Omega and the Shadowmen* (anthology)
Judith Gautier. *Isoline and the Serpent-Flower*
H. Gayar. *The Marvelous Adventures of Serge Myrandhal on Mars*
G.L. Gick. *Harry Dickson and the Werewolf of Rutherford Grange*
Delphine de Girardin. *Balzac's Cane*
Léon Gozlan. *The Vampire of the Val-de-Grâce*
Edmond Haraucourt. *Illusions of Immortality; Daah, the First Human*
Nathalie Henneberg. *The Green Gods*
Eugène Hennebert. *The Enchanted City*
V. Hugo, P. Foucher & P. Meurice. *The Hunchback of Notre-Dame*
Romain d'Huissier. *Hexagon: Dark Matter*
Jules Janin. *The Magnetized Corpse*
Michel Jeury. *Chronolysis*
Gustave Kahn. *The Tale of Gold and Silence*
Gérard Klein. *The Mote in Time's Eye*
Fernand Kolney. *Love in 5000 Years*
Paul Lacroix. *Danse Macabre*
Louis-Guillaume de La Follie. *The Unpretentious Philosopher*
Jean de La Hire. *Enter the Nyctalope; The Nyctalope on Mars; The Nyctalope vs. Lucifer; The Nyctalope Steps In; Night of the Nyctalope; Return of the Nyctalope; The Fiery Wheel*
Etienne-Léon de Lamothe-Langon. *The Virgin Vampire*
André Laurie. *Spiridon*
Gabriel de Lautrec. *The Vengeance of the Oval Portrait*
Alain le Drimeur. *The Future City*

Georges Le Faure & Henri de Graffigny. *The Extraordinary Adventures of a Russian Scientist Across the Solar System* (2 vols.)
Gustave Le Rouge. *The Mysterious Doctor Cornelius* (3 vols.); *The Vampires of Mars; The Dominion of the World* (w/Gustave Guitton) (4 vols.)
Jules Lermina. *Mysteryville; Panic in Paris; To-Ho and the Gold Destroyers; The Secret of Zippeliu; The Battle of Strasbourg*
André Lichtenberger. *The Centaurs; The Children of the Crab*
Listonai. *The Philosophical Voyager*
Jean-Marc & Randy Lofficier. *Edgar Allan Poe on Mars; The Katrina Protocol; Pacifica; Robonocchio; Return of the Nyctalope;* (anthologists) *Tales of the Shadowmen 1-11; The Vampire Almanac*
Xavier Mauméjean. *The League of Heroes*
Joseph Méry. *The Tower of Destiny*
Hippolyte Mettais. *The Year 5865; Paris Before the Deluge*
Louise Michel. *The Human Microbes; The New World*
Tony Moilin. *Paris in the Year 2000*
José Moselli. *Illa's End*
John-Antoine Nau. *Enemy Force*
Marie Nizet. *Captain Vampire*
C. Nodier, A. Beraud & Toussaint-Merle. *Frankenstein*
Henri de Parville. *An Inhabitant of the Planet Mars*
Gaston de Pawlowski. *Journey to the Land of the 4th Dimension*
Georges Pellerin. *The World in 2000 Years*
Ernest Pérochon. *The Frenetic People*
Pierre Pelot. *The Child Who Walked on the Sky*
J. Polidori, C. Nodier, E. Scribe. *Lord Ruthven the Vampire*
P.-A. Ponson du Terrail. *The Vampire and the Devil's Son; The Immortal Woman*
Georges Price. *The Missing Men of the Sirius*
Edgar Quinet. *Ahasuerus; The Enchanter Merlin*
Henri de Régnier. *A Surfeit of Mirrors*
Maurice Renard. *The Blue Peril; Doctor Lerne; The Doctored Man; A Man Among the Microbes; The Master of Light*
Jean Richepin. *The Wing; The Crazy Corner*
Albert Robida. *The Adventures of Saturnin Farandoul; The Clock of the Centuries; Chalet in the Sky; The Electric Life*
J.-H. Rosny Aîné. *Helgvor of the Blue River; The Givreuse Enigma; The Mysterious Force; The Navigators of Space; Vamireh; The World of the Variants; The Young Vampire*
Marcel Rouff. *Journey to the Inverted World*

Léonie Rouzade. *The World Turned Upside Down*
Han Ryner. *The Superhumans; The Human Ant*
Pierre de Selenes: *An Unknown World*
Angelo de Sorr. *The Vampires of London*
Brian Stableford. *The New Faust at the Tragicomique;The Empire of the Necromancers (The Shadow of Frankenstein; Frankenstein and the Vampire Countess; Frankenstein in London); Sherlock Holmes & The Vampires of Eternity; The Stones of Camelot; The Wayward Muse.* (anthologist) *News from the Moon; The Germans on Venus; The Supreme Progress; The World Above the World; Nemoville; Investigations of the Future; The Conqueror of Death; The Revolt of the Machines; The Man With the Blue Face*
Jacques Spitz. *The Eye of Purgatory*
Kurt Steiner. *Ortog*
Eugène Thébault. *Radio-Terror*
C.-F. Tiphaigne de La Roche. *Amilec*
Simon Tyssot de Patot. *The Strange Voyages of Jacques Massé and Pierre de Mésange*
Louis Ulbach. *Prince Bonifacio*
Théo Varlet. *The Golden Rock. The Xenobiotic Invasion; The Casta-ways of Eros; Timeslip Troopers* (w/André Blandin); *The Martian Epic* (w/Octave Joncquel)
Pierre Véron. *The Merchants of Health*
Paul Vibert. *The Mysterious Fluid*
Villiers de l'Isle-Adam. *The Scaffold; The Vampire Soul*
Philippe Ward. *Artahe ; The Song of Montségur* (w/Sylvie Miller) *Manhattan Ghost* (w/Mickael Laguerre)

MYSTERIES & THRILLERS

M. Allain & P. Souvestre. *The Daughter of Fantômas*
A. Anicet-Bourgeois, Lucien Dabril. *Rocambole*
A. Bernède. *Belphegor*; *Judex* (w/Louis Feuillade); *The Return of Judex* (w/Louis Feuillade); *The Shadow of Judex*
A. Bisson & G. Livet. *Nick Carter vs. Fantômas*
V. Darlay & H. de Gorsse. *Arsène Lupin vs. Sherlock Holmes: The Stage Play*
Séamas Duffy. *Sherlock Holmes in Paris*
Paul Féval. *Gentlemen of the Night; John Devil; The Black Coats ('Salem Street; The Invisible Weapon; The Parisian Jungle; The*

Companions of the Treasure; Heart of Steel; The Cadet Gang; The Sword-Swallower)
Emile Gaboriau. *Monsieur Lecoq*
Goron & Emile Gautier. *Spawn of the Penitentiary*
Paul d'Ivoi. *Around the World on Five Sous* (w/Henri Chabrillat)
Rick Lai. *Shadows of the Opera: Retribution in Blood; Sisters of the Shadows: The Curse of Cagliostro*
Steve Leadley. *Sherlock Holmes: The Circle of Blood*
Maurice Leblanc. *Arsène Lupin vs. Countess Cagliostro; Arsène Lupin vs. Sherlock Holmes (The Blonde Phantom; The Hollow Needle); The Many Faces of Arsène Lupin; The Island of the Thirty Coffins*
Gaston Leroux. *Chéri-Bibi; The Phantom of the Opera; Rouletabille & the Mystery of the Yellow Room; Rouletabille at Krupp's*
Richard Marsh. *The Complete Adventures of Judith Lee*
William Patrick Maynard. *The Terror of Fu Manchu; The Destiny of Fu Manchu*
Frank J. Morlock. *Sherlock Holmes: The Grand Horizontals; Sherlock Holmes vs Jack the Ripper*
Jean Petithuguenin. *The Adventures of Ethel King*
Antonin Reschal. *The Adventures of Miss Boston*
P. de Wattyne & Y. Walter. *Sherlock Holmes vs. Fantômas*
David White. *Fantômas in America*
Pierre Yrondy. *The Adventures of Thérèse Arnaud*

Victor Margueritte. *The Bacheloress; The Companion; The Couple*

SCREENPLAYS

Mike Baron. *The Iron Triangle*
Emma Bull & Will Shetterly. *Nightspeeder; War for the Oaks*
Gerry Conway & Roy Thomas. *Doc Dynamo*
Steve Englehart. *Majorca*
James Hudnall. *The Devastator*
Jean-Marc & Randy Lofficier. *Royal Flush*
J.-M. & R. Lofficier & Marc Agapit. *Despair*
J.-M. & R. Lofficier & Joël Houssin. *City*
Andrew Paquette. *Peripheral Vision*
Robert L. Robinson, Jr. *Judex*
R. Thomas, J. Hendler & L. Sprague de Camp. *Rivers of Time*

NON-FICTION

Stephen R. Bissette. *Blur 1-5. Green Mountain Cinema 1; Teen Angels*
Win Scott Eckert. *Crossovers* (2 vols.)
Jean-Marc & Randy Lofficier. *Shadowmen* (2 vols.)
Randy Lofficier. *Over Here*

ART BOOKS

Jean-Pierre Normand. *Science Fiction Illustrations*
Raven Okeefe. *Raven's L'il Critters; Rave's Faves*
Randy Lofficier & Raven Okeefe. *If Your Possum Go Daylight...*
Daniele Serra. *Illusions*
Randy Lofficier. *Over Here*

HEXAGON COMICS

Franco Frescura & Luciano Bernasconi. *Wampus*
Franco Frescura & Giorgio Trevisan. *CLASH*
L. Bernasconi, J.-M. Lofficier & Juan Roncagliolo. *Phenix*
Claude Legrand, J.-M. Lofficier & L. Bernasconi. *Kabur*
Franco Oneta. *Zembla*
L. Buffolente, Lofficier & J.-J. Dzialowski. *Strangers: Homicron*
Danilo Grossi. *Strangers: Jaydee*
Claude Legrand & Luciano Bernasconi. *Strangers: Starlock*
Thierry Mornet & Juan Roncagliolo. *Guardian of the Republic*
J.-M. Lofficier, M. Garcia, F. Blanco & J. Pima. *Strangers in a Strange Land*